IT CAME FROM NEVERLAND

Also available by Cynthia Pelayo

Novels

Vanishing Daughters
Forgotten Sisters

The Santa Muerte Series

The Missing
Santa Muerte

The Chicago Saga Series

The Shoemaker's Magician
Children of Chicago

Collections

Loteria
Crime Scene
Into the Forest and All the Way Through
Poems of My Night

IT CAME FROM NEVERLAND

A NOVEL

CYNTHIA PELAYO

CROOKED LANE

NEW YORK

Published in the United States by Crooked Lane Books, an imprint of The Quick Brown Fox & Company LLC.

Crooked Lane Books and its logo are trademarks of The Quick Brown Fox & Company LLC.

Library of Congress Catalog-in-Publication data available upon request.

ISBN (hardcover): 979-8-89242-444-8
ISBN (paperback): 979-8-89242-445-5
ISBN (ebook): 979-8-89242-446-2

Cover design by Marcela Bolívar

Printed in the United States.

www.crookedlanebooks.com

Crooked Lane Books
34 West 27th St., 10th Floor
New York, NY 10001

First Edition: June 2026

The authorized representative in the EU for product safety and compliance is eucomply OÜPärnu mnt 139b-14, 11317 Tallinn, Estonia, hello@eucompliancepartner.com, +33757690241

10 9 8 7 6 5 4 3 2 1

To Gerardo,
Meet me at the second star to the right.

Prologue

I LOVED HIM.

The boy with the ember hair and eyes the color of a forest, the green of bright moss. Or maybe the green of mold, of rot, of things left in the dark too long.

Mother once told me he was a dream, that no real child ever crept through nursery windows in the light of a London spring moon.

But he was not a dream.

He was a wish upon a star.

Something that shimmered behind a sky drowned in shadow.

Or so I thought.

Dreams do not leave scars. Dreams do not sing lullabies of love and delight in one ear while they speak of submission in the other. I argued this with him again and again. What he was giving me was not what he promised.

He didn't listen. He refused.

And when I returned home, the ultimate mythic betrayal, no one else listened either. Because I was just a girl, one who told stories. I was too much, just never enough. Too quiet. Too loud.

A girl who reveled in fantasy and story, yes, because stories are what make us human.

But the truth? My truth? They all waved it away with their hands.

That Wendy Darling, they'd say. She's made a complicated mess this time.

Her poor mother, they'd add.

Others would interject: It was her mother's fault, you know. She stuffed that girl's head with stories and now look at the poor child.

Wendy Darling, with such fancies in her head.

Wendy Darling, always spinning tales when she should be learning how to embroider, sew, keep a house tidy, and speak softly while minding her manners.

Such a strange girl. That Wendy Darling, claiming she'd been chased by birds with human faces.

They'd say all of those things and more, but I remember what happened because I remember his name. His name is the key that stirs all this up. His name is the crack of a hardcover novel in front of a crackling fireplace. His name is the wound in the words "Once upon a time." It reverberates there. Somewhere. In all of the "happily ever afters" to have ever existed, because not all "ever afters" end happily.

I remember his name, and I hold it over my heart like the cold lump of coal that it is, but it is real, and sadly, my love for him was—is—too. His smile is stamped on my mind. As are his eyes, and how they burned brighter than the summer sun at noon. That voice, how it rose over the sea like an anthem. I remember how the others cheered when he arrived over the hill, as if their savior had returned home. They hoisted him up on their shoulders, and smiled, and danced, with such fierce glee, welcoming their king back to his kingdom. I adored him more for that, for how their love for him made him more real, more golden.

In the quietest of hours, that smile still catches me. I feel my heart tug and then ache, because what I remember most days now is not just his smile, but the snares that followed.

How easily monsters trick us to fall.

And I fell, into that dark with him. In choosing to, I lost a piece of myself, the delicate fabric of my soul, and more.

I also lost who truly loved me, and I see them there still, dying beneath an ash tree.

I've been running through that forest path ever since, trying to hide, trying to shrink, fearing that once again I'll be spotted.

That I'll be seen.

Today, I hover between the girl I was and a woman still untangling what it means to survive between fairyland and the truth.

It's been over a decade. Twelve years. And still, I remember the height of that love. That terrible, dazzling height.

And the boy who taught me that in order to fly, one must first learn how to jump.

CHAPTER 1

AGNES WAS BURYING something beneath the elm tree.

From the window above the back stairwell, I caught the bent shape of her. The hem of her pinafore darkened with soil. Her hands moved quickly while working the earth.

I stepped outside. My boots sank into the lawn, damp with morning dew. Fog blanketed the perimeter of the grounds, and for a moment, it felt like nothing existed beyond the estate.

"Agnes?" I said, not too loudly, so as not to wake the rest of the children inside.

She didn't turn around.

Perhaps she didn't hear me. Or maybe she was just too busy at her task.

I crouched beside her. The soil seeped through my skirt.

"Hi, Miss Wendy." She turned to face me, her bright face flecked with dirt. The ends of her braids were darkened with mud.

"You should be asleep. What are you doing out here so early this morning?"

A tiny palm opened, revealing a bright white bird skull, delicate as fine lacework. Its hollow eyes were fixed on nothing and everything.

"Planting this," Agnes said, sounding very proud of herself.

"Planting?" I laughed, both curious and confused. "My dear, seeds are planted. Not bones."

"No," she said quite sure of herself. "This will sprout up. Bones are like seeds. If you bury them, they'll grow."

"Agnes," I said gently, "where did you learn that?"

She didn't pause her work. Instead, she dropped the bird skull into the hole she'd made. Slowly she began scooping up dirt from the mound and sprinkling it atop.

She looked up at me, eyes wide and unblinking. "From the boy in my dream."

"A boy in your dream," I repeated.

I turned back and looked at the timeworn manor, its stone walls fading into the morning mist.

"One of the children here?" I asked, thinking that's what she'd meant.

A smile formed on her lips. With the bird skull now covered, she pressed her hand on top of the mound. A final flourish, as if to say, *all done.*

"No, someone I'd never seen before."

"Miss Wendy?"

I stood up and brushed dirt away from my hands.

Rosie stood at the entrance, her apron flaring in the cold air. "Miss Eleanor would like to see you upstairs."

I nodded. "On our way." I extended a hand for Agnes. "Come along now."

She told me how she'd like to come back tomorrow morning and check if the bird skull had sprouted. I just nodded and continued listening to her, because that's what adults should do, listen to the stories that children tell.

It was then that I heard a great caw. My body flinched. The call of those birds felt like a strike, and no matter how often I heard them, their call was always a terror. I looked behind my shoulders and watched as it swooped low and landed on a branch just above Agnes's bird skull.

* * *

Miss Eleanor stood in the doorway.

As always, she was wearing black from collar to cuff. Her husband had died so long ago, leaving her this huge home. She grew lonely here. For some time it was just her and Rosie, the cook; Lucy and Hannah, who helped with the household duties; and Samuel, who maintained the property. She wanted life in this house, and so she opened the doors to children who had nowhere to go and whom nobody wanted.

The October sun caught the silver edges of her brooch, and for an instant when she angled her face, she looked less like a woman in her sixties and more like some sort of eternal magical creature.

I stifled a laugh, but as always, she spotted my mind as it raced to create a story.

"What's that?"

I cleared my throat. "Nothing, I just . . ."

The apartment was all warm wood and afternoon light. I crossed to the window seat and lowered myself there.

"Many will continue to arrive here over the course of the war, in different ways, for different reasons. Hunger. Loss of a parent. We'll make room for as many as we can." Her voice quieted.

I nodded. I suppose she stood at the doorway to give me a moment to imagine what this space would feel like if I made it my own.

The noises below grew as the children were awakened, gathering their things for the day. With their voices came the clamoring of feet and shouts:

"Who's got my socks?"

"Stop tugging at my hair ribbon, Beatrice!"

"Miss Lucy, I can't find my jumper."

The house came alive with the sound of children and the smells of breakfast. From the kitchen downstairs emerged the scent of porridge and cinnamon. I'd meet them soon in the classroom for their lessons.

Eleanor took a step forward and kept talking.

I shifted in the seat, my fingers brushing the worn leather strap of my satchel where it hung at my side. My journal sat inside. Just feeling its weight steadied me. Some people clutch rosaries or talismans for protection. I clutched paper.

The garden shimmered in autumn colors. Trees shrugged off gold and copper leaves, and for a moment I just let myself breathe. My fingers found the window latch before I decided to check it. *Locked*. Good. I pressed my palm to the glass and focused my attention on the garden below.

"Willie, you're going to hurt yourself!" Lucy said below.

I looked to the opened door.

A loud thud rattled the house. Shrieks, followed by laughter.

I stood. My satchel tumbled, sending all its contents spilling out. Books, chalk, my pencil case, all scattered across the floor.

Rosie called from downstairs. "It's just Willie jumping from the stairs again."

"That child," Eleanor muttered.

I crouched, gathering my things. "He's quite spirited, that boy," I said.

Noise swelled again from downstairs. I pictured Rosie as she herded the children toward the dining room.

Soon came the faint clatter of spoons against bowls and children's chatter, bits of dreams recalled, and sightings of rabbits spotted in the garden from the windows.

Yes, little ones arrived here carrying grief. Many cried for parents and siblings who could no longer care for them, or who no longer existed. But it was moments like these, the joyful chaos, in which I found delight. They all sounded as they should, like happy little children.

"Well," Eleanor said. "What do you think?"

"It's a generous offer."

My house was gray and silent. It was a home where laughter had lived at one time. Today, however, it felt more like a mausoleum. Yet I felt bound there, a guardian to a room I believed should be kept locked forever.

Eleanor's tone softened. "Take the time you need to consider," she said. "But we will need you here, Wendy. The children will need you here. All of us must prepare for the changes of the coming months."

She was right.

The war crept closer each day. More children would arrive at our door. Small faces stunned and silent. They'd ask when Mummy and Daddy were coming back. And I would have no answer except to say that they were safe here with us at Marigold House.

Something shifted then, in the light. A streak of shadow—no, not a streak. A shape. Moving wrong. Shadows don't move against their source.

I turned back to the window. A flicker drew my gaze upward. My stomach dropped. Against the dull gray, a bird. A crow. Another one. I said it aloud. "A crow." Not quite believing myself.

My fingers had already found the fabric of my wool skirt, digging into it. Twelve years of telling myself they were just birds was a very long time.

Eleanor's voice came behind me. "It can't hurt you."

"I know," I said.

That Wendy Darling with such fancies in her head.

* * *

It was there in my past, further back than That Place. The fear of crows. Flapping its wings. All my brothers could do was stare.

I ran. My shoes slipped in the wet grass until I came upon a giant tree. Its bark was slick and sticky with sap, but I climbed.

My brothers vanished through the garden gate, calling for Mother.

I climbed onto a sturdy branch, my whole body shaking, the tree shaking with me.

It landed right beside me. I remember how its talons curled around the bark. Sharp claws. Its feathers gleamed blue-black. It smelled of rain and dirt, and something else.

The crow tilted its head, moving an inch toward me. Inspecting me. Gathering me in with its shiny black marble eyes.

"Get out of here, you stupid bird!" In the depths of its eye I saw something behind me stir. A shadow. A boy's silhouette.

I gasped but was too afraid to look behind me.

The crow opened its mouth, and a whisper followed.

Wendy . . .

Its breath was so cold it felt like ice against my skin.

I gripped the bark, so scared to fall. The crow moved closer.

Come with me, Wendy. He's waiting, it said, though its beak hadn't opened again.

Mother's voice reached me and I exhaled relief. "Wendy! Get down here. It's only a bird. Just shoo it away!"

The crow jerked its head toward the sound of my mother. And then it extended its wings and was gone.

I scrambled down the trunk, slipping on the last branch, falling, stumbling, running into my mother's arms.

Even as she held me, and even as I cried, I still felt the cold breath of that black bird on my cheek. Sometimes I still feel it.

* * *

"Wendy?" Eleanor's voice drew me back.

"The bird's gone," I said.

My shadow seemed to be missing in the reflection of the glass.

"This entire flat would be yours," Eleanor said.

High plaster ceilings. Rich wood molding with detailed carvings, leaves and berries and pinecones. Light loved this room. It poured in through the windows in soft ribbons.

My gaze drifted to another window latch.

A lot of my time at Marigold House was spent checking and rechecking to make sure the windows were locked. There were those narrow windows in the hall. The arched panes in the classroom. The stained glass in the chapel. Each window was an opening. Each window could become a lifetime wound, so each window must always be shut and latched.

"You must start thinking of yourself," Eleanor said.

"I'm not sure if I know how."

"You can't sit in that house alone every night for the rest of your life, especially when we all want you here."

In the garden below, something shifted. A shock of color. A lavender blur caught in the blackberry thorn.

"Are any of the children missing a blanket?"

Eleanor's brow lifted. "No," she said. "None that I recall."

Her eyes followed mine. When she spotted it, she gasped. Without another word, she turned, out the door and down the stairs. Her heels echoing down the halls.

I followed.

The hallway carried the smell of fresh bread and soap and a faint hint of coal dust.

Downstairs, breakfast continued: spoons clinking, a kettle screeching from the kitchen, and children's voices rising and crashing against one another like waves.

We reached the back door. Eleanor pulled it open. Bitter morning air rushed in. She looked down.

A wicker basket sat on the step. Inside, a baby, pale, perfect, and damp. And yet, even with the cold, wet air, she slept peacefully.

Eleanor's voice fell to a whisper. "They all come in different ways."

My palm touched the child's cheek. "She's so cold." I picked her up and wrapped my scarf around her, waiting for a cry that didn't come. She felt good in my arms, my body remembering the rhythm of rocking a sleeping infant. I had rocked so many here when they were much smaller.

"Why isn't she crying?"

"She'll wake up soon, I'm sure." Eleanor stepped past me into the garden and crossed over to the blackberry bushes. She returned with the lavender blanket in her hands. "Thank goodness the fairies didn't take her," she said.

I wondered if it was a joke, but I remained silent.

Rosie appeared, her apron dusted with flour and her dark hair slipping from its pins. "My goodness, look at this sleeping beauty," she said, taking the baby from my arms.

Samuel appeared, standing outside beside Miss Eleanor. He grasped at his head in a panic, as if he were the one to have left the baby out there.

"I . . . I didn't hear a thing," he stammered. His eyes wide with awe and guilt and shock. "Is she all right?"

Rosie smiled. "She's fine," she said, brushing her nose against the infant's brow. "Just cold."

The baby stirred, a tiny fist breaking free from the folds. Her face tightened, and then she unleashed a glorious cry.

Samuel blinked, then let out a short, surprised huff of laughter. "I'll get back to it then."

"Oh, you poor darling," Rosie said, rocking her gently.

Relief coursed through me.

Every child who came to Marigold House carried a mystery. Some arrived without names. Others without memories. Each one had questions.

In all of my years, only one set of parents—mine—had ever returned to reclaim a child.

"I wish they would have knocked, whoever left her, but we found her and she's well. That's what matters. We'll call the doctor to pay her a visit, make sure she's all right, and she'll be staying with us," Eleanor said.

Rosie opened her mouth to say something else, but then—

Glass shattered.

We froze.

Eleanor's jaw tightened, a small tic flaring at her temple.

"I'll get it," I said, knowing it was a child who had gotten into something.

I stepped past Rosie.

Agnes stood near the pantry. At her feet lay a shattered jar. Honey pooled thick and golden around the shards. Her fingers glittered with it.

"Sorry, Miss Wendy," she whispered. "I wasn't stealing. Only . . . Rosie said there was new bread cooling and I thought . . ."

Her wide eyes flicked toward the hallway where Rosie and Eleanor rushed off with the baby. "I heard Miss Eleanor talking about fairies. That true? Fairies take children away?"

"It's just an old superstition," I said. Not wanting to speak more of things that children should fear.

"I heard her crying," she whispered.

"The baby will stay with us," I said. "At least for a while."

Agnes bent to gather the shards, but I reached a hand out quickly, stopping her before she sliced her fingers. Her braids swung forward, brushing the sticky floor.

"Because of the war?"

I gave a nod.

"Harold said lots of soldiers stay where they die. I suppose that means they become bones right there. Maybe they'll sprout too, like the bird skull I buried. Bones planted in the garden."

I opened my mouth to correct her, to say that isn't how death works. One can't just plant the dead and expect them to revive. But that felt too cruel to tell a nine-year-old child with no family at this early hour. There was no need for her to know the reality of loss right now. So I remained silent.

The honey smell thickened. Sweet, then bitter. It coated the air. I carefully brushed the shards into a dustpan.

Agnes wrinkled her nose. "Why does it smell like that?"

"Not sure," I replied, knowing I'd smelled this smell long ago, but trying to brush that from my thoughts.

"Go wash your hands," I told her softly. "We'll be starting lessons soon."

"I'm sorry again, Miss Wendy," she said before darting away.

I poured warm water on the floor and scrubbed until the honey loosened and washed away.

Down the hall, I heard the baby crying and children squealing with delight to discover they were no longer the littlest ones here.

Then came a tap. Quick. Measured. Like the tip of a finger against glass.

My body went still before I could tell it to.

I turned around and faced the back door. Perhaps Samuel had locked himself out. Perhaps one of the children was playing a trick. If so, there would be a face behind that glass.

There was no face.

What was there was a faint handprint on the surface. Small, faint fingers spread wide.

I stared.

Wind. It's the wind. Wind can press against glass. No, wind couldn't leave handprints. Maybe it was a child's print from earlier I hadn't noticed.

"It's just wind," I said aloud. Or even a twig that'd come loose and crashed against the door.

But still, I should check, because what if it was a child outside? It was almost time for their lessons and they should be making their way to the classroom.

I eased the back door open to brush away whatever had struck it. Cold air rushed in. *See, the wind.* Nothing more.

I looked down and staggered back before my mind could catch up. My hip struck against the counter.

A black bird. Small. Still.

Its feathers were stiff with honey, gleaming like amber. Where its eyes should be, only two dark hollows stared back.

A cat. It must have been a cat. Cats kill birds. Cats eat the soft parts. And the honey, maybe they found it somewhere? Maybe the bird died elsewhere and the cat dragged it here.

Hollow bird eyes watched me attempt to explain it all away.

I looked past it, into the garden, searching for something ordinary. The oak tree, its familiar shadow stretching across the lawn. This existed here, in a world where things behaved as they should.

The shadow lengthened. I watched it bend. Stretch. And then . . . *no.*

It unhooked itself from the trunk. Peeled away from its source like the skin from some fruit. It moved with purpose, slinking across the lawn toward the blackberry bushes until it disappeared out of sight.

I slammed the door, locked it, and pressed my back against the wood. My heart beating as if trying to crack through my ribs.

That Wendy Darling . . .

Your daughter should be sent to the Bethlem asylum . . .

I didn't see that. I didn't see that. I didn't see any of that.

It returned.

Tap. Tap. Tap.

I covered my mouth with both hands, trapping the scream that had lived inside me for twelve years. A scream I didn't think I'd ever need again.

My hands shook. My legs shook. I squeezed my eyes shut.

No. No. No. No.

This isn't real. You're tired. You've been reading the newspapers and sleeping badly because of it.

The tapping stopped. Silence pressed against the door.

And then, slipping through the seam between wood and glass, a whisper.

Wendy.

I didn't answer. I wouldn't answer. But my shadow answered for me.

It stretched across the kitchen floor, and flickered once, like something that remembered what I had been trying all of these years to forget.

CHAPTER

2

MORNING LIGHT CUT across the floorboards, catching the chalk dust that never quite seemed to settle in this room. I stood at my desk, facing rows of empty chairs, the blackboard behind me. In minutes they'd all rush inside in a tangle of laughter and chatter.

To my right was the trouble with this classroom, a wall of windows that looked out over the lawn. Outside, a soft shimmer of fog slowly lifted from the landscape.

My feet carried me to the first window. They were locked when I checked before class and after class. I would do the same today as I would do tomorrow and so on.

I reached for the latch.

Press. No give. Then to the next. Press. No give.

Working my way down the row, I pressed my thumb against each latch, until every window had been checked.

All were locked, and so we were safe.

Returning to my desk I stared for a moment at Roger's pocket watch. It sat where I always kept it, beside the inkwell, its face cracked, but its hands still moving.

It didn't belong here, just like parts of me didn't belong here either. Still, here we were working.

The door burst open and children poured in, laughter splintering the quiet. I couldn't help a smile as each one of them tumbled in.

Some huddled around me on their way to their seats, like a flock of chickens. It was difficult to tell where one voice started and the other stopped. There were "Good mornings!" and observations about the weather (Too cold this morning!) and breakfast (Rosie baked orange scones for us!). Of course, there were childhood complaints (Percy pulled my hair at breakfast!).

I returned the good mornings, offered my own comments on the weather, told Percy to apologize to Mabel. He did. She responded by blowing a raspberry and turning her back on him.

"See, I tried!" he said.

"I did see," I said, trying not to laugh. I waved them to their desks. "Children, to your seats."

Carol flew in, braids swinging. "Wendy! Miss Wendy!"

Charles entered last, rubbing sleep from his eyes.

"Charles had a bad dream," Carol sang.

"You don't have to speak of it," I told her gently.

That was the wonder of the children, so eager to share what they noticed, no matter how small. Somewhere in growing up we lost that, or it was stolen from us.

Charles gave a stubborn shake of his head. "I did not!"

"Let's give him some room," I whispered to Carol.

A wail rang from the corridor. The new baby making herself known.

"The baby!" Priscilla shouted, the rest of them showing interest and whispering about our new visitor.

"Yes," I lifted a hand to settle them.

Once their excitement faded, we began as we always did, with a story.

I reached for *The Water Babies*, then paused my fingers on the spine. A story about children who slip beneath the surface of the world and become something else.

It was the only thing I'd been brave enough to ask for the day my parents brought me here.

* * *

Eleanor's office had smelled of lemon and scrubbed wood. Portraits lined the walls: class photographs of children in neat rows and stiff collars. Their eyes wide. I sat beneath their images. My hands folded in my lap listening to the remaining years of my childhood be negotiated.

"Marigold House is better than St. Lawrence's Hospital," Father had said.

"Indeed," Eleanor agreed. "St. Lawrence's is also better than Bethlem."

Mother made a small, strangled sound.

"Wendy spent a week at Bethlem," Eleanor continued. "Constable Finch informed me."

"It was terrible," Father added. "Awful. A tomb for the mad."

But none of them knew how awful. Thin cotton dress. Cold stone floors. Crying and howling through the night. In the mornings I'd wake to find insects nesting in my hair. I spent my hours staring up at a slit of sky, a window so high up no one could reach it. I spoke to it anyway, as though I were speaking to him.

Eleanor leaned forward. "She spoke of missing children. Murdered children."

Father said nothing. Mother covered her face with her hands.

"Well." Eleanor turned to me at last. "What did you see, Miss Wendy?"

Father's fingers rose, a warning, but no words came.

Constable Finch. The doctors. The nurses. All of them told me to stop speaking about what I had seen. They said I would get in trouble. I would be locked away forever. I was a liar. I was bad. I had taken my brothers away. Where were the other missing boys? What had I done to them? I'd sit there through all of it, the scolding, the threats, and I'd shut them all out of my head. My eyes would drift to those high windows and my mind drift away to that faraway place. To him and me lying on the deck of that great ship. Hand in hand. Watching the moon in silence.

"Well, go on," Eleanor said.

I didn't take my eyes off Father, afraid I'd say the wrong thing. I didn't say much. "A treehouse. Children. Boys. Many of them."

"Go on."

"A black rock. The ocean. A forest."

"And what did you do there?"

"I read to the children at night."

Something shifted in Eleanor's expression.

"Then you'll help in the classroom," she said. "We also have a library. You can tend to that as well."

"If I'm to help . . ." I hesitated. "May I propose something?"

She smiled. "Go on."

"Can I start each class with reading a story to the students?"

Eleanor looked from Mother and Father and then back to me. "Of course."

She stood. The negotiation complete. "Mr. and Mrs. Darling, you may visit on Sundays."

They agreed under their breath, a promise all of us knew they'd never keep.

* * *

I cracked open the cover of the book, the memory dissolving like fog in morning light. Twenty children watched me from their desks. *Here. Now. Safe.* All of us needing each other. A family thrown together by circumstances none of us could really control.

I leaned against my desk and read.

I hadn't finished the first page when I noticed Frederick. His eyes fixed on something beyond the glass.

"Frederick," I said.

He didn't turn.

"Frederick."

"There was a man outside. He's gone now."

My hands tightened on the book before I could stop them. I crossed to his desk slowly and followed his gaze to the line of trees beyond the fence.

Nothing.

Of course it was nothing. Frederick had a fantastical imagination, much like the others.

"All right, children, let's get back to our story." But as I spoke, the light outside dulled. Fog thickened against the glass, and the windows became mirrors, reflecting the classroom back at us. The children and me.

I turned away from it.

"I saw him too!" George said.

Two children now. Two children seeing the same thing. It must have just been our reflection they were seeing.

"I'm sure you did," I said, entertaining their imaginations. "But he is out there and we are in here."

I glanced at Roger's pocket watch on my desk.

"Time for arithmetic," I said, hoping that moving on to the next subject would keep them focused.

"He's there!" Grace jumped to her feet, finger pointing at the window.

"Grace, please sit."

She rushed to the glass and waved. "Hello, man!"

Three children. All seeing the same thing. I should look again, but I don't want to. If I looked, I might see something. Their imagination, Wendy. It's just their imagination.

"Grace." My voice came out sharper than I'd intended. "Back to your seat. All of you."

Chairs skidded. Whispers scattered.

I opened *Longman's School Arithmetic* and approached the blackboard. The chalk was cold in my hand. The white lines squeaked as I wrote.

If a baker has twelve loaves and sells seven, how many remain?

Time settled after that.

Arithmetic bled into science, science into history, history into another reading. By late morning the children grew restless like they always do. Feet tapped. Pencils rolled. Whispers swelled as they made plans for which games they would play during break.

"Very well," I said. "Rosie isn't quite ready for you, so five minutes free time here, and then off to lunch when she collects you."

They erupted. Desks scraped against the floor. Chairs sighed. Groups gathered in bright pockets throughout the classroom.

A flutter of girls approached, and I could tell they were plotting.

Tom barreled forward, nearly colliding with my desk.

"I'll clear the board!" he announced, though everyone knew Tom enjoyed making a mess at the blackboard, which is why no one ever fought him for the duty.

Lillian placed her hands on my sleeve. "Miss Wendy, you have to cover your eyes."

"I have to?" I asked. "Well, all right then."

I covered my eyes, and immediately there was an eruption of giggles. "Don't make me regret this."

More giggles.

"You won't!" Lillian said.

"No peeking!" another one shouted.

"I'm not."

And then, the erasers began.

smack

A pause.

smack

Sharper this time.

Behind my closed eyes I pictured pale clouds of chalk dust swirling around Tom's hands.

"Humpty Dumpty sat on a wall," he recited between blows. "Humpty Dumpty had a great fall. All the king's horses and all the king's men, couldn't put Humpty together again."

"Open your eyes, Miss Wendy," Lillian said.

I lowered my hands.

Lillian stood before me, holding my hat as if unveiling a treasure. A new green ribbon circled the brim.

"It's beautiful," I said.

Head nodded. Cheeks bloomed pink.

Tom stepped forward, dust covering his hands.

"My mother used to wear a feather in her hat," he declared. "I saw a great big pile of them this morning. Big black ones. I'll bring you one. They sparkle."

I opened my mouth to say something, but I didn't quite know what to say other than "Thank you."

I thought of Agnes burying the bird skull early this morning. The dead black bird outside the kitchen door. *It's a cat, Wendy.* A cat prowling the grounds, hunting birds. That's all.

A bell rang from the hallway. Rosie appeared at the door. "Come now, lunch."

Voices merged, bright and cheerful.

I stood beside my desk and counted them off as they filed past.

"Florence. George. Harold. Lillian. William. Tom. Frederick. Agnes. David. Elsie. Edgar. Percy. Mabel. Henry. Grace. Stanley. May. Albert. Gladys . . ."

The room quieted as other parts of the house grew louder. Pots clattering in the kitchen. Distant footsteps. More children's chatter. One name was left to be called.

When I turned, I found Willie still seated. Shoulders hunched.

"What's the matter? Worried Rosie's still cross with you for leaping from the stairs?"

He shrugged.

Oh dear. He is upset about something.

I crossed over and took a seat beside him. The chair creaked beneath me. I noticed fresh initials gouged into the desk. I chose to ignore them, as I did small rebellions. Scolding children only made for unhappy adults.

"My father said he'd write," Willie muttered. "It's been three weeks since he left for Belgium."

I drew a deep breath. "I'm sure he meant to." But my heart ached with a truth I didn't want to think about.

Willie sniffled, rubbed his sleeve under his nose. "I even miss the twins, my baby sisters."

"Your mother must speak of you to them all of the time."

His chin trembled. "Mum said there wasn't enough food for all of us after Father left to fight."

And that's why Willie came to us two months ago.

"We'll keep you fed and safe. That's my promise."

He gave a small nod. "I'm twelve. I hear boys go to war at fourteen. That's not far off."

I cleared my throat. "Let's hope this terrible business is over by then."

"Why don't you live here, Miss Wendy?"

My mouth opened before I could think. "I used to."

His eyes lifted. Curious. "You did?"

"A long time ago."

"Why don't you now?"

I looked around the classroom. Strange to think I'd been Willie's age when I first came here. I'd spent hours in this room, reading, writing stories, and staring out that window.

"I grew up," I said.

That was partly true.

He swallowed. "I haven't been sleeping well," he whispered. "Lots of noises at night."

I lowered my voice. A secret between us. "I get frightened at night too. I sleep with the lamps on."

His eyes widened. "You do?"

"Always."

Light from the window shivered. For the briefest moment, I thought I heard it again, that faint, deliberate tap from the kitchen this morning.

"Told you," Willie murmured. "There's always funny noises around here."

"We mustn't give things that frighten us too much power," I said.

"What do you mean?" His small brows knitted together.

I glanced at the trembling window. "Try your best to ignore the scary thing."

Above us, a crash. I flinched.

Willie startled upright. "Wasn't me!"

Another sound followed. I glanced toward the ceiling. Something scraped above. Quick. Skittering. Beneath it, the unmistakable flutter of wings.

I rose at once, heart knocking against my ribs. I kept my voice steady, because that's what adults are supposed to do in times like these, act brave for the little ones.

"Come now. Let's get you to Rosie. Then I'll see to whatever that is."

We hurry down the corridor. The din grew louder with every step, clattering spoons, shrill giggles, the familiar chaos of children eating.

Inside the dining room, it seemed like none of them heard the commotion above.

"Wasn't me," Willie said to Rosie.

She gathered him in her arms. "Oh, I know it wasn't you, love." She smoothed his hair.

"What do you think that was?" I asked quietly.

Rosie's brow tightened. "Not sure at all."

I nodded and began to cross the room, but something flickered at the edge of my sight. A thin streak. Black. A shadow slithering across the far wall.

I scanned the room. Children seated. Bowls in front of them. Spoons in hands. No one standing to cast such a shape.

When I looked back, the dark shape was gone. A trick of the gaslight, surely.

Then I heard something rise from the noise of children eating. A low murmur threading between the clinking of cutlery and laughter.

A chant.

I paused. Listened.

The air shifted. Warmer. Thicker.

The voices grew clearer. Several children chanting in unison. Singsong and hollow:

And all alone by myself I go,
With none to tell me what to do,
All alone beside the stream,
Into the Land of Nod I dream.

For an instant, I felt it again, that iced breath on my cheek from that raven so long ago.

I didn't teach them that song. In fact, I don't even know where any of them had learned that poem. It seemed much too adult for children. Maybe one of the older ones had heard it at home. Memorized it and taught the others?

"Who taught you that poem?"

They burst into laughter.

"The Land of Nod," by Robert Louis Stevenson. The same man who wrote about pirates and buried treasure and maps. Yet, he'd also written that poem, "The Land of Nod," about the places children travel to in dreams.

Across the table, Agnes stared at me. Wide-eyed. Stunned. As if she'd woken up from a dream. She leaned close to Willie and whispered something, her hand shielding her lips.

"What is it?" I pressed.

Agnes hesitated. "He told us not to tell."

He.

Before I could ask, another crash echoed from above. Samuel shouting. Glass shattering, as though being swept into a bucket.

My breath caught. A warning screamed through me.

A window.

I turned and charged toward the stairs. The stairs groaned beneath my feet as I climbed.

I reached the second floor, library to my left, as well as the boys' quarters. Girls' quarters to my right.

"Samuel?" My voice came out breathless.

"Upstairs," he called back. Heavy. Unsettled.

Upstairs. Where Eleanor had asked me to move into this morning. I hesitated, not wanting to climb farther, but still, I did.

Eleanor inside the doorway of what would be my new bedroom. She held a handkerchief to her nose, knuckles white, shoulders trembling.

Samuel stood in the center of the room, pail in one hand, mop in the other. Motionless. As though afraid to take another step.

The window gaped like a broken mouth.

Shards of glass were strewn across the floor, glittering red.

Black feathers clung to the baseboards in sodden clumps.

And, on the far wall, a smear of blood, dragged downward in an uneven line. Thick at the top. Thin as a thread at the bottom.

I couldn't move.

A bird. A bird had flown into the window, punched through the glass and slammed into the wall. That was the only explanation. Birds did this sometimes. That's what Eleanor said.

But I had never seen a bird punch through the window like this.

My throat closed around a cry I couldn't find.

Eleanor reached for me with a trembling hand. "We're safe, Wendy. Please don't tell the children."

I nodded, but my gaze stayed fixed on the shattered window.

Cold wind pressed through the jagged frame, stirring a single feather near my boot.

We descended together.

My feet obeyed, but part of me remained in that room, staring at that window, wondering what else could come through it.

By the second landing, my breath had steadied. My hands had not. My fingers trembled in the folds of my skirt, my mind still assembling that image: bloodstained feathers, a twisted thing of shredded flesh crumbled in the corner of the room.

"When I first came here as a child," I murmured half to myself, "a bird did this. Flew straight into the window. You said . . ."

"Mistaking glass for sky," Eleanor finished.

The memory sharpens.

Nighttime. A dull thud. A burst of feathers. And me, racing barefoot through the halls, until I reached Eleanor. Her arms open to receive me.

"He's coming to get me!"

"No one's coming to get you," she'd reassured.

I slept in a cot in the library closet for the rest of my time here. For years, I was too afraid to sleep in a room with windows.

"They're just restless things," Eleanor said now, though I wasn't sure if she meant the birds or the memories.

"How does a bird do that?"

At the door, Eleanor studied me. "It's just a terrible accident."

"Just like in the book? A large black crow?"

Eleanor pushed open the door to her office. "That . . ." She paused. "That was not an accident." Her voice dropped. "And you must learn to stop living in the past."

I followed her inside. "This morning, I found Agnes burying a bird skull beneath the elm tree."

"Childhood games," Eleanor said, lowering herself into the chair behind her desk. She cleared her throat. "Are you still certain about the hospital?"

"Yes."

Yes, because I knew what it was to return from a foreign place broken in ways no one could see. And maybe I could provide some small comfort because I understood, in my own way, what they must be going through.

* * *

The afternoon's arithmetic lesson was meant to be easy. Something steady before the church bells began again, tolling for boys sent off to war.

I drew neat columns across the blackboard and then faced the room.

Rows of bowed heads bent. Pencils whispering in small, perfect unison. The rhythm soothed me, finally, something ordinary after a day streaked in darkness.

Except for Willie, who held a pen instead.

He sat crooked in his seat, shoulders hunched, as if trying to fold himself into the desk. His tongue pressed at the corner of his mouth, deep in concentration. Not on arithmetic. On a scrap of paper.

"Willie," I said, approaching. "Numbers, not pictures." Dried ink speckled his fingers.

I expected the unusual, houses, clouds, the wanderings of a child's mind. But the image stopped me midstep.

A boy with wings. Not white. Black and jointed, like an insect's. And the face, all sharp angles, as if carved with a knife rather than drawn with ink.

Willie's pen trembled, leaving a dark stream along the paper's edge.

"Who is he?" I asked.

Willie looked up. His brown eyes were solemn. Steady. "He told me not to say."

The same words Agnes had used.

I glanced across the room and found her watching us through the curtain of her golden hair. Her pencil hovered midair.

"Your numbers, Agnes."

Her eyes returned to the page.

A draft slipped beneath the window. Then a metallic sigh, followed by a click. The upper sash dropped several inches on its own.

Every eye in the room fixed on the window.

A single feather drifted through the gap. Black. It wavered in the air before landing on my lesson book.

Lillian placed a hand over her mouth, stifling a laugh.

My breath snagged.

What is happening?

My thoughts stumbled over themselves. Bird skulls. A dead bird outside the kitchen door. A bird crashing through an upstairs window. Now this.

I crossed to the window and shut it, fastening the latch until the metal bit into my thumb.

When I reached for the feather, it felt like ice between my fingers. I set the feather on my desk. I would deal with it later.

"Eyes on your work," I said.

Chairs shifted. Creaked.

The silver pocket watch at my desk clicked steadily away.

Beyond the glass, fog thickened, swallowing the lawn, the brick fence, all of London.

I turned to the blackboard and pressed a piece of chalk against the surface. A rasp. Once. Twice. Then I stopped.

A sound bled through the wall. Not the rush of wind. A whisper. A child's voice, lilting and sure:

He can fly.

I glanced over my shoulder.

Every head remained bowed. Every pencil midstroke. The voice hadn't come from any of them. It came from somewhere else.

The sound coiled through me, familiar as an old dream clawing its way up from the dark. I thought of his voice. That voice in the trees. That voice that promised me he'd always hold on to me, and he'd never let me fall. That voice. The very well who'd later commanded me to jump.

"Books away," I managed. The words came out hollow. "Early recess."

The children bolted for the door without asking why. Their laughter too high. Too sudden.

When they were gone, the quiet returned. Thick. Sentient.

Fog smothered the windows, swirling in ribbons.

The chalk in my hand split between my fingers. I opened my palm. White dust collected along my lifeline.

Then, a tap.

Soft. Deliberate.

Something was moving behind the blackboard. Tapping to gain my attention. But behind this wall there was nothing. Only brick, and then outside.

A sound unfurled, slow, rhythmic. The scrap and drag of wings against wood. Not frantic. Not trapped. Testing its boundaries. Learning its limits.

I stepped back. My heel skidded on the floorboards. My heart hammered against my ribs.

Another flutter. Then a tremor.

From inside the wall came a slow, rhythmic hum. A crystalline note, deep beneath the skin of the house. The beginning of a song I thought I'd forgotten long ago.

The house exhaled.

The blackboard rippled, its surface disturbed like a dark pool struck by a stone.

I backed toward the doorway, both hands pressed to my chest, as if commanding my heart to stay where it belonged.

Behind the wall, the sound intensified. Wings gathering. Stretching. Trying. Testing. Remembering how to fly.

The fog erased the world beyond.

And then, as quickly as they had begun, the noises ceased. I looked toward my desk, expecting to see the black feather. It was gone.

What remained was stranger. A thin scatter of tiny, sharp-edged glints, like powdered glass. They caught the dim light in quick silver flashes.

I stepped closer. Slowly. Reached out my hand.

Before my fingers could touch it, the shimmer shivered, dimmed, and slipped away, as though absorbed into the wood.

In its wake, the desk pulsed once. Faint as a heartbeat.

I pulled my hand back as if burned.

He was here. Not yet in the room. But close. Closer than he'd been in twelve years.

CHAPTER

3

CHIMNEYS EXHALED RIBBONS of smoke.

It was early afternoon and the streets were full of motorcars and people making their way home for supper. Women pushed well-bundled babies in prams. Men in dark coats and hats hurried along the pavement, evening paper tucked beneath their arms.

Somewhere, behind a shutter, a cough broke loose and lingered.

I pulled my hat lower on my head, fighting against the wind. The hem of my gray coat snapped like a restless flag. I didn't want to be late on my first day of volunteering at the hospital, so I rushed along, my lace-up boots striking the stones in a measured rhythm, but then I stopped. A crowd formed around the newsstand.

Men in heavy overcoats, women in plain wool, heads lowered, reading the afternoon's headline. Coins clinked together like bones.

My gloved fingers adjusted the strap of my satchel, and I pretended not to read what I was already reading.

The Times, London—16 October 1914

H.M.S. THORNLEIGH—OVER 500 LIVES LOST

News has reached the Admiralty that His Majesty's Ship *Thornleigh*, commanded by Captain Alistair M. Fenton, was struck yesterday afternoon by a torpedo from an enemy submarine while engaged in patrol duties off the coast of Aberdeen.

The vessel foundered within minutes. Rescue efforts by accompanying ships succeeded in saving only a small number of the crew. More than five hundred officers and men are feared lost.

Survivors speak of a sudden explosion, a great rush of water, and the ship listing heavily before slipping beneath the surface. Many had no time to don lifebelts.

The Admiralty expresses profound regret at this tragic loss of life and extends sympathy to the families of those who served.

No final signals were received before the ship went down.

Five hundred. I didn't even want to imagine it. A blast. Then bodies all lost at sea.

"Died so far from home," a woman whispered near the front of the line. "For what?"

The newsman nodded once. His fingers were blackened with ink, his eyes rimmed red. "Power," he muttered, to no one and everyone. "Little boys and men playing at it."

Boys. Men. Power

Boys and men, all seeking it. All wanting to wield control, at the cost of another.

And then, quietly, from somewhere deeper than thought, his voice rang in my head. Not aloud. Not here.

It had been years since I'd heard that sound so clearly.

You'll never grow up. You'll never grow old. You'll never die.

What about me? I heard my younger self ask.

Forever, he answered. Sweet as poison. You and me. Together forever.

The world blurred, as if I were seeing everything standing behind a waterfall. The street. Faces. Motorcars.

"Paper, miss?" The newsman's voice pulled me back into the cold.

London exhaled.

The omnibus engine sputtered. Boots clattered on the wet stone. People pressed close to the newsstand as though closeness to a stranger in this cold might offer some comfort from the horror in the ink.

Newspapers rustled in shaky hands. Every so often, a gasp emerged from someone who'd just read the headline.

"*Thornleigh* went down in minutes," a man murmured, collar pulled high. "Hit by a U-boat. Straight through her side."

"They died heroes!" someone shouted. A few others cheered.

A woman in a plum-colored hat spoke quietly. "My brother enlisted in August. Wrote to say it'd all be over by Christmas." Her chin quivered. "They all say that."

Someone behind her added, "Over a million men have signed up already. Clerks. Bakers. Can't walk down the Strand without seeing khaki."

"France. Belgium. Serbia. Russia." An older man with thick spectacles shook his head, his voice faltered. "Madness. All of it. Now sending boys off to drown."

"Miss? The paper?"

"No, thank you," I said. "I'm going to the hospital. To volunteer. I don't want to risk any of them seeing the news, in case they haven't heard it yet." I didn't want to drag in bad news on my first day with them.

The newsman looked up, his large coat threadbare at the seams.

"A teacher, then?" he guessed. "A kind voice will be welcomed in the wards."

I nodded. "I hope so."

He hesitated. His eyes narrowed, as if for a moment there was a second of recognition. I'm sure he'd seen my face in print many years ago, before our stories were changed by someone else into innocent children's tales.

As I turned again, the paper in his hand caught the wind. The headline twisted, warping as the sheet bent, letters slanting into a single word.

LOST.

Death was swirling all around us, closer than any of us had imagined. I wondered if that's why memories were stirring up. And I wondered if that explained the birds and the blackboard today.

Even if he was close, I wanted to believe that he could not reach me. There were rules. Old ones. Older than him. Older than stories told to frighten children.

There were rules even he had to obey.

Roger only knew a few of the rules, the ones he shared with me, but he was sure there were others. Everything Roger had told me lived in my journal, between its worn covers and ink-blotted pages. In the lines I'd written as a girl trying to survive that place.

Some words in my journal weren't just warnings. They were instructions. And they might be exactly what I'd need to stay alive.

* * *

The air in the hospital was thick with grief.

A nurse sat at the front desk, typing away quickly. Golden curls peeked out from beneath her cap.

She didn't look up when I said hello. She didn't even look up when I said good afternoon.

I glanced down at my boots, the edges covered in grime from the city streets.

"It's my first day," I forced myself to say, barely able to hear myself above the machine's percussion.

"Uniforms, second door on the left," she said, eyes fixed on the page in front of her.

"I'm not a nurse," I said.

The clacking stopped. The ribbon wheel spun once, then faltered. She peered over her wire rims. Her nostrils flared. "What are you, then?"

My fingers searched for the weight of the books in my satchel. Comfort. I pictured each of them: *Alice, Treasure Island, Grimm's Fairy Tales*, tucked close to my journal.

"I'm a volunteer," I said. "Here to read to the soldiers."

It had been Beatrice's idea. Her letter arrived one dreary morning.

They need voices, Wendy. Gentle ones. Someone to remind them the world still tells stories that have happy endings.

She'd arranged everything. I agreed without hesitation, because I believed my presence could make a difference. Perhaps there was an edge of guilt to it too. The thought of those injured men made me think of my own boys from long ago. If I could not bring my boys back, then maybe I could keep others from vanishing.

For an instant, I saw their faces again. Round cheeks. Eyes always set in the direction of adventure. I had once sworn to protect them all.

I failed.

The woman's mouth pressed into a thin line. "One came in this morning missing an arm and a leg. For three days he lay buried beneath a pile of bodies. What fairy tale will keep him from screaming at night?"

Her words struck something buried inside of me. I knew the small violences of a childhood gone wrong. Scrapes, cuts, gashes. I knew deeper wounds too, ones that demanded bandages tied in haste, tourniquets pulled tight to keep the bleeding, fevers and chills and rattled bones.

And I knew the stillness of a small hand in my own that would never grow any larger.

I folded my arms around my waist, digging into my coat to keep myself from coming undone.

"A story doesn't sew flesh," I said quietly. "But it reminds us of what it means to live."

The woman's expression softened. Barely. Then the typewriter began again, its teeth biting into the stillness between us.

She paused, lifted the telephone receiver, and pressed a hand over the mouthpiece. "Who are you here to see?"

"Beatrice," I said.

Her gaze swept over me. Deliberate and unimpressed. "Of course it's Beatrice," she mumbled.

She removed her hand and spoke into the line, her tone flat. "Beatrice to the front." She set the receiver down and returned to the typewriter.

Beatrice burst through the doorway, a sparkling warmth shining in a cold room. Arms outstretched, eyes shimmering. Her bright red curls cascaded from beneath her nurse's cap.

"Finally," she sang. "My beautiful darling."

She folded me into her arms. Her scent, rosewater and lavender, pulled me back into childhood. The world had changed, but she still smelled like slow summer days gathering bluebells and sneaking into the pantry to stuff our pockets with Rosie's tea biscuits.

"Just look at you," she said, holding me at arm's length. "Lovely as ever. The boys are going to love you."

She flashed a smile at the secretary. Beatrice was always all sweet on the surface and a fire beneath. "Margaret, did you know Wendy's going to be a famous writer one day?"

"Beatrice," I said, signaling her to please not embarrass me on my first day.

She continued, basking in Margaret's frown. "My darling Wendy here used to keep us up half the night at Marigold House. Stories of dragons, silver tears, moons made of sugar, and boys who could—"

"Beatrice!"

The typewriter whirred to a stop. Margaret cleared her throat. This was certainly a woman who had forgotten long ago how to laugh.

Out, her eyes said.

Beatrice yanked my arm. "Move, before we get sentenced to laundry duty."

We dashed into the corridor, our muffled laughter ricocheting off tiled walls. For a moment, we were girls again.

In those days at Marigold House, Beatrice had been my greatest healer. Her laughter, her rebellion against conformity, hair pins and pinafores, etiquette and manners. She was the proof that life after what had happened was possible.

As girls we'd race across the lawn. Climb trees in trousers we'd swiped from the boys. All of it. All of her. She taught me that what adults said, what others thought, those were all barriers to our own happiness.

And now, giggling as we rushed past authority, I realized I was still living in someone else's prison. Still shaped by who everyone thought I was, and who they thought I should be.

As my heartbeat settled, the hospital came into focus.

Each corridor buzzed with urgency. Footsteps echoed on tiles. Women's voices demanded more supplies while men moaned and hollered. The force of their pain shocked my ears.

Stretchers rattled past. Nurses in white hurried past us with towels and trays piled high with bandages.

It had only been weeks since the war began, and already everything felt so different. A light above us pulsed with a steady beat as we approached.

"I . . ." I began but didn't know what to say. I reached for Beatrice's hand.

She looped her arm through mine. "I know," she said.

There was no need to say anything more. Schools and parish halls were already being gutted and remade into wards. More were coming. All of us knew.

"I'll never understand any of it. Killing each other. All for what?"

"Those who make the decisions aren't the ones immediately risking their lives for it. So they don't care. Control and power."

A stretcher passed, pushed by two men in white. I tried not to look, but my eyes found the shape beneath the sheet. It remained still.

"Thank you for being here," Beatrice said softly. She sighed, her gaze drifting toward a doorway where another stretcher disappeared. Another white sheet. Corners limp. "It never ends."

"I don't understand how you do this every day."

"If this is too much, I'll understand."

"No," I said. Otherwise, I'd be sitting at home, ruminating on all that had happened at Marigold House today.

"I've missed you, my darling," she said.

"Me too."

She paused. Turned fully toward me. Her hands settling on my shoulders. Her eyes scanning my face.

"What's wrong?"

"I'm fine." I lied.

But I knew she could feel the lie in my pulse spiking and the way my fingers twitched. We'd grown up inside the same house, breathing the same air, dreaming of skies that promised us a life we could live by our own terms. She'd seen this fear before, seen me seated at the edge of my bed at night staring at our window.

"What's happening?" she said, blowing a strand of hair away from her face.

I wanted to tell her everything. About the feather. The voice. The way shadows seemed to breathe. But I hadn't told her then, and I wouldn't now.

Instead, I reached for what felt safe. "Eleanor's offered me the flat upstairs," I said. "Head teacher."

Beatrice gasped. "Wendy, that's wonderful!"

"But my house."

Her tone shifted. "It's old. It needs repair. Plus, Wendy, you're there alone so much, when Eleanor and I'm sure all of the children want you there with them."

I knew it'd be wonderful to be there. I could read to them at night before bed. I could turn the lights off and wish them goodnight, but what if something that was searching for me in turn found one of the children?

"You're not going to take the flat, are you?"

"I'll think about it."

She exhaled. "Come. I've got someone waiting for you."

From somewhere ahead, a low moan rose. Then the rush of hurried footsteps, and voices cutting through the corridor, calling for help. A stretcher appeared. Empty. Its wheels rattling as two nurses pushed it past us.

We rounded the corner.

Rows of beds, iron-framed, tightly ordered.

Nurses drifted between cots, their aprons stiff, the red cross on their front.

A group of soldiers sat near the far wall. Their shirts hung open, revealing bruised ribs, soft hollows of scars. A geography of wounds.

Some leaned over a crate between them, playing cards fanned out in their hands. A card struck the makeshift table with a slap. One of them barked out a laugh.

As if sensing my intrusion, one of them looked up. Dark-haired. Eyes bright. He smiled and lifted a hand in greeting. The others exchanged glances, and soon all of them were looking my way.

My breath stuttered. Heat flashed. I tore my eyes away.

Beatrice noticed at once and rolled her eyes. "Oh, love. You look like a schoolgirl gawking at a Greek statue for the first time."

My stomach tightened. Heat rising to my cheeks.

"They won't bite," she said. "They can barely lift a spoon, much less anything else."

She put an arm around me and gave a wave to the men at cards, and we continued on.

A man with half his face bandaged blinked one uncovered eye as we approached. "Pretty ribbon," he murmured.

I touched the green bow on my hat, Lillian's, and thanked him. His lids sank shut, surrendering to the morphine, or to the memory of what had taken him apart.

We moved on.

"They don't all seem of age," I whispered.

"They lied," Beatrice breathed. "No one checked."

I looked at the rows of young men in cots. It seemed like what we were doing was dressing them up as soldiers, polishing their shoes, and then sending them off to die. And for those returned, they were riddled with wounds, their faces stamped with a look I knew too well. It was the look that stared back at me in mirrors.

At the far end of the ward, doctors in white coats stood in a huddle, heads bowed close. I wondered what they did beyond gather and converse. So far, I'd only seen women offering care. It was the nurses who dressed wounds, shaved faces still shaking with fear, whispered comfort into ears that might never hear kindness again.

Humpty Dumpty had a great fall.

I thought of Tom. The classroom. The sharp crack of erasers. I wondered what sounds these men heard in the fields at night. Cracks or booms? Maybe it was louder than thunder?

Beatrice's pace quickened.

"I don't know if I can get used to this," I said.

"You will. Or you'll leave. There's no in-between."

Everything I was seeing was so awful, but I wanted to help. I needed to. If I could just help someone feel not so alone in all of this then at least my time here would have mattered.

Our footsteps softened against the worn gray linoleum. A door waited ahead, its frosted glass glowing faintly.

"He's right in here," Beatrice said, turning the knob.

The door opened to a small room. A single bed. A lone occupant.

Beatrice leaned against the doorframe, arms crossed. "We usually reserve these rooms for officers, but he's special."

"What's wrong with him?"

"He won't wake up," she said.

Won't wake up . . .

"We check his pulse a few times each shift."

Unlike the others, he didn't seem to have any marks. No cuts. No scrapes. No scars.

"Handsome, right?"

And he was. Beautiful. As if Sleeping Beauty were a man. There was color to his cheeks, his lips slightly parted, his chest rising and falling in slow rhythm. He was alive. But he was somewhere else.

"We don't know his name. Where he came from. What unit he was with. Many of them get separated out there in the chaos of it all. He has no wound. No fever. He's just . . . asleep."

The room pressed in around me. Above the door, a clock jerked its brass hands forward. Each tick reminded me I would be alone with this stranger, and that terrible humming light, as soon as Beatrice left.

"I shaved his face this morning," she said. "It was nice. I could just chat away, and he listened the entire time."

I took the chair beside him. It creaked under my weight.

My fingers searched for the flap of my satchel. I looked inside, deciding which book to read. My fingers glided along the spines. I knew their stories and the challenges within.

Alice's Adventures in Wonderland. Poor Alice, dashing after a rabbit, conversing with a Mad Hatter, all in an attempt to try to make sense of a nonsensical world.

Treasure Island. Jim trying to survive pirates and betrayal, struggling to decide who he wanted to be amid adult corruption and adventure.

The Secret Garden. Dear Mary and her journey through trauma and isolation, grief and anger. Her work reviving that hidden garden mirrored what she needed most, to heal her inner world.

Strange seeing these titles now, away from a bookshelf, out in the world. Making sense in madness. Navigating betrayal. Overcoming pain within. I could see it clearly now, how childhood could be distorted in treacherous hands.

I pushed the books aside.

That's strange. Something was missing.

I removed each of the books from my satchel and set them on my lap, rummaging through my bag.

It's not here.

My journal.

The air left my lungs.

Beatrice's head tilted. "Did you forget something?"

"My journal," I said. The room seemed to tilt. Bird skull. Feathers. Shadows. Words spoken from the journal could make all of these things manifest. It could bring him back.

Heat flashed across my cheeks. I misplaced it, that's all. I must have left it on my desk at school.

In all of these years, not once had I lost it. Or perhaps I'd left it at home? After the hospital I'd go home, and if it wasn't there, I'd return to Marigold House. It was somewhere. It has to be.

"I had it this morning," I spoke quietly.

She smiled. "You and your journal, always writing and reading. Well, it'll turn up. Things always have a way of finding you."

I turned back to the man. His skin was pale, but his lips were red, as if he'd just spoken and his words were still hanging in the air between us.

"Yes," I murmured. "They always do."

That book was more than paper. It was proof. Every line a thread binding me to what was real. To what everyone told me to forget, to ignore. When no one believed me, the only things I had left were the words I'd written myself.

Without my journal, I feared my memory would fray. That I'd forget it all, the shimmering seas and pirate ships and their crews who'd cheated death again and again. They were not just fairy tales. They were real.

I reached for my pocket watch and felt its cold metal face press into my palm. A small bit of relief.

Beatrice took a few steps toward me, her hands clasped in front of her. I sensed a lecture was coming.

"Wendy . . . after all of these years, you still hide behind your books. Your work. Your ghosts." She blinked, looked up, and then her eyes met mine. "You've spent so much time protecting everyone else, your brothers, the children you teach. Now you're here, and yes, I'm glad that you're here, but . . ." She paused. "When will you realize that your life belongs to you?"

I flinched. Not visibly, I hoped. But inside, something recoiled.

"Your life belongs to you, Wendy. Not to the past. Not to what hurt you." Her voice softened. "You can't keep mourning a life you haven't lived yet. The world's still out there, waiting for you to notice it."

Her words struck deep.

I wanted to tell her that I lived with the crushing fear and guilt that what killed him could still be out there. That my heart was twisted because at one time, I had loved him too. A killer. She didn't know what I'd lost. What I'd left behind. Their faces. Their embraces. All of my boys. I had abandoned them. Left them in the darkness.

I tried to smile. "Right, I agree."

It was better to acknowledge her words and move on.

From down the hall, a doctor called her name. "Beatrice? Where is that nurse?"

"I've got to go. I'll check on you later," she said "Don't vanish into your head again, darling. Promise?"

I nodded, though I wasn't sure I could.

"Good." She flashed a grin and was gone. White dress. Red cross. A blur vanishing into the gray.

I took a deep breath and finally introduced myself.

"I'm Wendy," I said to the sleeping man. "I'm here to read to you. I hope you can hear me."

I opened *Alice's Adventures in Wonderland* to the first page.

Somewhere in the ward, metal struck tile, a sharp, clanging sound that rolled through the hall.

My hands tightened around the book. "I know what it's like to go off somewhere in search of adventure and come back different."

I hardly knew why I was telling him this. It wasn't something one ought to speak of to strangers. Even my brothers refused to talk about it. They grew upset if I so much as mentioned it. Because of that, we didn't speak much these days. Especially after our parents died.

A draft slithered through the open doorway. Cold curled around my ankles.

Then, a too familiar sound. Soft. Steady. Fingers against glass.

Tapping.

My hands shook. I set the book on the table between me and the bed.

"Do you hear that?" I said to the man, knowing he couldn't respond. But I needed something to cling to. Something to keep from feeling so alone.

I looked toward the open door. The corridor seemed empty. No footsteps. No approaching figures. Only a low, gentle sound, wind. A window open somewhere.

Wendy . . . come away.

This time, the voice wasn't inside my head, like it had been at the newsstand. It was outside of me. In the room.

This was not a memory. This was his voice. This was him.

I closed my eyes tight, and every muscle remembered what my mind had tried so hard to overcome.

Sea salt on my tongue.

Morning dew on leaves, brushing against my skin.

The cold metal weight of a knife pressed into my hand, and his eyes commanding me to run.

Memory dragged me into its depths.

My brothers pleading: *Run, Wendy! Don't look back!*

I opened my eyes. "How?" I breathed.

We'd buried our childhood. And yet, that voice. That terrible, honeyed voice.

"Beatrice?" I called, hoping she was near.

A shadow stretched along the far wall, too quick for any person to cast.

The bulb above dimmed. Recovered. Dimmed again. Each flicker threw new geometries of shadow across every surface.

The clock ticked once. Twice. Then stopped.

The pressure in the room shifted. It no longer felt like I was surrounded by the weight of hospital walls, but an expanse of sky.

Then I heard him.

Roger.

I could see him. Long brown curls, a too-large coat with brass buttons.

"Just don't ever repeat the name carved on the Black Rock," he told me the day I nearly drowned. "After it goes to sleep, we don't want it waking back up too early."

"I don't understand any of this."

"Just promise me," he said. "When you leave, just don't say its name in your world."

"I promise."

"No. Not like that. Like a pirate." Tender. Serious. Him trying to make light of the threat of death.

"Aye."

Then he intertwined his fingers with mine.

* * *

Footsteps. Hurried. Bare. I was back in the hospital.

The sound stopped just outside of the open door. I waited for a knock, for someone to appear, but neither happened.

Light dipped to the color of weak tea. Behind me, the radiator hissed. A shock of white steam.

I stood and spoke to the doorframe. "Is someone there?"

The silence that followed my question was not still. Something was here. It leaned in. It listened.

I peeked in the hall. Nothing.

From somewhere, that voice found me. Not in my head. Not in my sleep. It was here. In this room.

"Wendy . . . you promised."

My hand flew to my mouth. Ice pooled in my stomach. My body trembled.

No.

From the top corner of the doorframe, a shape appeared. Slender. Black. A feather drifted down, spiraling once, twice, before settling on the floor in front of my boot.

At my feet, it shivered. Like it was still attached to a living bird.

Beneath the feather, black liquid began to form. It spread outward. Creeping toward me. Thin at first. Then thick. Ink. Oil. Tar.

"This isn't real," I said.

That Wendy Darling. She's made a complicated mess this time.

Behind me a sound. I turned. And froze.

The bed. Empty. He was standing, facing the corner.

Still. Straight. Feet bare. Trousers hung loose. Cotton shirt buttoned but oversized.

"Hello?" My voice came out thin. "I . . . I'll get the nurse." But I could not move.

He remained motionless.

Air swirled into the room. A draft. I realized a window was open somewhere.

The latches. The latches. *Something is undone.*

And the smell . . .

Moss. Damp earth. Something green and rotting beneath it.

That Place.

He was speaking to the wall. His voice faint. Cracked. A soldier's voice.

"Keep your head down. If I live, I'll never complain about the rain again." A wet laugh. "Shh. Listen. The shelling. It stopped. We were shelled all night. Guess they've grown tired."

His voice faltered. Then deepened. A different voice now, rougher, older. Another man speaking through the same throat.

"Stick with me. We'll make it through."

I pressed myself against the doorframe. My pulse charging through my body.

He's shell-shocked. Reliving the trenches.

The soldier turned his head. Just enough to catch the light. "My name? It's Edward. Yours, mate?"

His name. Edward. But no. *Who were you talking to?*

"Edward, don't talk to him . . ." I couldn't move. My legs were frozen in place.

Silence.

The bulb above buzzed. Once. Twice.

When he spoke again, I screamed.

"Peter." That name. *His* name. It came from Edward's mouth, but it was his voice. Peter's.

"No! Don't say his name! Don't say his—"

"Nice to meet you, Peter." Edward smiled. It wasn't his smile.

The shadow on the floor thickened, spreading across the room, finding the edges of the floorboards. Then it rose. Slowly. Deliberately.

I couldn't move. I could only watch as the shadow gathered into a mass, stretching, joining, forming, into the outline of a boy.

* * *

"How old are you?" I'd asked him the first time we met.

He avoided the question, turning it back to me. "How old are you, Wendy Darling?"

"I'm twelve."

A smile. The loveliest smile I'd ever seen.

"I'm twelve too."

I looked down at the grass beneath our feet. Except it wasn't grass. Not where we stood. A perfect ring of pale gray, soft as powder. The trees arched overhead, their branches woven so thick the sky had disappeared.

"What is it?" he asked, noticing my curiosity.

"We're standing in a circle. Is it . . . ash?"

"Oh," he said, as if it were nothing. As if circles made themselves. "I suppose we are."

He held out his hand. His fingers were cold when I took them. "Will you promise me something, Wendy Darling?"

I should have pulled away. But I was twelve, and he was beautiful, and no one had ever looked at me like I was the only thing worth seeing.

"Yes."

"Promise me you'll come away with me."

"I promise."

He smiled again. But this time, something moved behind his eyes. Something old. "Then we're bound. Shadows linked," he said. "You and I. Forever and ever."

* * *

I backed away, inch by inch. The door, that was the goal. My eyes fixed on Edward's back. My fingers trailed the wall, keeping me upright.

My back struck a surface. The doorframe.

"Don't trust it," I called to Edward. "It's not one of your mates!"

The bulb hissed. Flared. Then burst.

Glass rained down, tinkling like bells. Darkness swallowed the room, save for the corridor light glowing behind me.

"Wendy," said a voice. "Wendy Darling."

A hand caught my shoulder. Cold. Familiar.

I spun, and the world snapped back into place.

Beatrice stood there. Her smell, rosewater and lavender. I exhaled, wanting to fall into her arms.

"Is he awake?" she said, peering into the room. "I heard you talking."

I looked back. The corner was empty.

Edward lay in bed as before. Hands folded. Lips parted. A man deep in sleep somewhere between the battlefields and silence.

I scanned the floor, searching for the shadow. Instead I spotted the feather beneath the bed where Beatrice couldn't see.

"I was just reading aloud," I said fighting to keep my voice steady, my hands still.

"Are you all right, darling?" Beatrice pressed the back of her hand to my forehead. "You look feverish."

"The radiator," I managed. "It was steaming just a moment ago."

"Looks perfectly fine now."

She patted my back, then moved to Edward. She repeated the gesture, her hand to his brow. "Poor soul," she said gently.

Beatrice straightened, her attention shifting back to me. "You're pale, Wendy. Like you've seen a ghost."

I gave her a thin smile. "Just frightened myself with a story is all."

Her gaze drifted to the chair where *Alice's Adventures in Wonderland* still lay open.

"Falling down rabbit holes again," she teased. "Just promise me you'll find your way back."

"I was going to say . . ." I blurted, the words too fast, too eager.

"Yes . . . ?" Beatrice's brows lifted. Amused. Wary.

"I think I heard him murmuring for a bit. It sounded like he said 'Edward.' Perhaps that's his name. I think I'm going to call him that."

A blink. Then a smile. Half surprised. Half delighted. Each edged with curiosity. "Edward," she repeated, studying me. "My Wendy Darling and her stories. Very well. Edward it is."

From the corridor a stern voice called her name. "Beatrice? Where'd she'd run off to again?"

She sighed, then laughed. "I'll be back, love." She gave my arm a squeeze. "Don't vanish into your head again?"

Her footsteps faded down the hall, leaving me alone with Edward, and the ghost of where the feather had been.

A fine shimmer clung to the floor. When I knelt for a closer look, it vanished. Swept away by a wind I couldn't feel.

I sank into the chair, breath ragged.

"What's happening?" I asked Edward, knowing he couldn't offer a solution.

Above me, the bulb buzzed. Its hum faded slowly into something human. A low groan, and beneath it something familiar.

My name.

Soft as a secret. Just like the promise I once made.

And broke.

My eyes began to water. My mind tracing back all of our steps. Everything we'd done.

We had killed him. We had buried our childhood in that cursed place. How could it possibly come back?

But the dead don't whisper your name.

CHAPTER

4

As I walked home from the hospital, I thought of the children at Marigold House. Willie and Agnes, Harold, and Tom. They and Edward, all of them acting so strangely.

I ran through that day. The knife. The blood. We had broken the cycle, or so I thought.

Big Ben boomed. The sound rolling through all of London.

I moved fast, needing to get home and needing to hold my journal in my hands.

The streets seemed to vibrate with motion, men in overcoats and women clutching handbags against the wind. Above, the sky was brushed like a bruised plum, deep and violet.

Then something tugged at the back of my hair. I spun around.

Faces turned toward me. Glazed with exhaustion.

No one spoke. No one paused.

I lowered my hand. A few loose strands clung to my glove, static or wind, or . . .

No, just the cold and the wind.

Still, I stood there a long moment, watching the faces walk past, making sure no shadow detached from its source.

Outside Blake's Grocer, a group of children counted coins on their palms, their faces lit by hope. Mr. Blake leaned against the doorway. Then he saw me. His face faltered.

I looked away.

Once, that had been my brothers and me outside his shop, arguing over toffees, our chatter rising like startled birds. Mr. Blake would lean over the counter, feigning outrage as he let us underpay, winking as though goodness were a small secret we all agreed to keep.

At one time, everyone on this street looked at us with joy and kindness. Always so happy to see us. But soon after returning, the looks in their eyes changed. Smiles were forced when we crossed paths. Or, more often, they avoided us altogether. One day we were loved and cherished by everyone. The next, shunned.

We were looked at like we were wicked things. Things that spread spectacle and disease. No one outside of our parents or our maid Liza wanted anything to do with us. I learned too young that victims, in the eyes of the fearful, become indistinguishable from the monsters themselves.

London cheered for us when we returned. The lost Darlings.

In time, the stories we told began to crack under questions.

Where had we gone?

What had we seen?

How had we survived when so many children went missing and never returned? Or worse.

I told them my truth. About the sky that split open. A sea that sang. Wings that were not quite wings. But no one wanted to hear that. They only wanted comfort.

When my words failed to give them any meaning, their pens stopped moving. Notebooks snapped shut. Smiles stiffened. Applause collapsed into silence.

Not long after, J. M. Barrie penned his tale *Peter and Wendy*, a work of fiction that borrowed from my life, weaving our experiences into a narrative stripped of truth.

"Peter was not quite like other boys," Barrie hinted in his text.

Of course he wasn't. Because he wasn't a real boy.

Barrie took all of my words, and when he wasn't twisting them, he was laying my life out bare.

How could I ever trust anyone again after that? My parents. The constables who pressed me with questions. The reporters who recorded every word I said. And then Mr. Barrie, who took my story and made it his. A man who'd turn my own terror into his profit.

"It's a work of fiction" was all he'd say. And in time, everyone forgot about my account of pain and turned to his for joy.

My lungs tightened. I reached for my satchel, the worn leather steady beneath my fingers.

"Miss Wendy! Miss Wendy!"

I turned.

A boy came charging down the street, cap askew, boots striking the cobblestones.

"Willie?"

His grin broke through the dusk. And there, in his hand, my journal.

Relief and dread hit me at once. If I had lost it. If those pages had fallen into anyone else's hands . . .

"You dropped this, Miss Wendy!" He held the journal out. Proud as if he'd recovered buried treasure.

"You found it," I managed. "You found my journal."

I took it from him, hands trembling. The leather was warm from his grasp. Soap and sweat and street dust clung to it. I pressed it to my chest.

"It was under the bed in the flat upstairs! Agnes and Harold and me were playing hide-and-seek, and I was the best hider. I was! I felt it there by my elbow."

I remember now, my satchel falling this morning and the contents spilling out.

Guilt crept through me.

Why couldn't you just have left it back there in that faraway place? Why did you have to bring it with you? Your past clinging to you at all times? Maybe you should have forgotten. Forgotten it all. Forgotten all of them.

But I knew the answer.

Because it was mine.

Willie grinned. "Agnes said leave it be, but I knew it was yours. You always carry it. I said, 'Wait till Miss Wendy sees I found it, she'll be ever so pleased!'"

It's all here. Still real. The words. The truth. My memories. Not imagined. Not invited.

I had guarded this journal for years, never letting it leave my side. It was more than paper. It was the only thing that remembered what the world refused to believe. The cover rasped beneath my hands. I turned the pages. And then there—the pressed leaf.

Still green. Faintly luminous. Its veins caught in the lamplight and seemed to glow.

It should have browned long ago. Curled in on itself, shriveled into dust. But it hadn't.

The leaf from my childhood looked just like the day I had placed it between these pages.

The faint shimmer along its surface pulsed. *Breathe.* I placed it back in my journal.

"Where's that from?" Willie asked, leaning closer.

"A place very far away."

"Barbados?"

"No."

His brow rose. "China?"

"Farther."

He tilted his chin up. "One day I'm going to see the world."

"I'm certain you will. And you'll write to all of us at Marigold House about your adventures."

"Think so?"

"Indeed."

Before I sent him off to the house I had to ask. "Willie," I said gently. "Did you read any of it?"

His eyes traced the cobblestones. "I didn't mean to, Miss Wendy. Honest. It fell open."

"Of course," I murmured. "That's how you found it."

Willie nodded.

Behind me, a broom rasped against stone. Mrs. Crane, sweeping what didn't need sweeping, her eyes pinned sharp on me and Willie.

I stepped closer to Willie, my coat folding around us like a drawn curtain. "Tell me exactly what you saw."

He hesitated, breath fogging the air between us. "There were some words underlined," he said. "Just a few."

Oh no.

Above us crows shrieked in the sky.

"Willie, don't . . ."

But he was already saying it, just as I moved toward him. My fingers catching the shoulders of his coat, but those words were already leaving his mouth.

The crows went silent. Mrs. Crane's broom stopped mid-sweep. The street, the entirety of the city, all went still.

And the only sound I heard were those words that hadn't been spoken in years. Words carved into a black rock on an island that should not exist.

Peter, Peter, shadow eater.

Everything inside me went still.

The city continued its rhythm, the tram's rattle, the clock tower tolling the hour. Mrs. Crane resumed her sweeping, but none of it reached me, just those words. That name.

"Did I say something wrong?" Willie's eyes were wide and confused.

I didn't know what to do so I pulled him into my arms and held him tight.

"Are you all right, Miss Wendy?"

"Yes, Willie." My voice sounded so thin. "I just . . . you're just such a sweet child for coming all this way." I held him out at arm's length, studying his face.

"What does that mean?" he asked. "The rhyme?"

"Nothing," I forced a smile. "Just a silly thing children used to say when I was little. It doesn't mean anything."

But they weren't just words. They were an incantation. A summoning. And even if it was dead . . . I didn't want to test fate.

Names had power and I had been warned of that long ago, and Willie had just rung a bell.

* * *

"Just don't ever repeat the name carved on the Black Rock," Roger had told me once. We were sitting on the beach, our feet buried in the black sand, watching the tide roll in. "That rhyme is tied to his power."

"But that's not his name? Peter, Peter, shadow . . ."

He pressed a finger to my lips. "I said, don't say it." He waited until I nodded before lowering his hand. "And no, that's not his true name. His name is Peter Pan."

"Pan?" I frowned. "Like from myth? The god?"

Out of the corner of my eye, a ship crested the horizon. Roger stood, waving his arms back and forth, a waterlogged hat clutched in his hands.

"He didn't tell you?" He glanced back at me, surprised.

I shook my head.

"The god of wild nature. Of panic." He turned back to signal the ship. "Of hunger and appetite. Timelessness. He's not actually a god. Guess his maker thought that was a suitable name to give him when he came here. Pan."

Later, he brought me aboard his father's ship, one day to be his ship.

The deck groaned beneath my feet, the planks still warm from the day's sun. The smell of tar and rope. The metal tang of gunpowder. The crew stared as though they'd glimpsed an apparition. Eyes wide. Hands drifting toward swords and daggers, until they noticed my hand in Roger's.

As we passed each man, they took five deliberate steps backward.

"That's the captain's boy with . . . Peter's friend," one muttered. Awe and suspicion twisted into a single breath.

They gave me my own room. Grand. Gleaming. Paneled in a dark, polished wood that smelled of coconut palms and beach roses. Crystal chandeliers swayed gently with the tide. A closet full of gowns in jewel colors. Chests glinting with gems and gold, spoils from adventures I would never ask them to recount.

"Find whatever suits you best," Roger said, lingering in the doorway.

His gaze softened when it found me. Rugged. Sea-worn. Yet unexpectedly kind. He looked at me the way sailors look at land after weeks out on water.

"I have to go back."

"What do you mean? You're soaking wet. You nearly drowned. He left you for dead."

"My brothers," I whispered. "I can't leave them."

Roger stepped closer, lantern light trembling across his jaw. "We'll fetch your brothers," he said quietly. Fiercely. "And then you'll say with me. Here, you can have whatever you want. The land. The sea. I'll bring the sky down for you. I'll give you everything."

I'd fallen for this before. Promises from a boy that turned out to be lies. But from this boy . . . I believed him. Not because he seemed so sure of himself like the other, but because he seemed so sad at the possibility of me saying no to him. But I had to. I owed my brothers the safety of home.

* * *

Willie had said the name aloud.

And names were doors.

"Promise me something. Don't ever say those words again. Not aloud. Not to anyone."

He frowned. "Why?"

"It's part of a story," I said gently. "One I need to finish."

He hesitated, then nodded, crossing his small hand over his chest. "I promise."

"Good boy," I said. "Now, run along back to Marigold House. It's nearly dark and I'm sure they're all searching for you."

He grinned. Saluted. And then dashed off. Coat flaring behind him.

I remained beneath the gaslight, journal pressed tight against my chest.

I can hear Constable Finch's voice.

* * *

"Were there other children there with you?"

The room had gone still.

My parents stood behind him, pale, rigid, while the other officers loomed nearby.

"Yes," I said finally. "There were many children."

"Do you remember their names?"

I reached for my journal. My finger brushed its edge, the leather worn smooth.

Father pinched the bridge of his nose the way he did when pain overtook him. Mother's lips parted, then pressed shut.

"Their names?" Finch coaxed.

I flipped to the back of the journal, to the page where I had written them all. One by one.

I read.

"Tootles. Nibs. Slightly. Curly. The Twins. Stix and Patch. Moth. Cricket. Bram. Robin. Wren. Button. Chime."

No one spoke.

Then it came. A single laugh. Low. Disbelieving.

They didn't believe me. They were making fun of me.

Finch's jaw flexed. "And where can we find these other children?"

"Through the gate in the South Flower Walk. In Kensington Gardens. Past the man with the balloons."

A pause. He sighed. His boots struck the polished floor as he turned away.

The officers followed him out.

Only Father remained. He knelt before me.

"But those are their names," I said.

"Constable Finch just wants to find those boys."

"But they're there," I insisted. "Just past the gate. They're waiting. They're scared, that's all. But maybe the constables can fetch them."

He stood and crossed into the hall. The door remained slightly ajar.

Through the crack, their voices drifted.

"This many missing children," Finch said. "Something grave and terrible is happening."

"My daughter's told you everything she knows," Father answered. Clipped. Steady.

"It's disturbing how much she thinks she knows," Finch replied. "It may be childhood fancy, or something worse. I'll recommend she be sent to Bethlem Royal Hospital for observation. Then afterward to St. Adalbert's."

"No," my father snapped. "Absolutely not. She's done nothing wrong."

"You're right," Finch said, colder now. "Her parents have. The Magistrate's Court will issue an order. She'll be removed from the home and placed in Marigold House after she's evaluated at Bethlem and they deem she's safe enough to be around other children."

My brothers spoke less and less of it until they said nothing at all. As if it had been a dream we'd shared once, and I alone refused to wake.

Sometimes I think it was because I wrote it down. Because I made it real. And what is written cannot die.

Maybe Mr. Barrie knew that too, and a year later he wrote his book. Of course he couldn't choose different names. He had to choose ours. The Darling name. My name. There was no escaping what had terrorized me, because it was everywhere, in the book, in the play, in every hand that applauded our suffering as fantasy.

They thought we were pretending. They thought we were playing a game. None of it was a game. It was our lives.

My house waited at the far end of the street. Bricks dulled by soot and ivy climbing the walls. The windows clouded by years of dust.

Father had nailed the nursery window shut the night we returned, sealing the room, and everything it once held. That chapter is over, he'd said. Not another word about it.

But chapters don't always end so cleanly, and sometimes stories had a continuation, and I think that's where I found myself now in this part of the story.

A faint light flickered in the window above the door. Behind the lace curtain something moved.

Peter, Peter, shadow eater.

"There's more writing there," I remember telling Roger. The script carved into the Black Rock continued on under water.

"I've never noticed that before. These words were left here by the people who lived on this island before all of us. They left this warning, but I don't think Father knows about those words. I'll tell him. We have to go. The sun is setting."

* * *

Before I could knock, the front door opened.

Liza stood in the hall, dusting flour from her sleeves.

"How was the hospital?" she asked.

"Shocking. The ward was nearly full . . ."

"You look pale, love."

"I'm just tired . . ." I hesitated. "Were you just upstairs?"

"You know I don't go up there."

It was true. She only visited with me in the evenings now, to make supper and to sit a while. She'd made a promise too, to my parents. They'd left her a small sum for my care. I'd told her she didn't need to keep coming, but she insisted.

Liza followed as I made my way to the coat closet. She unpinned my hat, admiring the ribbon.

"Pretty," she said. "I thought you didn't like green anymore."

"Lillian pinned that for me."

"Such lovely children."

Dinah barreled in, paws skidding across tiles. I bent to kiss the top of her head. She smelled bright and fresh, with a hint of coal dust.

Liza reached for my satchel. I shifted it out of reach.

"School papers," I said.

"Michael's enlisting this week."

I froze.

I had known it was coming. But hearing it spoken aloud made it real. My baby brother, who lined up his toy soldiers on the windowsill at night playing at battle, would soon be going off to one.

"Margot's getting big. Three months now. I know John and Judith would love a visit from you. And Margot to finally meet her aunt."

"Oh . . ." I said. "Maybe soon. I just have a lot of work."

"They're your brothers, Wendy. All of you can't keep going on like this, sidestepping one another. Especially now. Especially with Michael off soon."

"I'll write them soon," I said.

"Wendy. Really? A letter?"

I sighed. Fine. "I'll phone them soon."

"Wash up," Liza said briskly, still not pleased with my responses. "I'll fix you a bowl."

The sconce on the landing flickered as I climbed the stairs. The frosted glass pulsed, dim, then bright again.

The floor sighed beneath my feet. The carpet, once rose-colored, had faded to a gray. Beneath the worn pattern, faint petals still showed through.

My hand skimmed the wall, the paper cool and ridged beneath my fingers. I could almost feel the wall trembling with the memory of us, the rush of our feet. Our laughter finding itself into each room.

At the far end of the hall, another light trembled. First dim, then guttering, the same faltering buzz the bulb above Edward's bed had made. I thought of the soldier in the hospital, standing in the corner. Asking for a name, and me begging him not to answer.

I moved down the long hall lined with photographs; their gilt frames dulled with age.

Mother and me by the pond at Hyde Park, her smile soft, mine uncertain. Michael in his bonnet, a white blur on a picnic blanket in Kensington Gardens, eyes wide as coins. All three of us once: John to one side, Michael to the other, my arms around Nana, our great shaggy guardian. Her fur always smelled faintly of summer rain.

Then the wedding portrait. Mother radiant, clutching her flowers. Father tall, already beginning to stoop. Their eyes bright with belief in something that wouldn't last.

After their funerals, I couldn't bear these faces.

I would walk this hall in darkness, afraid the photographs might turn to look at me.

My brothers had been polite at the wakes. Dutiful. Distant. There was no mention of our childhood. No mention of the newspapers nor of any of the vanished or murdered children.

We mourned, then poured our grief away.

By day, I belonged to Marigold House, laughter, and books. By night, to this home, silent and shuttered.

At the end of the hall, something flickered. A shift at the edge of vision, like the brief flutter of a wing behind glass.

When I turned, nothing.

Only my own reflection, lengthening across the wall. I moved closer.

The nursery door waited at the far end, still sealed. The brass lock had dulled beneath a film of dust. The key was tucked safely in Father's old desk, now mine. No one had entered our old room in years.

And yet, beneath the threshold, a pulse of light.

It quivered faintly, the color of candle flame seen through water. A ripple that breathed once, then vanished.

I held my breath. Listening.

The house exhaled around me: the tick of pipes, the distant groan of settling timber. But beneath it all, a sound too soft to name.

That room contained everything we had been. A history sealed in dust and quiet.

It was there John had lined dominoes again and again in perfect rows, toppling them just to hear them fall. It was there Michael had arranged his wooden soldiers by height and rank, the smallest ones always at the front, brave by necessity.

And it was there I'd sat between them, inventing stories so we wouldn't hear the silence outside.

The flicker came again. Brighter this time. Then gone, as if it had blinked.

I stepped forward before I could stop myself.

* * *

The air smelled faintly of cedar and something older. Something metallic, like blood gone to rust.

My palm hovered above the knob. Cold radiated from the brass, deliberate and alive.

I thought of the soldier, Edward, how he had stood rigid in that corner, eyes unfocused, voice trembling. Caught between worlds.

I drew my hand back from the door, pulse quickening. The light beneath the threshold had vanished. But the air still shimmered with what it left behind.

The hallway dimmed.

Shadows gathered.

I stepped forward and pressed my palm to the door. The chill climbed my arm, not the cold of neglect but of something deeper. The wood was dry beneath my cheek when I leaned close, yet it pulsed faintly.

My heartbeat stumbled in time with it.

Thud. Pause. Thud.

I listened.

The silence beyond the door was too whole. Not emptiness, but it felt like something was listening back. Listening to me.

Then came the sound.

A click.

A whir.

A breath of air slipped through the keyhole, cool, sudden, brushing my cheek. The window at the end of the hall was shut, yet the draft carried the faint scent of salt. Of tide. Of sand.

The doorknob trembled.

Once.

Twice.

Then began to rattle with purpose, as if a hand on the other side had remembered how to turn it.

My pulse faltered.

The hairs along my arms lifted. Not in surprise. In recognition. This isn't happening, I told myself. But I had stopped trusting denial years ago.

It had begun again.

Willie speaking that cursed name into the air.

Edward whispering to someone who wasn't there.

And now, here, the echo finding its way back to me.

The air thickened. The light beneath the nursery door flared once, sudden, searing.

I shut my eyes and pressed my back against the opposite wall, forcing myself to breathe. I tried to recall Eleanor's voice, the first night I arrived at Marigold House.

"Fear," she had told me, "is just a story we tell ourselves. And stories can be changed."

The rattling ceased.

In the hush that followed, something slid across the floorboards inside, soft, deliberate, like a child dragging a toy.

The light beneath the door blinked out.

And I was left in the dark, listening to the wind outside.

"Your food's getting cold!" Liza's voice rose from the stairwell, warm, ordinary. I blinked hard.

The hallway had returned to itself. Dim and still, the gaslight trembling in its glass. Yet something lingered. No scent. No sound. Just a feeling I couldn't name.

I stepped sideways toward the stairs, my body unwilling to turn its back on the nursery door.

The movement was gone. But it had been there. And it remembered me. I stood a moment longer, listening to the silence. Then I went downstairs, knowing Liza was right. It was time I got in touch with my brothers.

CHAPTER

5

THE DAY AT Marigold House passed in a blur of lessons and small emergencies.

Willie jumped from the stairs twice more, despite Eleanor's warnings. Each time he landed he had that same wild grin, as if gravity were a game he was winning. I flinched at the thud of his feet against the floorboards, my heart seizing before my mind could catch up. He stopped once Lucy told him he had to help her in the kitchen peeling onions.

Agnes was quieter than usual. I spotted her three times standing at the window, her breath fogging the glass, her eyes fixed on the elm tree in the garden. On the patch of earth where she'd buried her bird skull.

"It hasn't sprouted yet," she told me at lunch. "Maybe I need to water it?"

I didn't know what to say to that. So I said nothing.

Baby Jane was the only one who seemed at peace. I found her in Rosie's arms between lessons, her small fist wrapped around Rosie's finger, her eyes half closed and dreaming whatever dreams infants dream. She looked good, her cheeks round and pink. No trace left of the cold. She squirmed and reached for me.

"I think she likes you," Rosie said, bouncing her gently. She looked from Jane to me. Her eyes narrowed in that appraising look she got when an idea formed. "You know, she looks like you. Same hair color. Same eye color. Could pass as your own daughter."

I laughed at that.

"Well, why not? Especially if you move in."

"Eleanor told you."

"Of course Eleanor told me." She grinned. "We're all just waiting for you to say yes. And I'm sure Jane here would love having you around all day."

Jane gazed up at me with those dark brown eyes and stretched her hand toward my face.

I let her fingers brush my cheek.

"All I do know, Miss Jane," I said, "is that I'll read to you once I finish giving the children their lessons."

* * *

Afternoon came quickly and the tram ride from Marigold House to the hospital felt shorter. I made the journey without thinking, my feet carrying me through the familiar route, but my mind caught on Willie's reckless leaps from the stairs and Agnes's unwavering preoccupation with her bird skull. Then of course, there was darling Jane, how she fell asleep in my arms shortly after I read the words "Once upon a time," but still, I finished reading the story even as she slept.

The ward was quiet, many of the men slept and the nurses took their tea.

I pulled the chair closer to Edward's bed. Dust motes floated in the pale light from the window.

"I brought something different today."

I reached into my satchel and pulled out the thimble. I hadn't planned to bring it. I hadn't planned to show this to anyone, ever. But maybe I needed to talk to someone about this, anyone other than my brothers.

"When I was young," I said, turning it over in my fingers, "I told a boy I would give him a kiss if he liked."

Edward remained still, chest slowly rising with each breath. I knew he was listening.

"This boy, he didn't understand what I meant. He held his hand out, expecting an object. This told me he didn't know what a kiss was. I was a little embarrassed. My sewing kit was out so I reached for this and placed it on his palm. A thimble. He'd never seen one before. I could tell. So he decided it was a kiss. That was Peter, thinking that everything was something one could hand over. A thing someone could turn over in their hands."

Somewhere down the ward, someone coughed, and there was the soft percussion of footsteps.

"He gave me a button in return. An acorn button, from his shirt. He said it was his kiss to me." I closed my fingers around the thimble. The metal was warm now, from my palm. "The day we planned to leave, we were in such a hurry. I must've left it behind in the treehouse."

I sat there for a long moment, letting the silence settle.

"He didn't care about anyone but himself."

I slipped the thimble back into my satchel. My fingers brushed something else. Cool metal. A familiar weight.

I hesitated. Then I pulled it out.

I held the pocket watch in my palm. Its face clouded with age. Its hands still dutifully ticking. I had carried it for twelve years. Through every move of my day and every sleepless night. And those moments when I'd stand at the Thames thinking of him and the sea . . .

"This belonged to someone else," I said quietly.

Edward didn't move. Didn't respond. But I kept talking anyway. For so long I'd told others' stories, and this was the first time I'd ever told anyone this story.

"His name was Roger. A pirate's son. I know how that sounds. Believe me. But it's true. He lived on a ship. I was supposed to bring him back here to London . . ." I couldn't finish.

The watch ticked in my palm. It shouldn't tick. It hadn't been wound in twelve years.

"He was so kind," I said. "That was the thing about him. He was kind in a place where kindness got you killed. He brought me food when I was hungry. Showed me where to hide . . . when the other one was angry. He taught me which berries were safe to eat and which paths to avoid, and he showed me the way home."

My throat tightened. I swallowed against it.

"He gave me this watch. It comes with me everywhere. And sometimes I hold on to it like I'm holding on to him."

* * *

I turned it over. On the back, scratched into the metal were two letters: R.H.

Roger Hook.

"He died saving me." I couldn't finish.

The ward was silent around us.

I looked at Edward's face. At the stillness of it. The peace.

"He was the most real thing that has ever happened to me, and sometimes I feel like I can't move forward because parts of me are stuck back there on that island."

A tear slipped down my cheek. I wiped it away with the back of my hand.

"I've never told anyone that," I said. "Thank you for listening. No one ever wanted to listen to me . . . not really."

I sat there for a long moment, the watch in my palm, the tears falling faster now. I didn't try to stop them. There was no one here to see. No one to judge. Just Edward, silent and still, holding my secrets.

I slipped the watch back into my satchel. Pressed my palms to my eyes. Breathed until the shaking stopped.

When I looked at Edward again, he was the same. Unchanged. Unhearing. Or so I thought.

His right hand had moved. Just slightly. Just enough that his fingers now rested at the edge of the bed, reaching toward where my hand had been.

I stared at it.

"Edward?"

No response. No movement.

But his fingers stayed there, extended, as if waiting for me to take hold.

I reached out and held his hand.

And somewhere deep in the corridor, I thought I heard something faint. A child laugh.

* * *

Back at home at my desk, I twisted open the fountain pen. My hand shook as I thought about what to write.

The clock ticked. Slow. Steady.

Liza had gone hours ago. She'd left an extra bowl out on the kitchen table. "I fear you'll be up late, and so in case you're hungry there'll be something for you in the kitchen."

She was right. I didn't know when sleep would come.

The light beneath the nursery door. Edward's voice whispering into nothing. My journal in Willie's hands. Birds and feathers and shadows that moved wrong.

I turned to the page and began to write the letter I dreaded to send.

Dear John,

I'm worried and I think we three need to talk, you, me and Michael. I know you don't like to speak of it. You'd said long ago that dead things stay dead, but I don't think that's true. Not anymore.

I paused, the pen hovering.

The fire hissed, collapsing inward. I pressed on.

Strange things have happened all day. So much I don't even know how to tell you, but I have to tell you this. At the hospital today, a soldier said his name, and before you think to yourself that yes, this is a name that others may have known, that I'm sure of it. I know who he was speaking of.

My hand faltered. If I wrote more, I would make it real. But it had always been real. We were all just encouraged to forget, and I was forced not to speak of it.

Beside my hand on the desk, Roger's pocket watch lay open.

Beneath the scratch of my pen, I could hear it ticking. Each tick a pulse.

I brushed my thumb along the rim, tracing the faint groove worn by his fingers. The metal was cool, familiar.

We were so close, Roger.

I closed my eyes, willing the memory of him, and I was there again. Not in the horror of what came after, but just before it, when we had some moments of magic on the island.

* * *

Salt wind filled my lungs, brined and sharp. The sea licked my lips. Ropes creaked, gulls called, and the ship swayed gently on the open water. Above us, the black flag snapped in the wind, white skull grinning down at nothing. Beside me, Roger swung his legs over the edge, face tipped to the sun.

"Is that where you got your name?" I pointed up at the flag.

He smiled. "When Father brought me aboard, he gave me a new one. Named me after the flag." He glanced up at it, squinting against the light. "Jolly Roger. I like it. Suits me better than whatever I was called before."

"Father's been good to me," he went on. "Taught me how to read the stars. How to map storm lines on the horizon. How to hold a course when the sky grows dark and the sea turns against you." He picked at a splinter on the rail. "Soon he's going to show me how to navigate the black waters."

"How old are you?" I asked.

He shrugged. "Father thinks I'm fourteen."

Roger looked quickly and rubbed his eyes. He seemed on edge. As if trying to brush a memory away. And it was then that I knew. He had also belonged to Peter once.

"I'm sorry. I didn't mean . . ."

"He left me in the swamps," Roger whispered. "Said I'd slowed the story. Father found me there. Half of me was in the mud. When Father reached in to pull me up, well, that's when it happened. He sacrificed a part of him to save me."

A shadow lengthened over us.

A tall shape, hat slanted, an arm at one side, and the other arm ended in that polished curve of iron. For a heartbeat I remembered Peter's warning: That pirate pierces the necks of children with the hooked hand.

My body went rigid.

Roger hopped off the edge and stood at my side, tangling his fingers in mine.

"Father . . ."

The man stepped into the light. His wind- and sun-burned face more sorrow than fury. He removed his hat, pressed it to his heart, and bowed.

"Miss," he said, then he placed the hat back on this head and was gone.

The deck swayed. My breath caught.

"Peter said he was a terror," I whispered.

Roger's head shook once, sharply. "Peter is the terror. He lies. He steals from the other world. He brings children here to feed the story that keeps him alive."

A chill threaded down my spine. My brothers. I couldn't leave them there much longer.

Roger leaned closer, his voice lowering to something barely human. "When a child stops amusing him . . . he doesn't simply let them go. He consumes whatever wonder is left in them. He drains it. Leaves them hollow. That's when their body returns to the other side, all dried skin and bone."

My stomach clenched.

Roger kept speaking. "And if the story grows hungry, he takes more. Every twelve years, he goes on and fetches a new group, one by one. Once he's taken all he can, he goes back to sleep and begins again."

"Why every twelve years?"

"I don't know. Maybe that's the age when a child starts realizing they're leaving true childhood behind. Maybe there's some meaning in it. So many stories just don't have all of the answers."

Something inside me snapped taught.

I needed to get back to my brothers.

Before Peter got to them.

* * *

"Tomorrow," I whispered. I'll post the letters tomorrow.

The clock struck midnight. I placed the letters together on my desk and watched the lamplight.

For a moment, the house was still.

Then, a sound from above. A slow, deliberate creak from the nursery.

Another, and another.

The pen slipped from my fingers and rolled across the desk.

I held my breath, listening.

Then came another sound. Softer. Nearer.

A footstep.

No. It can't come in. Not this far. There are rules.

I rose from the chair. I wasn't dreaming. I wasn't a child. And I hadn't invited it in.

That was what it needed. Permission. To enter your life. And I would not give it. Not this time.

The air had changed. Faint. Sweet. Metallic. Sugar and rust. The smell of nursery toys long after a child had stopped playing with them.

A floorboard creaked somewhere. Then another one.

Halfway up the stairs, I saw it. Small. Deliberate. Waiting.

A toy.

A wooden flute, no longer than my hand. The carvings along its length were crude but familiar: feathers, wings, the faint curve of a laughing mouth etched into the grain.

My pulse faltered. I knew this was his. I'd seen him play it before. How was he doing this? How did he get in? I would not call out. I would not address him because that was what he wanted. My acknowledgement. My attention. And I wouldn't give it.

I bent down, hesitated to reach for it, and then it dissolved into a fine mist. A dark shimmer left behind on the step.

Before I reached the top of the stairs I heard it, the nursery doorknob jerked and twisted, as if someone were trapped inside.

Then came music.

* * *

I listened closely, approaching the door. With each step I reminded myself I hated him for what he did to me. For what he did to my brothers.

The doorknob turned again. Then stopped. Laughter. Not loud. Just clear enough for me to know that there was someone in that room.

Music played.

Jack, Jack, Jack-in-the-box,
Playing your music—when will it stop?
Jack, Jack, Jack-in-the-box,
You're all wound up—time to pop!

John's jack-in-the-box.

I could imagine it behind the door. The painted clown bursting free, red-cheeked, glass-eyed.

The jack-in-the-box went on. Wheezing. Someone was turning the crank.

A flicker of gold unspooled at my feet. Not lamplight. Not gaslight. It moved across the floorboards, restless. Alive. A glow too warm for fire. Too deliberate for flame.

Campfire.

The word surfaced before I could stop it.

I dropped to my knees. The chill bit through my nightdress as I pressed my ear to the floor, trying to looked through the seam beneath the nursery room door.

From beyond came a faint crackle of embers. And then, a voice. Sweet. Cruel. Impatient.

"Wendy. It's time to play."

I flinched, but he wasn't talking to me, not me here in this house right now.

I pressed my eye close, trying to see, and what I saw was not my house. Not the nursery. Not London. A forest.

The trees pressed close, bark slick with sap, roots threading through soil that glowed red-orange in the firelight. And in that glow, movement.

Children. Over a dozen of them.

My boys.

Their names rose in my throat. All of them at once. But I couldn't speak. I wanted to call out. I wanted to pull them through the door and hold them and tell them that I was sorry. I was so sorry. I should've gone back. I should have brought them home.

They spun around the fire barefoot and shrieking, their bodies smeared with soot, streaked in crimson. Animal pelts clung to their shoulders, fox, wolf, boar, over their heads, the skulls of beasts too large for their frames: hollow eyes, curved bear jaws, a crocodile's grin splitting open a boy's face.

Blood glistened down their necks. Some held bones as flutes. Others slapped their thighs, the rhythm, primal, didn't want to stop. But their laughter wasn't really joy. It was worship.

And at the center of them, standing before the fire, more like god than boy—

Peter.

His shadow stretched too long, too sharp, flickering in ways no fire could explain. His face was still a boy's, perfect, radiant, but his eyes held something older. Something that had never been young.

He lifted a hand.

The children stilled. Their skull masks gleamed in the firelight, breath fogging the air in quick, shallow bursts.

"Shhhh," he said.

The forest obeyed.

I felt it then, the pull. The same enchantment that had once bound me to his voice, his stories, his games. It threaded through me before I could stop it.

"Wendy . . ."

He smiled.

"Boys," he murmured. "It's time for a story. Right, Wendy?"

The fire snapped. The children shifted, small, eager. The soft thud of bare feet against damp earth.

They gathered in a circle around the flames. Their skulls glowed. Their small hands clutched together.

Then, softer, another voice.

A child's.

Mine.

"Why are you whispering?" a younger me asked, low and teasing.

"Because there's a monster in the forest."

Laughter followed. Thin. Musical. The kind that circles when you listen too long.

"And if the monster finds us?" little me asked.

"Maybe she's watching us right now." Peter paused. Smiled. "Aren't you, Wendy?"

I flinched. My stomach turned to ice.

The others laughed with her. With me.

My brave, beautiful boys.

I pressed closer to the floorboards. My pulse hammered in my throat.

I'm sleeping. I'm not really seeing this.

Then, Peter's voice again. Softer than breath. "Once upon a time, there was a girl who forgot her promise."

The flames bent inward. Every child turned toward the door. Toward me.

"No," I said aloud.

The light shifted. I searched the seam beneath the door, but Peter was no longer there. Where had he gone?

"Don't be afraid, Wendy." The voice slipped through the keyhole. "You know I would always find you."

I froze. My breath thinned. My body remembered what my mind refused to accept.

Beyond the door, the celebration twisted into frenzy. Children's cheers rose. High. Sharp. Piercing.

Then, through the seam, I saw it. A blade. Small. Sharp. Gleaming. Lifted.

A cry tore out of me. I squeezed my eyes shut.

A squeal followed. Not laughter. Not human.

The light beneath the door flared red.

Iron and smoke. Blood and ash.

"Dinner!" Peter's voice rang out, bright with delight. "I told you I'd catch that pig! A great big marsh pig!"

The children erupted in cheers, high, breathless, unrestrained.

Little Wendy's laugh joined theirs.

Then came the sound. Wet. Rhythmic. Deliberate.

The pig screamed, shrill, uncanny, like a child being chased through reeds. Not quite animal. Not quite human.

The laughter swelled.

I pressed my palm against the door. It vibrated faintly beneath my skin. "Stop," I whispered.

Something warm began to seep through the seam.

A thin trickle at first, winding between the boards, touching the tip of my shoe. Blood, thick and hot, reeking of copper and swamp rot and smoke.

It slid down the curve of my foot in a slow, deliberate ribbon.

My body refused to move.

A nightmare. This is a nightmare. But the heat was undeniable. The smell, a horrid truth.

Then, movement.

A shadow slipped through the seam where the blood had seeped. Rising slow as smoke.

It coiled around my ankle. Cool at first. Then it tightened.

I gasped, pushing back, but the dark followed, climbing my leg like a searching hand.

"Wendy." Peter's voice, closer now. Almost tender. "You belong here. With me. With the boys. Forever."

"No," I hissed, jerking free.

My skin still burned where the shadow had touched me. As if marked. As if claimed.

Then, a bark. Sharp. Alive. Defiant.

Dinah exploded down the hallway, a woolly storm of gray and white paws thundering against the floorboards. Her growl tore the silence open, low, primal, furious. She hurled herself toward the nursery door, teeth bared, fur bristling.

The shadow recoiled, the blood vanished, and the light snapped out.

I gasped, palms pressed hard to the boards. "Good girl. Good girl."

She padded over and licked my face, tail wagging.

"It's all right," I lied, voice shaking. "It's over now."

But I knew better.

He had found me again. And I feared he wouldn't leave empty-handed.

The shadows in the corner swelled, then receded, as if the house itself exhaled.

The rules, I reminded myself. *He cannot come in. not this far. I am awake. I did not agree to play.*

Then the telephone rang downstairs. Shrill, abrupt. I startled, then stood and made my way down.

I lifted the receiver.

"Hello?"

"Wendy."

Michael's voice. Older now, roughened by years and distance, but still carrying that fragile, boyish tremor, the same one from when he used to call for me in the dark.

I gripped the cord tightly. "Michael?"

How many years has it been?

I almost asked, but I remembered. Since the funeral. Since the accident that took Mother and Father together. A derailed trolley on a bright summer day.

"I just had a nightmare," he said quietly.

The words struck like a match to kindling.

"Me too."

The line hissed. Crackled.

Went dead.

For a long moment, I listened to the silence breathing back through the receiver. I stood there staring at the front door, thinking about the windows. Wondering how long they would all hold.

And in that quiet, I heard something faint. Not static.

Wings.

CHAPTER

6
Michael

MY FLAT ALWAYS smelled of coal and tea.

I'd long ago gotten used to it. No choice but to.

The scent clung to everything, curtains, the bread tin, the pages of whatever book I'd left open on the table.

I liked to keep the room tidy. Out of habit. Not really out of comfort. I liked knowing where everything was. It helped me feel steady, grounded. I also didn't own much, which was just fine with me. That made it all the easier to leave it all behind.

A narrow cot tucked against the wall. A small table with more books, all of them borrowed. The only bit of decoration in the entire place was a horseshoe hung above the door. Thanks to Wendy.

Though, tonight the whole place smelled off.

Putrid. Like something had crawled behind the walls and died there.

I rushed over to the windows and threw them all open. Cold October air rushing in, along with city noises from below.

The clatter of tram wheels. Boots marching home, or maybe some away from home. Someone below shouting "Good night!" Perhaps after a few too many pints. Then, farther off in the distance, a man scream-shouted-slurred the words to "It's a Long Way to Tipperary." I wonder how many he'd had to numb it all.

I fell into the wingback chair by the window and looked down at my hands. Blue ink stained my fingertips.

The words from the contract burned behind my eyes: *Enlistment. Service. Purpose.*

The gas lamp outside sputtered once and died, shooting shadows across the room.

I shut the windows and eased back into the chair, closing my eyes, drawing a long breath.

I'd go see Wendy and John tomorrow. Of course I would. I was leaving soon. I know we didn't speak much, but still, I loved them, and goodbyes were owed.

A drip echoed from the kitchen sink, slow, metallic, steady. A lone man's lullaby.

Soon enough I'd be somewhere that never slept, where the noises never ceased, where quiet was a luxury, maybe a lie.

What else was there to do? *Enlistment. Service. Purpose.*

Something sharp creaked in the corner. I opened my eyes. Listened.

"That's strange."

The only thing that sat in that part of the room was an old toy chest. It was the only thing I brought here from my childhood home. I set it in that corner the day I moved in and never touched it again.

I felt stupid some days having it there, but I reasoned, Wendy had her journal. I had this.

Sometimes remembering the past isn't about being stuck in it. Sometimes remembering the past is a reminder of what happened, what was learned, and how we can continue forward.

From the chair, I could see it clearly, the brass hinge catching the lamplight, and the lid . . . open just a crack.

"That's . . . very strange." I straightened up in my chair.

And now, the smell of the room shifted. Of wind carrying hints of river water.

"No," I whispered to myself, but it was already too late.

My mind was there, and I could hear John. Sharp. Frantic. "Toss those things in the fire, Wendy! Burn them!"

"No! I can't!"

"We can't take anything back—"

And then the memory sharpened: Wendy, on her knees. Roger, on the ground, legs splayed out in front of him. His back against a tree trunk, eyes closed.

Nearby, Peter . . .

"Wendy," John pressed, voice breaking. "We have to go."

She was sobbing. Her arms around the neck of a dying boy. Her face buried in his jacket. His long dark hair resting on her shoulders.

Her fingers clutched her journal one hand, and in the other she held a pocket watch, glinting in the sun.

My face was covered in tears. My hands and feet caked in dirt. From running. From falling.

"John . . ." I whimpered. "I want to go home."

John looked at me. My big brother. Eyes so sure. "We're going to get you home. All of us."

Something stirred. Shifted. The ping of something metal dropping onto a wooden floor.

I sat up, pulse leaping. I looked around the dark room. It was so small I could see every inch in moments, and there was nothing out of its place.

My eyes moved back to the chest . . . and my breath snagged.

The lid had been pushed fully open.

Before I could step forward and look inside, my eyes shifted downward, where I spotted the impossible.

Tin soldiers.

Not scattered. Not toppled from age or gravity. Neatly arranged in perfect formation.

Each soldier's shadow leaned inward, their dark silhouettes converging on the same point.

The lamplight glinted off of their bayonets. Their helmets tipped forward in a posture that wasn't accidental. They were at the ready.

A low hum prickled up my arms.

A grown man shouldn't be unnerved by toy soldiers. But I was.

My hand trembled as I reached for the nearest figure. Its chipped head gleamed back at me, its eyes worn away a long time ago.

I'd forgotten how light they were. How sharp their bayonets.

"How . . ."

Something rumbled beneath my feet, beneath the floorboards. As if someone were running upright on the ceiling below.

The platoon quivered.

One soldier shifted to his side with a tiny scrape of its boot against the floorboard.

I stared, noting their position. And then it all clicked into place.

They weren't guarding anything.

Every face. Every rifle. All of them, they were turned directly toward me.

"Bloody hell . . ."

They weren't arranged in a position of protection. They were lined up as if they'd just set sights on their enemy. Me.

"Michael . . ."

The voice was a spear dug straight through my ribs.

I spun around. There was nothing there. My chair. The window.

"Michael, you left me."

"I refuse to believe in you anymore," I said. "I've grown up." I took a step back.

The floor gave an uncertain creak beneath my heel.

I dragged my hands over my face. I'm tired, I reasoned. It's nerves. I leave in days. Off to another country, it might as well be another world.

The lamplight shuddered, sending a shock of shadows across the walls. I monitored them, one by one, moving like no shadows should. They swirled against the surface of things like a drop of ink dropped into a glass of water.

And it was in that moment I realized: We may try to forget our monsters, but they won't forget us.

"We killed you."

Laughter erupted in the room followed by a boy's scream.

"I remember," I told myself. Again and again.

Wendy bursting through the trees. Breath ragged. Roger right behind her. John and I waiting for them on the forest path, where it forked. One way toward the treehouse, and the other . . . home.

Peter was there waiting. Eyes furious that we had discovered the way back home.

"We have to go." Wendy stepped forward, and that's when Peter snatched her wrist and pulled her close.

My sister screamed. Crows cawed and Peter laughed.

I cried, "Wendy! Leave her alone!"

John knelt and looked me in the eyes. "If I tell you to run along, you do. You go, quickly. I'll bring Wendy. We'll be right behind you."

* * *

I stood in my flat now, frozen, half man, half child, but fully a ghost.

We were not the only thing to emerge from Kensington Gardens that day.

There were bodies. Some John's size. Others mine. All desiccated and darkened by the sun.

A balloon vendor heard us crying, and it was he who called for the constables. The Darling children were found.

Now I see, we never really did kill that story. It'd just been sleeping this entire time.

A toy soldier tipped sideways. Then another. A slow cascade. As if some unseen child's hand was knocking them down one by one.

Toy rifles and bayonets skittered across the floor. Helmets rolled in uneven arcs. One soldier snapped straight clean across the middle when he hit the floor. Severed at the waist.

Fear pinned me upright.

"Still playing soldier, Michael?"

I swallowed hard, throat dry. Unsure what to do. Where to go. Every corner of the room felt alive.

Just as the toy soldiers had done. Just as boys on the battlefield would soon do beside me.

I feared not only the wrong command but making the wrong decision.

"Who's there?" I managed.

A child's giggle responded.

Beneath my boots, the floorboards began to hum again with that vibration, of someone running. Pacing. Moving.

Then the floorboards began to move and lift as if hands below were pushing them up. Hard.

Wooden boards bowed upward. Loud splintering cracks filled the room. I took a step back away from the path of wood bulging.

A tremor crawled up my calves, and I could move no farther or look away.

And then, slowly, a thin gray finger slid through a break. Wrongly thin.

Its nail split straight down the center, exposing white slivers of bone like ivory needles.

Another board cracked, sharper. And then a whole section of floor splintered open.

From that black pit below I heard a small child snickering.

A small hand appeared, blue, twisted, the skin puckered with red and yellow sores, cut open in places that had never healed.

A child's hand. It waved toward me.

I could not move. I could not close my eyes.

The hand continued to move, splitting and breaking floorboards wide until it reached me, and hooked one finger into the bottom of my trouser leg, tugging once, soft as breath.

"Don't leave us again, Michael. Come with us."

The voice seeped up through the boards, soggy, soaked, echoing with years.

My stomach dropped into ice water. I begged my eyelids to shut, but they would not.

Another crack, faster now. The floor giving way in a jagged line.

Within that gap, an eye appeared. Small, gray-white and set deep in a child's face that should not have been able to move.

The face rose slowly through the gap, pale, swollen, blue-white cheeks dusted with dirt. I remembered him.

A dozen years ago.

A boy. About my age at the time. Nibs. Nodding in the direction of the swampy lagoon. All of us had gathered there for a game.

Peter had dared Nibs to swim across it.

"I can do that!" Nibs blurted, eagerly.

"You sure?" Peter teased. "There're crocodiles in there." And the way Peter said it, so excitedly, felt wrong.

Nibs jumped in the water, the sun shining on his golden hair.

Small arms paddling, and it took no time. Seconds maybe before they all gathered.

Massive, scaly beasts. Their bodies slick and green. Mouths snapped open. White bone. Dark throats. Green dark water churning.

Nibs didn't even have time to scream.

A soft sound escaped me, a gasp and a sob.

Fingers clawed at the inside of my skull searching for an explanation, for sense, exhaustion, war, the fog.

The telephone rang. The sound of brass bells screaming for attention.

I stared at the candlestick telephone for a moment. Something so normal in this madness. When I looked back to the floor the toy soldiers, the dead little boy, the torn-up floorboards, it was all gone.

I stumbled over to the phone. Lifted the receiver and then I heard her.

"Michael?"

Her voice sounded so faint. So distant. A dream I was trying to remember.

"Wendy?"

Static.

"I had a bad dream."

Static.

My mouth tasted of copper, as if I'd bitten down on my own fear.

"Me too," I managed.

The line hissed, cracked once, and went dead.

I stood there, holding the phone in my hand, listening.

Outside, a tram clattered. An automobile honked. And I overheard the bright laughter of young women.

I looked toward the chest. The lid was down. From here, it didn't seem special at all. Just a battered old toy chest with a few worn toy soldiers inside. Objects a man clung onto to remember that at one time he was a child and at one time his life was full of imagination and splendor, and not the weighted worry of stepping onto a battlefield.

I set the receiver down and returned to my chair. My hands shook. My feet shook.

Tomorrow, I wouldn't just call.

I'd go. To my sister. To Wendy.

I'd tell her all I'd seen, and let her know that I remembered.

CHAPTER

7

John

THE BABY WAS crying. Not from hunger. Not from dampness. Judith had checked twice. Moving with that slow, shaky exhaustion that only a new mother knows, before she finally collapsed into bed.

But the crying didn't stop.

It remained, a steady tempo. Pressing on, then thinning for a few minutes before it rose sharp and then deepened.

Our baby, Margot, just a few months old.

Her cry stretched itself into something that sounded older than a child. The way she shrieked, it didn't feel normal.

It gave me a chill, that raw and painful cry.

"Judith," I whispered. Guilt pricked me, not wanting to wake her, but still needing her to know I would check on the baby. "I'll go to Margot." I brushed a kiss on Judith's brow.

I swung my legs from the bed, the floorboards cold.

"Margot," I said, her name tumbling out of my mouth before I reached her door.

The gaslight in the hallway shook.

"Just frightened," I said. "Poor darling." That's what it was. She woke with a fright and found herself alone in the dark.

"On my way, darling."

Her wail shifted. It pierced the walls and threaded through the beams and pipes of this house, and for a moment it seemed as if all of the portraits along the hallway shook with the force of her cry.

Partway down the hall I paused. The cold bit my nose and cheeks. I turned around, half expecting to find the window wide open, but it wasn't. It was closed and latched. A wreath made of hawthorn and St. John's wort hung just above.

Judith had seemed displeased when she removed the tissue paper from the box to discover it.

"That's quite beautiful," I said. "Very thoughtful of Wendy."

She gave me a forced smile, "And look, with instruction as to where she wants us to hang it."

I slipped the letter from the package before Judith could read it. Wendy had a way with worry that made others . . . uncomfortable, but that I understood.

John, please hang this in the hallway by the window. Hawthorn and St. John's wort to protect the baby. This will keep it away.

Even after all of these years she worried. Every now and again Michael and I would receive little packages in the mail, pots of honey, iron keys. Goodness knows we each had horseshoes sent to use on several occasions. But even if a part of me thought these superstitions silly, I never once failed to put them to use.

Just in case.

The flame flickered, sending a strip of shadow across the ceiling. I steadied myself against the wall.

Margot's cry rose and dipped, this strange sort of warbling that did not sound at all like the wail of a baby. The crying fractured, echoing strangely, once above me, once below, somehow close and impossibly distant.

A trick of this old house. Maybe.

The crying stopped.

Another noise. Thin. Fluttering. Leaves rustling the wind. Wings flapping, finding their way.

And then, as if startled by something, the baby—a fierce cry erupted.

I pushed forward.

The floor groaning beneath my feet, the creaks not in step with my movements, instead like a child beating erratically on a drum.

A small draft stirred a mix of smells. Ones that did not belong here.

I stopped, my limbs confused by those scents that didn't belong within the walls of a home.

It smelled not just like outside, but like a forest pounded by rain. Wet leaves. Rain sliding off gigantic palm leaves.

This wasn't the smell of London in fall or even spring. This was the sense of a place so far away it didn't even have a name. We just called it that Far Place.

The baby's cries reached me in the dark, ivy weaving itself through my fingers and yanking me back.

I shut my eyes and pressed my palms against them. No, that was a long time ago, but still . . . I slipped into my thoughts.

Wendy, her eyes affright.

"John . . ." Her eyes flicked from my hands back to my face. "Whose blood is that?"

I looked at my palms in the dark hallway.

"We were hunting boar, and Peter pointed and said: 'There, quick!' I drew my arrow. I . . . I didn't . . . it was Tootles behind the bush. I listened to Peter. I trusted him."

"Colic," I said to myself. Margot has colic. She's fine. Just needs her father.

Deep within my ribs I felt something shuddering, dislodging itself: fear.

It had snatched me and my siblings from our nursery, and it dropped us so very far away from home. It promised us a childhood of laughter, games, toys, and sweets.

Within days, I believed we'd die there.

The doorknob to Margot's nursery felt hot in my palm. I pushed it open. The door sighed. Hinges squealed.

Moonlight washed the room in silver. Dark shadows rose in corners.

"Margot," I whispered. "Papa's here."

The room was quiet. Still.

I approached her crib, and there she slumbered. Her tiny fists tucked beneath her cheeks. Her chest slowly rising and falling.

I pressed my hand gently on top of her head. Her hair so silky and fine. She was deep asleep.

But . . . I'd heard her crying?

A single floorboard moaned behind me. That smell returned. Pine sap. Wet leaves. Damp soil, and something else . . . harsh and coppery.

I turned around and flinched, startled by the sight of myself. My reflection looking back at me from a mirror.

Its frame, oval and chestnut, was simple and ordinary, but tonight, in this light, it seemed out of place. The surface wavering, as a breeze rushing over a body of water.

Behind me, in the mirror, I could see the entirety of Margot's room. From the curtains it seemed as if a form emerged.

"Who's there?" I shouted.

Laughter. Soft. Childlike.

The room was quiet. I searched behind the curtains. I crouched beside the crib. There was nothing.

Perhaps I was dreaming, I thought. Dreaming of her crying. Dreaming of all of this.

I reached for the doorknob to return to bed, and then I heard it.

A child's whisper. Thin and singsong.

It was coming from that oval shape.

I returned to the mirror, and in that surface, I saw a streak of black unraveling itself from the edges of the mirror.

Peter, Peter, shadow eater.

There was no one who lived on this earth besides me and my siblings who should know those words.

Wendy said the wards would work, just in case, and here I was . . . just in case. Iron above our front door. Wreaths made of wild herbs, those which it detested. But still—it made its way back.

"This is impossible . . ."

I had seen her drag a blade across his neck. Blood splattered onto the forest floor in sheets. He collapsed to his knees and toppled over. Frantic fingers clawing at the widening gash as though he could put himself back together.

Her face had gone white. Her eyes vacant. Unreachable.

"Wendy, give me the knife."

She stood there, trembling. Holding the blade out. Her fingers slick with blood.

My gaze followed hers, to Roger.

Peter's blood continued to pour. Pooling. His skin shifting from green to black.

"Wendy, give it to me."

Quiet tears lined her face. We both looked down to find what had become of Peter, a heap of bone and blood and leaves.

"John . . ." her voice broke. "How did I allow myself to fall . . ."

"Don't blame yourself. He tricked you. He wore a boy's mask. A boy's promise. He lied because all he wanted was to steal your happiness, to make himself whole while making you hollow."

Above us a crow cawed. And another.

I took the knife from her and flung it deep into the forest. "We have to go." I took her hand, reached for Michael, and the three of us ran, not looking back.

* * *

The shadow unraveled across the mirror's surface. Unfurling like a flag. A black smear loosening from the corners of the glass. It curled, recoiled, like a ribbon of smoke trapped under ice. It slid quickly in nervous spirals. Movements defying the rules of light.

I shook my head no, again and again, because he could not be here. I had seen him die.

But here he was. In my infant daughter's bedroom.

Not behind me, but there, inside the glass.

A boy with stars burning in his eyes. His red mouth curved into a smile too bright, too sweet, a child's grin mocking the whole of innocence.

The taste of rotting leaves and dead flesh filled my mouth. My stomach turned.

Peter.

That name was an abomination of time and memory.

His eyes glimmered like winter stars, his lips still set in that dreadful, perfect smile.

"I'm . . . sleeping. A nightmare," I stammered.

He stepped through the mirror as if stepping through a curtain.

"Are you dreaming, John? Are you dreaming of me?" He tilted his head, inspecting me. Studying me. His eyes piercing.

He looked of ruin and remembrance. Dressed in green. Leaves that had died long ago covered his clothes. Each one shivered faintly against him, their edges quaking and clicking and snapping like insects pinned to his sleeves and trouser legs. They lifted in faint, restless tremors. Fluttering. Though no wind blew. It was as if each leaf attached to him breathed on its own.

Light bent around him, and the black shape that trailed him, that dreaded shadow, stood taller than me, as tall as the room, brushing against the ceiling.

Now I understood with a clarity that shocked me cold. The past had not just been real.

It was here.

His hair was the glow of embers in a dying fire.

His face was beautiful but wrong. Sharp, delicate features, and with fine white teeth, of which his incisors tapered into slight points, strong enough to bite clean through raw meat.

My face flashed hot. This was not a little boy. This was madness and monstrosity that relished our pain.

Every time I had cried, Peter laughed. Every time I begged him, *please, no more adventures*, we went, and for every game we played we returned missing another child, his body left to rot in a cavern, a marsh, or heaved onto a canoe and rolled out into the sea.

Once I tried to go back, to give one of the boys a proper burial, but I found him surrounded by marsh pigs. Nothing left but crunched-up bone.

"John, I missed you." His voice wasn't a single voice, but something layered, reaching, searching, as if trying to remember which one belonged to him.

I tried to speak. To curse him. To drive him out. To muster even a shred of sound, but nothing came.

My chest cinched tight as though invisible fingers were logged behind my ribs squeezing.

His smile unfolded slowly. A boy's smile. Soft. Guileless, but behind it, a devil's bite sharpening with delight.

My pulse stuttered. The room tipped sideways.

For a moment, I wasn't in London at all but back in that impossible forest, where the only warmth we had was Wendy, seated in front of the glow of that firelight telling us stories.

It was Wendy's tales that transported us, her stories, lullabies, nursery rhymes, and fairy tales.

It was her words that soothed us and made us feel that magic, good magic, was real and kind. That is when we were the most childlike when we were there, when she transported us elsewhere with her words.

Peter, his games, his adventures, all of it, all of him was illusion. A lie, where laughter was forced by day to hide how we'd all collapse into bed at night smelling of death.

"I . . . didn't allow you in," I stammered, the words shaking apart as I spoke them.

He was not supposed to pass through doorways protected with iron. Or pass through windows with salt sprinkled on their sills.

"You're right, I can't come in those ways, but I can come through your mind. I'm in your memories, John."

"You're not really here then . . ."

He nodded no, then yes. A devious look. "Not yet, but I'll keep getting stronger and then you'll let me in."

"Never."

He raised his eyebrows. "No?" He nodded toward the crib. "Maybe she'll let me in then."

Margot.

My stomach dropped. Panic rushed up my spine, seizing every part of me at once. My hand trembled. And all of me became useless. Unable to move. Unable to grab him and fight him.

"I can enter any home that has a child," he said, mocking. "As long as they believe in me. Babies dream about in-between places all the time. And I'm always there listening."

"She's a baby! My daughter!" The protest ripped out of me like a wound being torn back open.

My child. My daughter.

Every single nightmare I thought I'd outrun surged back, swift and merciless. He would never have her. He would not lay a single wicked shadowed finger on her golden head.

"I've missed Wendy so much," he said softly. "You and Michael too, of course. But Wendy . . ." His eyes brightened. "She was the first girl I ever brought to the island."

He leaned in, boyish and eager, as if sharing a secret he'd been saving for centuries. "She's special. There's a spark inside of her. It makes people feel safe. Warm. She makes them forget when they're afraid, when they're hurt. She makes all of their worries fall away."

A shadow crossed his face.

"I hate that she does that for other people. That shouldn't be for other people. That's just a waste on them. It should all just be for me."

His voice lowered to a whisper.

"I know she can't help it. Carrying that light and belief. But I can smell it. I can taste it. It tastes like forever."

He smiled. Wide and wrong. Every single part of me strained, trying to move. Wanting nothing more than to charge at him.

"I'll get more boys. Then she can be their mother and read them stories and tuck them in at night."

His breath hitched, hungry. "Then she'll tell me stories. Every night. Every story. All of them. Then I'll be able to taste all of the pieces of her. Every single one."

He met my gaze with a stillness I'd only seen in snakes, moments before they lunge for their prey.

The rug seemed to shift beneath my feet, a subtle drag as though the floor itself recoiled. The walls of the bedroom leaned inward, sending slithering shadows tumbling forward.

And the smells. *Those dreadful smells.* Moss and wet stone. Logs burning on the fire, and something else.

That other place. The name we'd all promised to never utter again.

I forced my mouth to open, to make out words. "Leave us alone," I choked, barely recognizing my own voice. My muscles slowly awakening again. "We killed you. You're nothing. You're not real."

He took a step forward, arms loose at his sides, as though this were all play.

"Maybe I'm not real," he mused. "Maybe I'm just wood smoke and mirrors. Maybe I've been living inside of your brain this entire time."

That awful, dreadful smile of his sharpened, and I wished no more than to tear it off his face.

"Or maybe I'm realer than you, John. Why? Because I can fly. I can fight. I never stopped. And I've been waiting for my Darlings to open the door."

His gaze swept over me, cold, appraising. "What did you do with yourself all these years? Hmm?"

A tilt of the head. "Was it worth growing up? You've gained a bit of weight, I see. You lost some hair atop your head too. Let me guess . . . what did you grow up to be?" He tapped his chin theatrically. "An accountant."

He shook his head before I could answer. "No. A barrister. You studied the law. Why is that? Is it because you broke so many?"

"Shut up!" The words tore out of me. "I didn't hurt anyone!"

"You didn't?" His head angled, owl-like. "Nibs? Jax? There sure were a lot of accidents when you were around."

He laughed. Delighted in the torment he trapped me in.

"Get out!" I cried. "Get out!"

Peter's laugh morphed, birdlike, a warble between crow and child. A sound that scraped down my spine like claws.

"Oh, John," he cooed. "You're a miserable old thing. But don't worry. We'll get you back home, and you'll see, everything will be wonderful again. Better than it ever was."

He leaned closer, voice dropping low, almost tender.

The mirror rippled, the entire surface shifting to a scene from so, so long ago. Me kneeling on the ground, arms covering my face, because I could not bear to witness him looking like that. *Jax.* His head twisted in a way it shouldn't. His neck bulged. Sharp, shattered pieces of bone jutted out from his legs.

"Jax actually was quite a bore," Peter said, looking at the scene. "You, though, John. You are a great pal to join me on adventures. I can't wait for you all to return home. Soon. Soon."

The glass turned black, waves crashing into one another. Slowly, gracefully he stepped right through and he was gone.

I fell to the ground and stared at my reflection. Eyes wide. Face colorless, a sheen of sweat on my forehead. Hands pressed to the sides of my head, willing for all of what I'd just seen to be unseen.

I had to phone Michael. I had to see Wendy. They had to be warned. Peter was back . . . and somehow, he was able to get in. Not feigned flesh and blood like before, but a phantom, with plans to gain strength.

I staggered to my feet, my hands steadying on the railing of the crib. Margot, still asleep.

Michael. Wendy.

He would not touch my daughter, nor my brother, nor my sister. Peter had destroyed enough lives, and we barely escaped with our own.

I shut my eyes tight. Hating him. Hating what he'd done to us. We had emerged from that blackness and returned partly broken, and we would not be dragged back.

CHAPTER

8

Wendy

THE SMELL REACHED me first. Smoke, thick and acrid.

I lurched awake. My cheek tore free from a scatter of papers on my desk, stuck to a pool of half-dried ink. My hand was still locked around my pen. My knuckles white. Each finger ached as I uncurled them one by one.

I winced. A sharp pain shot down my neck and radiated in my shoulders. I had fallen asleep at my desk, not in my bed.

The fire pulsed weakly in the grate.

My vision adjusted. I traced the contours of every shadow in the room. Watching. Waiting for any movement that couldn't be explained.

I sat there for what felt like hours, monitoring the stillness, before I trusted myself enough to look toward the window.

A silver veil clung to the glass. The world beyond looked bleached white.

Fog. Just fog. Fog can't hurt me.

But it made me feel adrift. Cut off. The way he had once cut me off from everything I knew.

That was what he did. He tore me away from myself when I was younger. And now he was threatening to tear me away from what I loved.

My children at Marigold House.

For years I believed I owed penance. I cared for the little ones because I thought I had to. But loving them never felt like service. It felt like the most natural thing I could do. It gave me joy. It gave me meaning.

Marigold House had taught me that I could heal. That my life belonged to me, not him. That I could become something new.

I stood, opened the door, and peered down the hall.

The nursery door was closed.

I exhaled.

Soon the children at Marigold House would be stirring, feet padding down the dormitory floor, hands shaking shoulders, bodies bounding on beds.

Awake! Awake!

I could almost hear them now.

They were my tether to this world.

I could hear Eleanor: *You're safe.*

I could hear Rosie: *Your life belongs to you.*

* * *

And I could hear Roger, explaining what I hadn't wanted to understand.

We stood at the bow of the ship. The sun dipping low over the horizon.

"What does he want?" I asked.

"Your light, Wendy. That's what he feeds on. Hope. Promise. Innocence. Joy." Roger stared out at the water. "That's why he wants children. He drains us of all our possibilities until all we're left with is fear and despair. That's when he discards us. That's when we die. He'll keep doing it until forever."

He paused.

"You could stay with me," he said quietly. "But I can't promise I could keep you safe. There's no true safety when he's near."

"I have to go back. For my brothers. Then I have to set it right."

"Then promise me something."

"What?"

"Promise me that as soon as you get your brothers you'll leave here and forget this place."

* * *

Movement caught my eye. The grate. Something was burning in it. I looked from the desk to the fireplace and back.

My letters. No!

I rushed to the hearth. The letters I'd written to John and Michael—both of them, curling in the flames.

"How did this happen?" I said to the empty room.

I knelt, watching the flames engulf my words. The pages curled inward on themselves, blackening at the edges. My handwriting twisted as if trying to escape.

Melted wax pooled at the grate. Ink bubbled and blistered. I reached for the poker, trying to drag whatever I could out.

Sparks scattered. Pieces disintegrated in my hands, collapsing into brittle curls.

Only one small scrap survived. Its corner trembling in the draft.

I'm afraid the shadows are creeping closer. I don't want to die. You and John are the only hope I have. I want to live my life, one where I'm not always looking back, searching for him in dark corners. Please help me.

I placed it on a log and watched my words dissolve. Behind me, the steady tick of Roger's watch. I set the poker back and stood, wiping my hands on my skirt. When I looked at them again, my palms were stained with ink.

And then I remembered.

I had sealed those letters in envelopes. Folded them. Pressed them with wax. *The fire was nearly out when you fell asleep. You didn't put them there.*

My stomach tightened.

Somehow, Peter had learned to reach into my life without being invited in. and that was as dangerous as having him here.

I looked at the walls. The ceiling. "I don't know how you're going to do this," I said aloud. "But I'm going to write them again. You won't stop me."

The curtains swelled inward, the pale fabric filling for a moment with the shape of someone.

Then they settled.

"I will never allow you back in."

On the desk lay my journal. Open. Waiting.

Beneath the smell of burning paper and ink, another scent rose. Dead leaves rotting. On the tip of my tongue, the hint of crushed mushrooms, freshly plucked from dirt.

A rustle through brush. A faint child's laugh.

The air tightened around me. My eyes began to water.

Animal noises now. The chirrup of birds. The clicking of insects.

"Fine," I said, snatching the journal off my desk. "If you want to hear what I wrote, then listen."

I opened to the first page.

Today, I met a boy I really like. He has fiery red hair and green eyes and he climbs trees, and he's marvelous.

"But that was a lie. You were the lie. A mask." My voice shook. "You're not a boy. You're something else altogether, and you tricked me."

I flipped to the place where I kept the leaf. There it was, glowing. Its pulse faint, but undeniable. Everything in that other place lived and breathed.

I brushed my fingertip against it and wept. My shoulders heaving. I turned to the fireplace. Looked at the journal in my hand. Back to the flames.

I couldn't do it.

If I burned these words, I would be destroying both of them, the monster and the memory. This was all I had of Roger. And all I had of that pretend other boy I'd loved, if only for a little while. The one who helped me climb trees. Who held me as we watched ships come into port at sunset. Who walked me to the edge of the beach to see the great departure of newly hatched turtles.

That was the wound. Loving someone who wasn't really real. He was only real because I was real. And it was because of him, that monster with the red hair and green eyes, that I had found Roger. Or, really, Roger found me.

I snapped the journal shut and sat on the edge of the bed.

And I let my thoughts take me back.

* * *

Kensington Gardens. Late afternoon light. Brass music drifting across the treetops.

The air smelled of roasted chestnuts and peppermint, mixed with coal smoke.

Children darted past trailing ribbons and balloons, their shrieks rising and falling.

Women in fine dresses and hats watched as a vendor tied green string to a blue balloon. It was John who spotted the Round Pond first.

"Look! The boats!"

"Here," Father said, pressing a shilling into John's hand. "Go play," he said from behind his newspaper. "Stay away from the gardens!"

Mother and Father sat on their bench and waved us away.

I reached for Michael's hand, and the three of us hurried toward the water. The pond's surface shivered, a bright mirror reflecting the sky.

Toy yachts glided across the water, brightly painted, their owners standing by looking proud. Children leaned over the banks like miniature admirals, shouting predictions as their boats drifted past.

John and Michael joined in, cheering each vessel along.

"I want to look at the balloons," I said.

"Later," John replied, barely glancing at me.

"Michael . . ."

"I want to stay with John."

I huffed. "Fine. I'll be back."

The man at the balloon cart stood alone now. The women in their pretty dresses had moved on. He wore a spotless white uniform to match his equally white cart. A cluster of green, red, gold, and blue balloons rose at this side.

He lifted a red one. It glowed like a drop of blood held up to the late sun. "Would you like a balloon?"

But there was something in that red, that deep, pulsing red, that felt wrong.

I shook my head.

The vendor's eyes followed me. Heavy. Steady.

"Be careful," he said. "Fairies like to snatch little children from those gardens."

I pressed my teeth into my lower lip and then said, "Maybe I want to disappear."

The man laughed, a strange sound, somewhere between human and crow.

I drifted toward the edge, where the trees stood in solemn ranks. A soft wind blew, and leaves whispered, almost musical.

For a moment, I wondered how they did it. How did fairies make little children disappear? Was it through magic? Could they slip into shadows and come out somewhere else?

I stood there, listening to the leaves. The absence of everything else.

No one had come looking for me. I wondered how long it would take for anyone to notice I was gone.

I had grown tired of watching after John and Michael. Tired of helping with the sewing and cleaning. I'd overheard Mother tell Liza that it was time I learned how to cook. Cooking. For whom? I didn't want to care for my brothers for the rest of my life. I wanted my own life. I didn't want to get married. I didn't even want children, especially when there were so many running around alone, sad, without any proper parents. Those were the ones who needed caring for. The ones who didn't have anybody.

"Maybe I'll just disappear forever," I said aloud. "Run off with the fairies myself, and we'll see what you all think about that."

I just wanted to feel seen. Chosen. Important. Maybe I just wanted a friend.

That was when I felt it. Not a sight, a presence. A knowing that something had shifted in the air around me.

Then movement in the trees. A glint. Something green. Something gold.

A single leaf drifted from above, spinning slow, and I reached for it, without thinking. Its veins glowed faintly in my palm, as if lit from within. Warm. Alive.

The world stopped.

The noises from the park ceased. Birds no longer flew overhead. The only sound was my pulse beating in my ears.

A creak from above.

I looked up and gasped when I met his eyes.

"What are you doing up there?" I demanded to know.

He tilted his head. Curious. Confident. Amused. For a moment, he looked like an owl, obscured by leaves and branches, not quite there unless you were looking for him.

He crouched in the crook of an oak, like a creature grown from bark and shadow. Sunlight threaded through his hair. Not quite flame-red, but the color of deep autumn.

His eyes were the green of river water. "My name's Peter," he said.

I felt the air change. The trees leaned closer.

Heat rushed to my cheeks. I turned away, unsettled by the sudden need to stay exactly where I stood.

"I have to find my brothers," I murmured.

When I looked back up, he was gone from the tree. When I looked down, there he was. Standing inches away.

He was a boy, but not, because he was so still. So precise. A statue. A painting.

I stared. He didn't seem real. He seemed *written*. A character from a story. A fairy tale.

"It's rude not to introduce yourself," he said.

"Well, it's rude to crouch in trees above girls."

He laughed.

I eyed him. "My father told me to stay away from here. He said many boys have gone missing from this place."

Peter's eyes brightened. "And still, knowing how dangerous it was, you came."

"Of course. I'm very brave."

"I agree. You are."

His lips curled. Slow at first. Then certain. "The boys aren't missing," he said. "I can show you where they are."

His hands hung loose at his sides, but his fingers twitched, like he was listening to music I couldn't hear. His eyes glittered. Green. Bright. Endless.

"Would you like to come with me?"

A breath. A dare.

"I can take you to them now."

"You're not listening. I told you, my brothers."

He studied my face like he was trying to memorize it. "You can bring your brothers too," he said. "There's room."

I looked up to the treetops, thinking I'd spot the missing boys there. "Where are they?"

"Somewhere for us. Where adults can't find us."

"A . . . treehouse?"

"We have one," he said. "And a waterfall. And a lagoon. And a beach."

I laughed. "Impossible."

"Everything is real," he said, stepping closer, "if you believe it is."

"Prove it."

"I'm here, aren't I?"

His scent reached me, wild, mineral, like a forest after rain.

"What about parents? Yours? Theirs?"

"We don't need those." He took another step. His breath grazed my jaw. "What do you say? Come away with me?"

"I . . ." I couldn't stop looking into his eyes. Green and glittering and bottomless. I could drown in them.

A crow called above us, and he tilted his ear toward the sound as if it were speaking to him.

"Tonight," he said. "After you've all gone up to the nursery."

My breath hitched. "How did you know?"

Another tilt of his head. A sly smile. "I know everything about you."

Another crow called from somewhere I couldn't see.

"If you know everything, then why do I have to introduce myself? What's my name?"

"You're Wendy . . ."

Another caw.

"Darling. Wendy Darling."

Something fluttered inside me. Bright and terrifying. I ached for escape. For possibility. For a world beyond this narrow one of rules and roads already drawn.

"Leave the window open tonight," he said. "I'll find you."

I tried to form a question, but the words tangled on my tongue.

He reached out, caught a strand of my hair between two fingers, lifted it to his nose, and inhaled.

Then he looked at me through his lashes. "I'll be there tonight," he whispered. "And then we'll fly."

Fly?

The wind circled him. Leaves stirred at his feet. Shadows bent and stretched toward him, long and thin.

For a moment, just a moment, I forgot who I was. I forgot the world. I forgot everything but him.

He was the first beautiful lie I ever wanted to believe.

And he was ruin, though I didn't know it yet.

He smiled, releasing my hair. "I know," he said.

"You know what? I didn't say anything."

"You didn't need to." He stepped back. "I'll see you tonight."

The wind slid through the trees.

And then he was gone.

* * *

I snapped the journal shut and slid it into my satchel.

Outside, dawn had come.

I washed. I dressed. I wrote new letters and sealed them with wax.

I went to the telephone and dialed John. It rang. No answer. I dialed Michael. It rang. No answer.

I sat on the kitchen floor next to Dinah as she ate her breakfast. I drank my tea.

"You may have to stay with Liza for a little while," I said, stroking her back. "Thank you for taking care of me. But I don't want you getting hurt. I don't want anyone getting hurt, and whoever I can keep out of his way, the better."

Outside, I locked the front door and stood there for a moment, hand still on the knob.

Maybe last night wasn't real. Maybe I'm just tired. Worried. There's so much change happening. We're at war, sending young men off to die. Boys, really. Perhaps it's just that . . .

Then, faint, impossibly faint. I heard it.

Jack . . . Jack . . . Jack-in-the-box . . .

CHAPTER 9

THE GATES TO Kensington Gardens stood open. It's just a shortcut to Marigold House, I told myself. Just for today. Once I entered, the air shifted. It grew heavier here.

The gravel path crackled faintly beneath my feet. Wet leaves clung to the bottom of my boots. I walked briskly, keeping my gaze low. When I turned left, I stopped. Confused, feeling spun around. The Round Pond stretched before me, its surface pewter-colored and perfectly still. But this wasn't where it should be. That wasn't the path I'd taken, but still, here I was.

That's the thing about fairy stories. Sometimes a path changed while you were on it.

A boat slid close to edge. Its wooden hull, pale and worn. Its mast snapped clean through, as if something had seized it midplay

A streak of red ran across its side. Paint, I insisted. A spill. An accident.

Doubt tugged inside of me, and then I tasted it. Salt water. Bitter and briny. No. Not this. Not now. Not another slip into my past. I needed to get to my children.

* * *

Peter's hands tight around my waist. Him shouting at me. Telling me what I had done wrong, yet again. That I had run off to the pirate ship with Roger, but that was not the truth. Roger saved me from drowning.

And Peter?

He didn't mention any of what he had done, that he was the one who abandoned me at sea, when I asked again if we could go home. He said if I were so determined to do things on my own then I should learn to fly, and then all I remembered was water.

Tears rolled down my face, fat and hot. I tried to break free from his hold, but he was just so strong.

"You're not to leave the house. Ever again. I worry . . ."

"Peter . . . please, you're hurting me . . ."

"Promise me you'll never leave me again. Promise me!"

"Peter, please . . ."

"You belong here. You belong to me. Say it."

He squeezed tighter. It felt like my ribs were about to crack.

"I promise. Anything. Please. Stop. Let me go!"

And then, he did.

An embrace. A smile.

"Come, read us a story," he said.

Later, he'd say he was just playing. He said I was confused. That of course he didn't mean to scare me or hurt me, *he* was just teaching me to fly and I must have slipped. I must have fallen. That I was the bad one for going off with Roger. Bad form, he said. When I should have just waited for him . . .

That is what he told all of the boys. All of them agreed with him about what my story should be.

He was rewriting me.

But Roger wasn't.

* * *

The present snapped back around me. Round Pond. I was at Round Pond, on my way to Marigold House.

The boat drifted across the water.

A light drizzle began to fall. Beads of rain clinging to the boat's mast.

"Pretty morning, isn't it?"

Behind me, a man stood at the edge of the trees. Tall and too thin. Dressed in white. His cart behind him, also white.

His coat was soaked through, as if he'd walked straight out of the water. In one hand, he held a single red balloon, its surface gleaming like a bead of blood.

"You're the same man," I said. "Who was here that day."

He smiled. Wide. Off. "Take it," he said. Soft. Coaxing.

Fog rolled through, curling around us like fingers.

He tilted his head. "Be careful in the gardens. Many boys have gone missing in these gardens."

That tilt. So achingly familiar. A gesture that lived on the edge of my nightmares.

"No one ever leaves," he murmured to himself. "No one ever gets away from him."

Cold cinched at my throat.

The red balloon swayed, slow, its surface expanding and contracting.

"Would you like to come away with me?"

Words that hit like a blow.

He's just a man. He's just a vendor. But my body knew. It was early morning. Why would anyone be set up in a park right now . . . selling balloons.

"No . . ."

A wide-mouthed laugh. Wild and loud. Something from an animal. I stumbled back and screamed.

In the pond, a boy floated face down. Ribbons of red outlining his frame.

"He didn't last too long," Peter's voice said behind me. "Not much joy in him to take. War does that. Strips them of glad things and happy things. That's all right though. I can dig deep and take what I can. It just means I'll need to move quickly. And then they'll return here faster."

The man with the balloons was gone. Only dense fog remained where he stood.

Shadows flickered above me. A balloon drifted upward, twisting lazily in the air, and then, *pop*!

My boots skid on gravel.

A crow settled on a branch above me. It cocked its head once. Twice. Then it opened its beak. A sharp warbling emerged, like a child's laugh.

I remembered those black points, me on the branch, and the shadow I spotted in the reflection of its eyes.

"You've been following me a long time," I said.

I ran.

If Peter was here this morning, he wasn't here just for me.

He was here for them.

* * *

Rosie stood at the kitchen table stirring sugar and flour in a wide bowl.

The wooden spoon clicked against the rim. A steady, metronomic rhythm. Her sleeves were rolled; her forearms dusted with flour. Gray strands clung damply to her temple where the kitchen heat had caught her.

She didn't look up when she spoke.

"Eleanor's in her office." She lowered her voice. "Consulting with a family. Father's enlisted. Wife can't keep up with all the little ones."

"We'll take care of them here," I said.

"You all right ?"

"Didn't sleep well last night."

"I don't know how any of us are supposed to get any sleep. Belgium. France. Bombed. Papers keep saying we should prepare. Prepare for what? How does anyone prepare for any of this?"

The spoon stopped mid-stir. "It's a strange thing," she murmured. "The war takes the men . . . and children follow."

Her words hung in the air.

"There's always room for one more," I said.

She resumed stirring, the rhythm slow and deliberate.

Outside, the fog scraped gently against the glass.

Voices drifted faintly from down the hall, soft, overlapping murmurs, punctuated by laughter.

"The children should be done with breakfast soon."

I nodded and poured myself a cup of tea, my hands trembling. The cup rattled against its saucer.

Rosie looked at me from above her work. "Just don't look up at the sky," she said.

I knew she imagined my fears were about the war. And they were, but not only that. I thought of the children. I wondered if Agnes had checked on her bird skull, and if Willie continued his drawing, if Charles slept well.

It was all there. I could see it, but I'd ignored it. Peter slowly creeping into our world.

From somewhere in the house a baby cried. The long, soft wail.

"How's she getting on?"

"Doctor said she's healthy. Eleanor gave her a name, Jane."

Jane.

"That's beautiful."

A thump shook the house. Followed by a delighted squeal.

Rosie frowned. "Willie!" she called, hurrying toward the hall. "Stop that or you'll break your neck!"

"But I can fly!"

The cup slipped in my grip. Scalding tea splashed across my wrist, but I didn't feel it.

"Wendy . . ." Rosie pressed a tea towel to my hand.

"I'm fine . . . go check on Willie."

My lungs tightened. My vision blurred.

From the hallway came the swell of children's voices, rhythmic and rising. Almost chant-like.

I can fly. I can fly. I can fly.

My heart kicked hard against my ribs. Their laughter mixed with the shriek of the kettle.

Rosie's footsteps hurried down the corridor. "Enough of that now! Off with you lot! Go wash up and get ready for your lessons with Miss Wendy."

The chant cut off. Silence fell.

The hallway to my classroom was lined with children's drawings, crooked houses, stick figures, skies painted in impossible greens. Skies only children could still believe in.

Behind me, I heard it again.

"I can fly!" Willie shouted.

For a blink, the sound didn't belong to him. It was older. Hungrier. Wilder. Chaos in an impossible forest that morphed to jungle then beach and sea on a whim.

Peter's voice. Slipping into a child. He did that at the hospital with Edward.

I spotted him on the stairs. "Willie," I called. "Come down from there, please."

He only grinned, too bright, too sure. He bent his knees deep, as though the ground beneath him were moving and he needed to keep steady.

"Willie," I said. "You heard Rosie. It's not safe. If you've already washed up after breakfast, then go straight to the classroom."

He just stared at me and then he jumped.

A thud followed and rattled the bones of the house. For one terrible instant, I thought he had broken something. Shattered a knee. Or even dislocated an ankle.

My heart seemed to stop beating, until he laughed.

"I'm fine, Miss Wendy!"

More children appeared. Some clapped. Others raced down the hall, toward the classroom.

All of them continued with that terrible chant.

I can fly.

I can fly.

I can fly.

Those words coiled through my head, and I remembered. The sound of wings. The window blowing open, and the night-time breeze rolling into the darkened nursery lit only by the moonlight.

* * *

At my bedside, something black. Shifting. Twirling. Expanding. It was like the whole of midnight given shape, dotted with millions of shiny points. Stars. Planets. Within its canvas, the sparkling lights of shooting stars.

I knew what it was. A part of him, but not.

"That's my shadow," Peter said, appearing at the foot of my bed. His eyes caught in the moonlight.

"Why isn't it attached to you?" I sat up.

He didn't answer. And I never asked him again.

"Can you help me sew it on?"

I climbed out of bed and fetched my sewing kit. He held the shadow still against the dresser. When I took it from him, the cold shocked through my fingers, up my arm, and into my skull.

Wendy . . .

I paused. I heard him inside my head.

"Everything all right?" he asked.

"Yes," I said, even though I was sure of what I'd heard, his voice in my mind.

Stitch by stitch, I attached his shadow to him.

When I was done, he told me thank you. His voice low, soft, a secret. "You trust me?"

I nodded.

"I'll take you to the beginning of stars." His smile was boyish, yes. But his eyes, they were anything but a boy's eyes. They held their own light. "Where sun and moon touch the sea."

His hand found mine. His thumb traced my palm.

My breath slowed and far in the back of my thoughts something screamed to pull away, but I couldn't.

He stepped closer. He smelled like the earth after a storm. "I'll take you past the second star. Then beyond. Where stories go. Where they never end."

He was inches from me now. His free hand rose, fingers sliding into my hair, curling at the base of my skull. His grip tightened.

His lips brushed mine, barely there. Cold. Dry. Not a kiss. Something else. A promise. Or a warning.

"Now, we fly, my Wendy . . ."

I blinked. "My brothers . . ."

We woke them. They rubbed sleep away from their eyes, yawned and asked where we were going, and I told them to trust me, because I trusted Peter.

John, behind me, always so fearless. Michael, so little, clutched his bear in one hand and me with the other.

The air howled around us. My breath vanished. Ground snapped away. Chimneys and shadows. All of it slipping, dissolving into fog.

My heart thrashed in my chest. Wind stung my eyes.

In that first moment of weightlessness, in that impossible thrill, I believed in all of the possibilities of him. That he could give me everything I had ever wanted. That he could make me whole.

Peter looked back. His grin didn't belong to a boy. "See?" he called over the wind. "You're safe with me."

Stretched across him, his shadow. That blanket of black stars writhed, detached, alive. It slithered through the air like smoke across a ceiling. It reached for me. Eager. Trembling. As if it has been waiting centuries for me. Peter glanced back as if scolding the shadow and it retreated.

Even as I smiled, and told my brothers that they'd be all right, that I'd be all right, something lingered. As the city fell away in silver and black, I thought of that shadow of a kiss and what its promise meant.

* * *

The memory shattered.

I found Agnes seated cross-legged on the floor of the classroom, surrounded by books she'd pulled down from the lower shelves. Not reading them but stacking them and building towers. She'd constructed a fortress, buildings and ramparts fashioned from stacked volumes.

"What are you building?" Sitting beside her. The floorboards creaked beneath my weight.

"A castle."

She carefully positioned a copy of *Grimm's Fairy Tales* and *The Railway Children*. The tower wobbled.

"That's very clever," I said.

"My father used to build things." Her voice softened. "Before the war took him."

She reached for another book and paused. Her hand hovered over the spine.

The Little White Bird. Gold lettering, faded but legible.

"Where did you get this?" I asked.

"The library."

I had put this book on the very top shelf. There was no way she could have found it on her own.

"I had a dream where to find it," she said as if reading my thoughts.

I opened my mouth to say something, but I wasn't sure what exactly when I heard children's laughter. Closer this time.

They entered the classroom one by one. I told Agnes to put her castle away and get to her desk.

Rosie appeared in the doorway, wiping her hands on her apron. "That should be all of them."

"Thank you, Rosie."

The children shifted in their seats, whispering, giggling.

"What's so funny this morning?"

No one answered.

"Secrets, I see," I crossed my arms. "All right then, take out your readers. We'll begin with—"

A black blur flew past the window.

More laughter. Chatter. Whispers.

"It's just . . . a bird," I said, trying to convince myself.

I stepped closer to the window. Morning fog clung to the grounds, sweeping across the lawn, curling through the trees.

A heavy blanket of white swept across the lawn and curled through the trees, and then I spotted it . . . a deep hole where Agnes had buried the bird skull yesterday. It looked as if someone had dug it up. Or it had clawed its way out.

I found Agnes watching me.

"What are you looking forward to learning today, Agnes?"

She pressed a finger to her cheek and looked to the ceiling. "I want to learn all about birds."

"Maybe there'll be time for that," I said. "Today we'll start with our story, then science, reading, and . . ."

"Why not a rhyme?" Harold blurted, half standing, his hand shooting up too late to matter.

"Or a lullaby!" Mabel chimed, bouncing up so hard her braids thumped against her shoulder.

"A fairy tale!" Frederick called from the back, his chair skidding as he leaned forward.

"A child's story!" Gladys said, kicking her heels together beneath her desk.

The room buzzed, voices overlapped.

I couldn't tell if they were mocking me or simply being children. Mischievous, unstoppable. Alive with impulse.

Only William seemed to sit still and quiet. Hands folded neatly on his desk.

"Nice to see that you don't have a preference," I said to him.

He blinked once, then lifted his chin. "I guess I don't know which one I want because I don't know the difference between those types of stories, Miss Wendy."

"A rhyme," I said, "is a little song made of patterns. It repeats so you won't forget it. That's what makes it comforting."

They leaned in closer.

"A lullaby is gentler. Something sung to keep you safe as you fall asleep."

Mabel giggled.

"A story," I went on, "is a path. It has a beginning, a middle, and an end. We follow along with it on its purpose."

"Children's tales." I felt every eye on me. "Those pretend to be harmless, but they hide teeth beneath their sweetness. You think it's one play, until it isn't."

Their fidgeting stilled.

"And a fairy tale," I said, "is older than all of these. Older than us. Older than our city. Fairy tales know what children fear. And the cost of their wishes. They promise wonders, but they always ask for something in return."

The room was completely still. Quieter than I have ever known them to be.

From the corner of my eye, movement. Out of the window.

I thought I spotted someone beyond the fence, but Samuel wouldn't go that far. That was off the property. My eyes strained. Scanned. A dark tall figure.

That Wendy Darling . . . such a strange girl.

I blinked and he was gone.

Behind me, a rustle of pages.

"Miss Wendy?"

"Yes, Agnes."

"You're staring out the window."

I exhaled. "You're right." I moved to the board and grabbed a piece of chalk.

Believe in goodness, I wrote on the blackboard, more to prove that I could still move.

When I looked behind me the children were still silent. Still staring. Not unkindly, but it was as if they were waiting for something to make its announcement.

A gust struck the windows. The panes rattled.

Willie laughed. "He's here," he said.

"Who?"

Willie grinned. "Peter."

The chalk slipped from my hand and struck the floor, splitting cleanly in two.

Wendy Darling . . . with such fancies in her head . . .

"Who gave you that name?"

The children looked to one another, silent conspiratorial glances.

Outside, the mist pressed low across the lawn, swallowing the hedges, blurring the path to the gate.

I leaned closer. Shapes gathered. Small figures. Hand in hand. Forming slowly in the fog.

It's a trick of the light, Wendy. The mist playing games.

My hand lifted toward the glass and stopped, refusing to touch it. I pulled my hand back.

The shapes were still there. And I knew them. Each and every one. I knew the slope of those shoulders. The height of each boy. I knew how the twins always held hands.

The mist thickened. Their outlines softened.

A bright voice broke the spell. "Miss Wendy."

"Yes, Agnes."

"Do you see my bird?"

"Your bird . . . ?"

"Yes, the big black one," she said. "I found him in the garden this morning. He grew very big and very fast. He told me his name is Solomon, and he said—"

A shadow swept across the window. Quick. Low.

The children gasped. One of them cried.

"We're safe, children," I said. My hands shaking. Eyes darting to the window latch.

The room dimmed as if we were doused in shade.

You can't have them, I said to myself. *Leave them alone.*

Agnes sprang from her seat. "My bird!" She ran to the window.

I surged forward. Keeping her away from the glass. "Agnes, honey. Get back to your seat."

But she pressed closer.

"Children," I said. steadying my voice, "let's take a short break. Tell Rosie to get you some biscuits. That I asked. Please."

"Look!" Lillian smiled. "He's back! The man!"

"Lillian, please . . ."

"But he's right there, Miss Wendy."

She was right.

I controlled my tone. "A break. Go. Now. All of you."

They filed past me. Heads bowed.

I met Agnes's eyes. "You too. Run along now."

She nodded, eyes wide. "Yes, Miss Wendy." Her voice barely a whisper.

Willie paused in the doorway. His lips parted to say something.

"Willie," I said. "You mustn't believe that the things you dream are real."

"He said you'd say that."

"Willie . . ."

And then he was gone.

Half-whispered voices slipped through the corridor. *Did you see it? Maybe it was an angel.*

He was certainly no angel.

The door closed with the last of them. Only quiet remained. The fog swallowed the world beyond.

My reflection wavered in the glass. Trembling at the edges. And then another shape formed beside it. A darker outline. Motionless.

Through the blanket of mist I saw him. He appeared like a ship on the horizon. From here I could see the glint from the brass buttons on his jacket.

I gripped the windowsill to steady myself. This was not a shadow. He was there. This man was real.

How?

How could he have made that impossible journey?

He remained still. I imagined he was as shocked to see me. So many years and worlds had passed between us.

Then his outline thinned, wavered, and all that remained was my reflection in the glass. Ghost-white. Shaking. A woman who had seen and lived the impossible.

Behind me, something shifted. A draft slipped through the room, carrying a scent I knew too well.

Salt. Rust. Blood and memory.

Far off, a bell began to toll.

I pressed my hands on the desk, trying to hold myself upright, and knocked over the box of chalk.

White pieces tumbled out, shattering on the floor and bursting apart. I knelt to gather them, though my hands shook.

The door creaked open. Rosie's voice drifted in. "Miss Wendy? You all right? The children said there was a man outside. Samuel's on his way to check."

"Thank you, Rosie. I just needed a small break." We all did.

She stepped closer, finding me hunched over scattered chalk. "You shouldn't be on the floor," she said gently. "I'll fetch the broom."

"No, I'll do it. Where can I find the broom and dustpan?"

"Library," she replied. "I was tidying in there earlier."

A shriek erupted from the dining room. Then the unmistakable thud of a ball bouncing and rolling.

"Tommy hit me!" Elsie shouted.

Rosie spun toward the hallway. "All of you! None of that in the house! Tommy, no hitting Elsie. Or anyone, for that matter!"

Silence fell behind her, brief and trembling.

I was left alone with chalk dust clinging to my fingers.

* * *

The stairwell groaned beneath my feet. Each step a reminder that Eleanor had just offered me a chance to leave my past, my childhood home, behind and move in here to be near the children.

But part of that past had been standing outside moments ago.

When I reached the landing, I found the library door ajar.

I could smell the paper before I pushed it open. The aged sweetness of old pages and ink.

I stepped inside. Books towered in uneven rows. Spines bowed with years of handling. Dust motes spun in the dim light.

The broom leaned against the far wall. Before I reached for it, something caught my eye, a slim volume half buried beneath a scatter of books on a table.

Its cover was familiar in the way heartbreak is familiar.

Green cloth. Gold lettering.

PETER AND WENDY

Our names. Forever entwined.

I thought I had gotten rid of all of these copies, but I knew it was impossible, in a way, to completely sever my name from his. We had been bonded forever in ink.

I moved toward the book.

I had read it years ago, Mr. Barrie's fictionalized version of what happened to me and my brothers. What he wrote was a story of delight and fancy. What he left out were the missing children, their dried-up bodies appearing in Kensington Gardens weeks after they'd vanished.

The cover flew open. Pages turned and flipped by themselves, until the book settled open on a page.

Air escaped my lungs.

No windows were open. There was no breeze coming in from any corner. The air was still.

I stepped toward the table and reached out. The book was old, its spine cracked, its edges feathered with use.

It had settled on a chapter title: ***The Flight.***

The illustration, nearly faded, showed a boy suspended in midair. His shadow stretched unnaturally long beneath him, curling at the edges.

Beneath him, three children leaned out of an open window, their faces wonderstruck. So naïve as to what he really was. All of them unaware of how easily a childhood wish could become a snare.

I lowered my gaze to the line beneath the image: *"Second to the right, and straight on till morning."*

My fingertips brushed the page. It was warm, as if someone had just been holding it.

Wendy.

His voice.

Lights flickered overhead.

Shadows shifted in the corners. Dust swirled. Pages fluttered on shelves, like wings awakening.

Something brushed against my shoulder. Something else seized in my chest. It felt like the entirety of the floor in the library were tiling.

I spun around, expecting to find someone there, but all I saw were shelves and books and the ladder, its wheels crooked on the rail.

When I looked back at the table, the pages flipped again. A new chapter heading waited.

Wendy Returns

My legs nearly gave out.

That chapter did not exist. Not in Mr. Barrie's story. I knew each and every word of this book. I'd committed it to heart, and this chapter was not there.

In the margin, in dark ink:

Every story is a doorway. Some cannot be closed.

Light trembled overhead. Dimmed. Then steadied.

The pages turned again, fluttering, flipping, then settling near the end of the book.

My eyes found a line:

When you return, you will be yourself again.

The letters seemed to rearrange themselves. Ink bled, spreading across the page.

When you return, I will never allow you to leave again.

The sound that escaped me wasn't a scream. It was smaller than that. The sound of remembering things I had forced myself to forget.

Lights flickered again, longer this time.

I stumbled back. My skirt brushed the ladder. Its hinges groaned.

Wendy.

My legs gave out. I caught myself on the ladder, fingers white around the rung.

* * *

I wanted to scream. to tell him to stop, to leave me alone, but I knew he wouldn't. And so I said nothing. I had to figure this out with them, my brothers. I knew he was getting stronger each day, and we had to stop him before he did something awful.

Dust stirred. Another page loosened from the book. It rose, weightless, and drifted through the air like a feather and landed at my feet.

The house shook and from downstairs I heard screams.

I was already moving down the stairs, hands skimming the banister. Feet slipping on the runner. Screams. More screams. Shrieks.

Willie lay crumpled at the foot of the stairs.

Not fallen. Broken. The front hall was too small for what lay in it.

His limbs were bent at wrong angles, folded, twisted, as if someone had forced them past where joints were meant to go. One arm pinned beneath him.

A splintered femur bone jutted out of his leg.

His head lolled to one side, blood trickling from his nose and sliding into his hair.

The children had gathered at the threshold but would not cross. Florence stood with her hands over her mouth, silent. George stared at the walls as if reciting something to himself. Agnes cried silently, and Lillian's face was pressed into her shoulder. No one moved.

Humpty Dumpty sat on a wall . . .

My stomach heaved. Black feathers drifted all around him. Around all of us, like confetti.

Some landed in his blood and clung there, sticking to the floor.

My legs buckled. And my knees hit the floor before I realized I'd fallen. Shock shooting up through my legs.

"Rosie! Eleanor! Someone, call the doctor!"

He did this to you. His sick game. He's a monster.

Heads pressed into my shoulders. Trembling arms threw themselves around my neck. Cries were muffled on my sleeve.

"Willie . . ." small voices said.

"Willie . . ." others cried.

Someone was saying my name. I couldn't answer.

I couldn't do anything but kneel there, frozen.

"Willie," I whispered, leaning close. "Can you hear me? Love, it's Wendy. We're going to get you help. Please. Hold on."

His lashes fluttered. Lips parted.

Please. Please don't die. Children aren't supposed to die.

Scattered words escaped him.

"Come . . ."

"Away . . ."

His gaze drifted past me. Past the staircase. Past the ceiling. Past the house itself. His mouth softened into a smile. Then his eyes rolled back.

"Willie!" I pressed my hand to his chest. His heart still beat, faint, fluttering, but there. "He's alive! He's still alive! Rosie! Samuel! Please, someone help!"

A cold gust knifed through the hallway. Feathers scattered and spiraled into a storm. They lifted and circled over his broken body.

Then Rosie was there, knees hitting the floor beside us. "Dear Lord," she breathed. Her eyes swept the room. Children. Feathers. Blood.

Agnes was closer now, a fistful of feathers clutched tight in her small hand. Her eyes wide. Unblinking. Her face drained of color.

"He told me to go outside and gather them," she whispered. "He said they would help Willie fly."

Lillian sobbed into my shoulder.

Rosie pressed her fingers to Willie's wrist. Waited. Her face shifted, not blank, but urgent.

Her hands moved with practiced calm, checking his neck, his spine. "Don't move him. Don't touch him."

Somewhere beyond the house a bell tolled.

Eleanor appeared in the doorway, rigid, pale, hand clamped over her mouth. Behind her came the nursemaid, Lucy, Hannah, Samuel. Everyone wide-eyed. Shaking.

"Get them out," Eleanor choked. "All of them."

The doctor was on his way, Eleanor said, and she sent Samuel outside to anticipate his approach.

Rosie and the girls herded the children away, voices trembling. They clung to each other, crying, hiccupping, upstairs to their rooms.

Only Willie remained here with me. Still.

His last words. *Come away.*

Peter was keeping one of his many promises to me.

If you ever leave me, I will tear through everything you love to find you.

* * *

I wept. I cried for Willie. I cried for me. I cried for all of those little boys I could not save.

Eleanor put a hand over mine. Cold. Shaking.

"He'll be fine," she whispered.

"It's my fault." The words scraped out of me. "I did this. I—"

"My darling, no. This is no one's fault."

Eleanor caught my shoulders, held me firm. Her breath trembled, but her gaze didn't waver. "This is certainly not your fault."

She eased back, hands still on my shoulders, studying me, really studying me, as if memorizing the shape of me before the next blow came.

"The constable is on his way." Her voice dipped.

I don't understand. *Why is the constable coming . . . why . . . I didn't do this. I told you all the truth. I told you all the names of the boys.*

Wendy Darling, always spinning tales . . .

"Wendy, do you understand? I'm trying to protect you. The doctor is on his way. I had to. The constable will come, will see that this was a dreadful accident, and he will leave. But he will be here and he will be asking questions, and you need to go. Now."

I understood. The telephone rang from her office, sharp as a crack, and she retreated to answer it.

The wail of the constable's car rose in the distance.

I raced to my classroom, snatched my satchel from its hook, and slipped out the back door before the siren reached the street.

Cold hit me hard, but I moved fast.

I thought about the constable, and I wondered what he would see and say. I wondered if he knew that I worked here.

That should be no crime. But of course . . . they always considered me a suspect, that I had something to do with all the boys who disappeared, who were found dead.

I stopped and looked at the house. Something stirred in an upstairs window.

A shadow. Not moving. Not hiding. Simply watching.

Last time, when I was young, I didn't fight so much as flee, but this time, I would do all that I could to stop him.

"Leave them alone," I said to the thing in the window.

I hoped that when I returned in the morning, he had not hurt another child . . . or taken another one.

CHAPTER 10

I HIT THE WATER hard. Cold slapped the breath from my lungs.

I sank. Hair whipping around my face like tangled weeds. The world became a blur, and in that moment, I grew so tired and my limbs began to grow so still.

It was quiet here. Peaceful.

And then, hands.

He hooked his arms beneath mine and hauled me up through green light. We burst through the surface, both of us gasping, water splashing, kicking, coughing.

"I got you!" I heard him shout above it all . . . but . . . who was he?

He dragged me toward a slick black rock rising from the shallows. Its face gleaming like oil, like something alive.

We collapsed across it. He patted my back, hard. I vomited seawater. Cried, and shook. The world existed at an angle; it was cold and cruel. When I lifted my head, I saw words carved deep into the black stone. Sharp and jagged. Forced into the surface with fury.

I whispered them: "Peter, Peter, shadow . . ."

"Don't say it," he said.

The boy who saved me was lying on his back and looking up into the sky.

"That's what he is," he rasped. "That's what he does."

Long dark hair fell past his jaw in salt-stiffened tangles. A faded coat with brass buttons, sleeves rolled to the elbow. A dagger on his belt. A thin gold hoop in his ear, not the mark of a sailor, something worse.

When I realized who it was, I glanced back to the water, wondering if I should jump back into the sea.

He caught my movements. "Please don't jump back in, or I'd just have to save you again."

"You're his son."

"I do have a name." He sat up, facing me. "Roger."

I didn't move. "I'm Wendy."

"You shouldn't believe everything you hear," he said. "My father's not a monster. Nor am I."

His hair clung to his forehead in wet strands. His eyes held that last feverish green of the sky.

"You don't know anything about what he tells me."

"I know he almost killed you," he said. "And he'll try to do it again."

"It was . . . an accident."

He arched an eyebrow. "An accident?"

"A game."

Roger went still. His jaw tightened. "What an awful game to play."

I was lying to myself, because I didn't want to admit how bad it'd gotten. I didn't want to admit how I feared every time he and all of the boys, and John and Michael, went off on "adventures."

Why was it that they always returned without one or two of the boys? Why was it that they returned covered in mud and grime, scrapes and deep cuts, and their eyes far and distant?

Each time they returned, it was as if another speck of them had been taken, stripped away. And each meal was quieter, each bedtime a little more still, and the sparkle in their eyes faded more and more.

I lowered my voice. "Can't he hear us here? What we say?"

"No, not out on the water. Not on the ship either. He can't access any of our thoughts here or there."

Roger reached for his belt and unhooked a dagger. He turned it over, offering me the hilt. It shimmered with tiny emeralds, each one catching the dying light.

I didn't move.

"What do I want that for?"

"You have to kill him, Wendy." His voice was flat. Certain. "If you don't, the next time I find you out here it may be too late."

My hands shook. "I can't do that."

"You can. You must."

"I don't understand."

"Listen to me." He leaned closer. "Don't forget what I'm telling you, because it's already happening. You're forgetting who you are."

I shook my head.

"Do you remember your mother?" he asked. "Your father?"

"Of course I do."

"What do they look like?"

I laughed. Sharp. Defensive. "What a stupid question. Mother . . . she has . . ." I reached for an image. Searching. There was nothing.

"And your father? What does he look like?"

There was nothing there.

The dagger glinted between us. My hands were still shaking, not just from the cold water but something else.

"Do you remember where you're from, Wendy?"

I looked at the sky, searching, for what . . . ? Buildings. Yes. There were buildings there. A bell. A tower.

"London."

"Good. You're still there. Whatever you do, don't forget. The unraveling starts in the forgetting."

I stared at him, the boy who had dragged me from the mouth of death.

"Stab him in the heart and tell him he's nothing. He's only a story, one that feeds and lives off the lives of others."

I stared at the dagger.

"To get back home," he continued, "there's a fork in the forest. A path overgrown with vines. If you look hard enough, you'll find a great tree with a hollow in its trunk. Looks almost like a little house carved right into it. Follow that path. Keep walking. Don't turn back."

"What lived in there?"

He flashed a smile. "What *lives* in there, you mean." The smile faded. "Don't disturb it. They get angry. They don't like children much." He paused. "Just follow the path home."

"What about you?" I whispered.

He faced the sea, where the waves hissed Peter's name. The entirety of this place buzzed with him, was made of him.

"Forget me too. Forget all of us," he said.

I had a thought. I don't know why, but it felt like it was the first clear thought I had had in so long.

"You should come with me. When I leave."

His mouth fell open, and he angled his head, as if he were hearing a song for the first time.

"Why would you offer that?" he asked, still surprised.

"Because this isn't our home. Neither of us. And we deserve a proper home . . ."

When I returned to camp, Peter and my brothers embraced me. Peter told me how worried he was about me. He went on to tell the boys all about how I landed in the water. No one challenged him. Why would they? This was his world he forced us all to live in.

I tucked the boys in that night, and that's when I noticed how Peter's shadow curled around his body like a loyal animal.

As they slept, the sky burned green. Black feathers fell like rain, soft and weightless.

In my journal I wrote, furiously, about all that had happened. The water. Roger. The warning. I wrote and wrote, so I would not forget. Each word a stitch toward the murder I planned, and escape.

* * *

I almost didn't come today.

The walk to the hospital felt longer than usual. The streets were the same, the same gray buildings, the same gray sky, the same gray faces of people going about their gray lives, but something had shifted. The shadows seemed darker, like dark black pools. Every few feet the crows seemed to multiply, on rooftops, lampposts, and bare branches.

I was being watched. I knew it by the prickle at the back of my neck as if someone's eyes were boring down on me.

* * *

But still, I had to be here, because the only one I could talk to about any of this was Edward. He wouldn't give me those looks of concern the doctors and nurses had given me once. Or worse, a sneer of contempt like Constable Finch gave every time he saw me. Edward wouldn't ask me questions that were meant to lead me into another stream of thought. Edward wouldn't make me think that what I was saying held no weight and did not matter. Because Edward did not talk, not at all.

The ward today was busier. New arrivals. Young men whose eyes had aged decades. Parts of them bandaged, wounds seeping through the fabric. Beatrice was assisting in surgery. I'd see her later. I nodded to the nurses and made my way to his room.

Edward lay as he always did. Still. Silent. Face turned toward the light.

But something was different.

I stopped at the foot of his bed. Studied him. Tried to name what had changed.

His color, maybe. He looked paler than before. Almost gray. There was something around his eyes, a darkness, a hollowing, as if the skin had thinned overnight.

"Edward, it's Wendy. How are you feeling today?"

I moved closer. Sat in my chair and reached for his hand.

His fingers were cold. Ice cold, despite the warmth of the ward.

"Edward, can you hear me?"

Nothing. The same nothing as always. But it felt different now. Heavier. Like the silence was listening back.

I pulled my hand away. Rubbed my palms together to chase away the chill.

"I thought I'd read some Tennyson today," I said. I stared at his chin, nose, mouth, waiting for movement, but there was none.

I turned the pages to "Sweet and Low."

Sweet and low, sweet and low,
Wind of the western sea,
Low, low, breathe and blow,
Wind of the western sea

I paused and glanced at him. His lips were moving.

Maybe it was a twitch. Maybe it was a tremor. But I saw it, the faint motion of his mouth forming shapes around words.

"Edward?"

I leaned closer. My heart hammered against my ribs.

His lips moved again. Barely a whisper.

I bent until my ear was inches from him.

And I heard it, an exhale and with it came my name. *Wendy* . . .

I jerked back. The chair scraped against the floor.

"You hear me, Edward. Yes, it's Wendy. I'm here."

His eyes were still closed. His body was still motionless. But then . . . his lips curled at the corners. Just slightly. Just enough.

A smile.

But this was someone else's smile. I knew that for certain. This was someone wearing Edward's face and smiling at me.

I stood so fast the chair toppled behind me. My satchel fell, spilling books across the floor. I didn't stop to pick them up.

Beatrice. I needed to get Beatrice. I can't be here alone with *him*. Not again.

I walked, I didn't run, couldn't run. The nurses would ask questions.

I heard them before I looked. Squawking. Screeching. At the window I spotted two of them, then three. Black crows swooping across the sky.

And then the worse thought came to me: *How long had he been listening?*

The thimble. Roger. Everything I'd whispered to Edward in the dark, thinking no one else could hear.

Peter had heard it all.

CHAPTER

11

THE CHAPEL WAS cold, even though warm sunlight leaked through the stained glass windows. Fractured jewel colors, reds and blues and golds shifted across pews.

Dust drifted though beams.

A single day had passed since the fall, and already my world here felt so different. Our safety threatened.

Willie was alive. But the doctors expected he'd be in the hospital for some days, and worse, they were unsure if he would be able to run and jump and play as he once had. How awful it was to have the freedom of childhood movement stolen from him.

Each child held a white feather in their hands. It was Agnes's idea, which I tried to deter, but Eleanor told me they're children, and they grieve in their way. What I wish I could tell her was that this idea seemed to come to Agnes from someone else, but I remained silent.

I stood near the back, hands folded together, unable to think clearly.

Eleanor stood at the front, her voice steady despite a tremor in her hands. She spoke to the children of love, of patience and kindness. She told them how Willie would need us when he returned and how we must be gentle with him.

Rosie and Helen dabbed at their eyes. It was then Eleanor informed us that Lucy would remain with Willie at the hospital to assist with his care until he returned.

My thoughts continued drifting in and out. I kept hearing Willie, seeing him. The angle of his arms and legs.

He did this. Peter did this and he would do it again.

The feathers in the children's hands caught the light and my attention returned to Eleanor's voice when she spoke of recovery. She said it would be scary for all of us, as Willie would be in bed many days and in pain, and when people are in pain they may scream or moan or cry. And how it was important we all helped to alert one another so we could make sure we were doing all we could to keep him comfortable.

* * *

The world folded in on itself, white feathers dissolving into white light, all brightness and blur.

When the light dimmed, I was kneeling inside the treehouse. Its walls smelled of sap. The air was humid, heavy.

Curly lay on a bed of moss, shivering. His teeth chattered. Blankets were piled on top of him.

His lips cracked. A sheen of sweat covered his face.

I had been wiping his forehead for so long the cloth had gone warm. Behind me, I heard someone enter.

Peter's shadow touched me first, sliding over my shoulder like a cold hand.

"You're supposed to make him better," he said.

"I'm trying. I don't have any medicine to give him. All we have is rest and water and time."

I pressed the cloth to Curly's burning forehead. "I'm doing everything I can."

Peter tilted his head. Puppet-like.

His smile arrived a heartbeat later, forming into place, as if he had to remember how. "You're their mother," he said. "And mothers fix things. That's what you're here to do."

I could not fix this. What he had dragged back to me was a boy who had eaten a fistful of poison neverberries, on a dare. By him. For fun. For play.

Life and death are all a game to Peter. And we're the only ones who can die.

Peter crouched beside me, so close his knee brushed mine. An accidental touch, but the air between us grew warm.

"If he doesn't get better," he murmured into my ear, "it's your fault."

"I didn't do this."

He leaned closer, his lips pressed to my ear.

"Why are you crying?"

"I'm not."

But the tears had already gathered at the corners of my eyes, blurring my vision.

Peter took my chin between two fingers, pressing his nose against mine.

"You are," he said, smiling faintly. "You always are."

"Peter, please . . ."

The smile vanished so completely it was as if it had been wiped from his face.

He removed his hand from my chin, not gently but with offence. "Don't tell me what to do." His words were too soft and measured, like a threat.

The walls of the treehouse seemed to flinch.

Then his quiet rage slipped away. "Go rest, Wendy. I'll take care of everything."

And I believed him. Why did I believe him? Because I was just so tired.

I pushed myself upright, my legs shaking as I moved toward the door. The treehouse shifted and swayed with my every step.

At the door, I paused. Days had gone by since I'd seen Roger. Or heard from him. He'd told me he'd write, send me messages attached to his pigeons.

"Peter," I whispered, hand on the frame. "Have you seen Roger?"

The name fell like a stone into deep water.

Peter's smile faltered.

For one suspended beat, everything stilled, the air, the leaves, even Curly's strained breath.

Then the change came. A twisting. A turning. As if some hidden strings inside him had been yanked taut.

A ripple slid beneath the surface of his skin. Subtle. Unnatural. Bristling at the sound of Roger's name.

Light warped around him.

"Roger," he echoed. "It's always Roger now, huh?"

He rose with impossible grace. Movement too fluid to belong to flesh and bone. His eyes darkened, a hunter's green.

For a moment, I thought he might strike me. Not with fists. Not with touch. With that look, the one that made me feel so small, like I owed him an apology for speaking. For existing.

"Don't worry about Roger," he said at last. His words low, tender, but venomous.

He stepped closer. Close enough that the air thinned. Close enough that I could smell copper on his breath.

I should have fled. I should have known.

He looked at me with that impossible beauty, that false softness that made me forget how easily he could strike down a boar, gut a marlin with fevered strokes. How he sat in silence, face blank, when one of the boys returned with their body pierced by swords. Their blood-soaked clothes tossed into the fire. Their bodies laid in the forest.

"Go sleep," he whispered again, brushing his thumb across my cheek. "You'll feel better in the morning."

So I went.

And in the morning, Curly was gone.

Peter told us he had run away to live with the mermaids across the island in the lagoon. He said it with an easy smile. Bright and cheerful. Words no one dared question.

But I knew.

The sea was loud that morning. Its waves beating the shore like something pleading to be heard.

And Peter knelt by the stream, whistling, as he washed blood off his blade.

* * *

Cold wind brought me back. The door to the chapel was open and children were filing out, Eleanor guiding them along.

And there remained Agnes in the front row, staring at the feather in her hands. Head bowed. Shoulders shaking.

"Willie said Peter was coming," she cried.

Rosie moved toward her. "Hush, love."

The bell above us tolled again and again.

At the window, a feather clung to the glass. Not white, but black. I approached, and just beyond the pane, in a large oak tree, sat a great black crow.

Its coal-dark eye fixed on me with a terrible, knowing stillness.

CHAPTER 12

DAYS WENT BY in relative quiet.

Today, the air outside the hospital bit sharp. Smoke and antiseptic mingled in the fog.

Ambulances rattled over the cobblestones. Men pressed up steps, some limping, some carried on stretchers.

A woman in the waiting room clutched her newspaper tight. The headline read: BRITISH FORCES SUFFER HEAVY LOSSES AT THE FRONT

And beneath it: FEARS OF BOMBINGS IN LONDON GROW

"Margaret . . ." I said, rushing past the secretary. The typewriter clattered behind me as I entered the corridor.

"Wendy!"

I found Beatrice waiting for me. She grabbed my hand and we hurried along. Her cheeks were flushed. Her apron streaked with gray smudges. Her gaze swept the hall, a quick defensive sweep, before she took hold of my hand and pulled me along.

"We're running low," she said.

The inside of the hospital felt like a scream. Movement. People bumping into one another. Moans. Pleas. It smelled of iron and sweat.

"On what?"

"Everything."

Inside, the space throbbed with motion. The air reeked of bleach. Orderlies surged past, arms stacked with towels, bandages, sheets. Somewhere down the hall a man screamed, a low, dragging howl. Everything here vibrated with pain.

She spoke low. Quickly. "They're saying the trenches are full. With the wounded. With the dead." She brushed a loose red curl from her face. "Officers are just leaving boys out there to die."

She squeezed my hand tighter. "Boys"—her voice went thin—"just boys playing soldiers."

The thought lodged beneath my ribs. Boys played war on the island too. Their endless battles all turned to bloodshed, all for sport. No one ever grew old enough to survive them all, except of course Peter, who planned all of the adventures.

"They're saying we're to prepare to be overrun, but we already are," Beatrice said. "Dozens more are coming tonight. Hundreds. I just don't know what we can do for all of them."

She hesitated. Her voice shifted, gentler now. "I'm sorry . . . How are you?"

"It's difficult. I just . . . need to be there for the children. They're all so confused by it all. I . . ."

I stopped. What could I truly tell her? That I feared what would happen to the rest of them? That I was beginning to wonder if I was capable of protecting anyone at all. Including myself.

Beatrice's face softened, reading something in my silence. "Please tell me you've spoken to your brothers . . ."

"I've written them letters. I've called. Nothing. Michael answered once, but said nothing. They're not writing back. No one is answering my letters."

"Pay them a visit."

"I just . . ."

"Go to their homes, Wendy. Walk up the stairs and knock on the door."

"I will. Today. I promise."

"Good."

Beatrice stopped walking. She turned to face me fully, and something in her expression hardened, not with anger, but with the kind of fierceness that comes from watching too many people give up.

"Wendy." She squeezed my wrist. "Learn to take up space. You're allowed to do that. You don't have to shrink. You don't have to live small."

Her eyes searched mine.

"My love, your life belongs to you."

My life belonged to an ash ring. To a promise. To a boy who took and took and called it love.

"Beatrice," another nurse called. Breathless. "We need you. A bad one's come in and we're shorthanded. Doctor says surgery now."

Beatrice rolled her eyes. "I'm so tired," she said. "I just came from surgery." She reached to the wall to steady herself.

"Go," I said. "I'll see to Edward."

"Thank you, dear. I'll . . . I'll see you later."

A stretcher screeched past me, wheels squealing. A man lay upon it. He looked just a few years older than Willie. His face turned away. Head dangling over the edge.

Somewhere deeper in the wing, a doctor shouted for more clamps. What followed was the wet unmistakable snap of bone setting.

Farther on, a man with a bandaged head sat alone on a bench, staring at his empty hands as if mourning something taken from them.

I continued making my way to Edward's room, surrounded by screams that pitched and dulled.

When I turned the corner, my breath hitched.

Light and shadow shifted at the far end of the corridor. A small shape stepped forward, moving into the light. It faced me.

A little boy, no taller than my ribs. Curly. Or more like the idea of him.

He wore animal skin. A lion's pelt draped over his small shoulders, the great cat's head lolling against the little boy's own.

Fresh blood slicked the fur. It was smeared across his cheeks and wrists, staining his shirt in dark, tacky streaks.

His hair veiled his eyes, and then there was that familiar tilt of his head. I had seen it too many times.

"Peter misses you."

My blood went cold.

That Wendy Darling . . .

It was her mother's fault, you know. She stuffed that girl's head with stories and now look at the poor child.

"Curly's dead," the shape of that little boy said. "You left him and because of that he died."

Laughter roared through the corridor.

Lamps guttered. Air thickened. The smell of that other place charged in, earth, moss, rot.

The boy tilted his head again, as if listening to someone just beyond my sight.

"Come away . . ."

And this time, it was not Curly's voice. It was *his* voice.

I clapped a hand over my mouth.

My knees loosened beneath me.

Curly's dead. Curly's dead. Curly's dead.

The figure smiled. Lights blinked on and off, and the form of that little boy unraveled into shadow before collapsing in on itself.

Gone.

By the time I reached Edward's door, my hands were shaking.

I found him writhing beneath the thin cotton sheet, his limbs jerking as if yanked by invisible strings.

His eyes strained toward the darkest corner of the room, rolling so far back I could only see thin crescents of white.

Foam formed at the corners of his mouth.

I turned around, looking back to the door, to the empty hallway. I knew there were no doctors available. Nor nurses.

I held my hands out, not knowing where to start. What to do. I'd done this before. I've calmed children with convulsions.

When I approached, that's when I saw it. On the pillow beside his head lay a feather. Black and slick. It glistened in the lamplight.

I reached for it and tossed it to the floor.

"Edward," I whispered. "Edward, look at me."

His lips parted. A rasp slipped out.

"Edward," I tried again. "It's Wendy. Your friend. I'm here with you."

". . . Wendy."

He blinked once. Deliberately. And when he opened his eyes, they shone green. Glimmering.

Not Edward's eyes. Peter's.

On the wall behind me, my own shadow shuddered.

Something seized in my chest. I coughed, hacked. I felt like I was choking. Like something had lodged itself in my throat. My hands went to my neck.

"He's come for your shadow," Edward's voice said.

My shadow.

Every lamp in the corridor flickered, blinking in and out. Something creaked in the far corner of the room.

His gaze slipped past me, upward, toward the ceiling. I followed, and saw them, all of the shadows pulling apart from their source in this room and gathering above us.

"... you promised ..." Peter's voice.

My breath broke. I gasped, pulling in a deep breath.

I backed away from the bed. "I would have never gone with you had I known what you were! You lied to me! You were never good!"

The room shrank. Then green fire in Edward's eyes burned.

"Let him go!" I said. "He doesn't belong to you."

Then, just as suddenly as they appeared, the color bled out of them. Green tears slid down his cheek.

Edward's eyelids fluttered. His body seemed sagged back into the pillow.

But his eyes . . .

They were open. This was him. Edward. He was awake now.

"Wendy?" he rasped. His own voice.

I sobbed and threw my arms around him. "You're awake."

He placed a weak hand on my back. "It's dark . . . I heard gunfire . . ."

A nurse. A doctor. I needed to find one. Now. "I'll get a nurse. To help. I'll be back. Don't move. I mean . . . I know you can't. But please . . ." I didn't know what to tell him. Be cautious of shadows and green-eyed boys. None of his world was making any sense.

A knock at the door. Beatrice.

"He's awake." Beatrice smiled and put her hands on her hips and looked from me to Edward. "I knew you couldn't stay asleep that long with a pretty girl by your side."

She pressed close to me. "Miss Eleanor called."

"What?"

"She left a message at the front desk with Margaret. She needs you there straightaway. Agnes is missing."

* * *

At Marigold House, I found a young constable in the nursery, tapping the windowpane with the back end of his pencil.

Tap. Tap. Tap.

"What are you doing?" I demanded.

"This is an investigation, miss. I can't divulge information to you."

I knew that if Agnes had left on her own accord, she would not have done so in silence. She would have woken everyone up to tell them her plans. That was Agnes.

The latch was locked. That's what I'd come here to check. If she didn't leave this way, she must've left another way.

Another constable, stockier, gloveless, stood by the bookshelf. His hat sat low over his face. His fingers moved slowly, leafing through books I kept here for the children. *The Water Babies. Hans Christian Andersen's Fairy Tales.* And then, I saw what he was holding in his hand: *Peter and Wendy.*

My stomach dropped. *Who brought that down here?*

The constable flipped through the pages. "My children love this story," he murmured to himself.

I turned and walked downstairs. A chorus of spoons against bowls rose from the dining room, the children eating their supper. This time, in relative silence. I passed Helen in the hallway, carrying dirty dishes back to the kitchen. Her eyes were pink from crying.

"It's just so awful," she said beneath her breath. "All of it."

* * *

I found Eleanor in her office standing behind her desk. Her composure rigid. Hands clasped at her waist, looking at past portraits on her wall. Children who had come and gone so many years ago, many of whom found great joy here and later success. Going on to study and travel. Not allowing stories of abandonment and pain to dictate their life's path.

My eyes moved to the man in the seat in front of her desk.

Him. Again. Constable Finch. Older, wider, but with those dead blue eyes all the same.

"What is she doing here?" he asked. No greeting. No courtesy. Just the flat blade of disbelief.

"You've got a good memory, Detective Constable Finch," Eleanor said. "You haven't laid eyes on Wendy Darling in over a decade."

Detective constable now. He'd moved up in rank.

With that familiar dry, clipped tone he said, "I'd know that face anywhere."

"I work here," I replied, keeping my voice level.

Eleanor stepped forward. "Miss Darling doesn't have much time. She needs to get home and rest so she can teach in the morning." Her voice was firm. "And I'd appreciate you refrain from speaking to my staff as if they were criminals."

"She doesn't live here?" He looked from Eleanor to me, scanning my hand, finding no wedding ring. "That's peculiar, don't you think? A single woman living on her own?"

"Detective Constable Finch," Miss Eleanor said. "It is improper for a man your age to scrutinize the personal life of a young woman in my school, especially when the pressing matter is a missing child. Ask your questions, please."

His gaze stayed fixed on me. "Where is Agnes?"

The question landed hard.

"I don't know," I said.

"You have a history," he murmured. "A record of being . . . overly involved with missing children. And now one child is grievously injured and another is missing at Marigold House." He paused. "Strange, isn't it, Miss Darling?"

Strange.

Such a strange girl. *That Wendy Darling, claiming she'd been chased by birds with human faces.*

Something inside me recoiled. The measured meanness to his tone. I'd heard it all from him, from other adults when I returned.

* * *

That Wendy Darling. Strange. Mad. Unusual.

I heard she was seeing things.

She told the paper that she could fly.

I heard she was speaking to people who weren't even there.

Her poor, poor mother. I just can't imagine the scandal. A child speaking of dead children.

You know what they say, she may have been involved with them being missing. Maybe even their murder.

* * *

"You should be looking for Agnes. Not here interrogating me." My voice cracked, but I recovered and steadied it. He would not intimidate me. Not anymore. My focus had to be on finding Agnes.

Beside me, Eleanor made a sound, *hmm*. Sounding impressed with my words.

"Where do you think she's gone to, then?" he asked.

I had to choose my words carefully. Otherwise they would haul me to Bethlem Royal Hospital again where they locked away women who dreamed strange dreams or spoke truths men couldn't bear to hear. I imagined that the wards didn't look too different today than from my visit there long ago. Tile floors scrubbed raw. Locked doors. Nurses with pity on the surface and steel beneath. They would force a diagnosis on me to keep me there trapped: hysteria, delusion, exhaustion. Anything to make sure I'd never leave again.

"I don't know," I said. "That's your job to attend to. We'll do all we can. Search the house. The estate. We'll do our part, but we need you to do yours."

From the corner of my eye, I saw a warm smile grow on Eleanor's face.

"If you'll excuse me, I need to go home so I can be prepared for my students in the morning."

In the hallway, I found the other constables making their way downstairs. I ducked into the parlor and watched as they entered Eleanor's office.

I had time, but not much.

I rushed up the stairs.

In the girl's dormitory, past Lillian's bed, past Elsie's and Florence's.

Agnes's cot was the third from the end, always near the window, where she liked to be. To whisper to the trees before she fell asleep, she'd once told me.

Her bed was not made. Sheets creased. Blankets folded back as if she'd merely risen to use the lavatory and would return any second. The pillow was on a strange angle. Beneath the pillow, I thought. She's hiding something there.

When I lifted it, there it lay. A black feather.

I raised it to the light. In my hand it felt warm, alive, and as I looked closer it pulsed as if it had its own heartbeat.

Outside the window came a riot of noise.

In the treetops I spotted dozens of black spots dotting branches. Crows. A great many of them. And all of them seemed to be screaming in a tangle.

I thought of Agnes's bird skull, and how she said dead things could rise. Be made new again. Maybe that's what Peter was. Maybe he was dead for a time. Asleep. And now, after a long slumber, he was awake, ready to fill the island with more children.

I approached the window and looked down and saw a little boy staring up at me.

Jax. Another boy from that faraway land. His neck still held that bulge the way necks shouldn't. It was the last image of him I had.

Birds descended on him in a single, terrible hush. Black bodies, sharp-beaked, their wings wheeling. Dozens. More. All spinning around him, and he disappeared in a blur.

Behind me, the dormitory erupted. Children clutching their nightgowns.

"You're right. It is bedtime. I need to run home."

"Miss Wendy!" They gathered around me, arms wrapped around my arms, legs, waist, squeezing me tight.

"Can you read us a story?"

I tapped the tip of Mabel's nose. "Just one. Go get *Grimm's Fairy Tales*, please."

Easing onto the window seat, I glanced once more outside. Everything was still. No birds, no wandering boys.

Mabel pressed the book into my hand, and the children gathered around me on the floor, seated cross-legged. Eyes bright. Wanting a bit of magic before bed.

I turned the pages, until I found "The Golden Bird," settled in and read:

"A certain king had a garden, in which stood a tree that bore golden apples. When the apples were nearly ripe, they were counted; but one morning one was missing. The king became angry and ordered that someone should watch under the tree every night to find out who was stealing them . . ."

In the morning, I would try again to reach my brothers. If that didn't work, I would walk to their homes and pound on their doors.

I didn't care if they found discomfort in speaking of the past. It was speaking to me now, and if we all didn't face it together, that past, that story, would consume us all.

CHAPTER

13

I PULLED MY COAT tighter.

My boots struck against the pavement, but even that was unable to soften the rush of wings overhead.

Streetlamps flickered. One by one. And all along my path crows landed on lampposts near me and watched in silence.

At the river crossing, the wind had died, and the city stood motionless.

Water lapped at the bridge pilings, slow and uneven. It even seemed like the Thames was trying to remain still. All of us on guard for shadows.

The loudest sound came from the pocket watch ticking inside my satchel. Roger always near, always reminding me to keep time, to keep moving. To keep watch.

I kept moving.

I'd already let Liza know not to worry, that I'd be home late. She seemed pleased by this, thinking that maybe I'd be out with girlfriends. Or maybe I'd be meeting with a man. Can't imagine she'd expect my delay due to being interrogated by Scotland Yard for suspicion of kidnapping.

My eyes adjusted to the dark that engulfed the end of the street. My stomach fluttered when I saw them.

Two figures. Standing in the street just outside my home. Each looking up at the windows.

I slowed. My throat tightened. They seemed so absolutely unreal. There. Them. Together.

My brothers.

Were they ghosts? Was this Peter playing tricks?

Or had they really come home after all these years?

John and Michael.

John stood tall, rigid, hands clasped behind his back. Sharp. All angles. Handsome in a dark suit, which caught the lamplight. He looked older than I remembered. Gray threading throughout his temples. Lines bracketing his mouth. Just like Father.

Beside him, Michael. My baby brother, though he wasn't a baby anymore. A grown man, broad through the shoulders. Jaw squared and stubbled. Posture carrying that particular alertness I'd seen in the soldiers at the hospital. He was eighteen now. His hair was fairer, like Mother's.

They both looked up as I approached. And in that instant, the tension in my shoulders eased, and I felt like I could breathe.

John's posture softened. Michael's face brightened with relief.

"Wendy," John said. My name suspended between reprimand and gladness. "You've kept us waiting."

Michael, my baby brother, charged straight at me, scooped me off my feet, and spun me in the air in the middle of the street.

"Wendy!" he shouted. "I've missed you!"

"Michael, please don't drop her," John teased.

"Be quiet, you boring, ol' barrister. I could've done that too, you know, become a barrister, but I'm going to go see the world. Make things with my hands."

Mrs. Crane's blinds snapped open across the way.

"Oh, dear," John said. "We have company."

Michael stopped and set me down. I leaned on his shoulder. "That's great. I love company," he said.

Michael raised a hand in greeting and boomed, "Good evening, Mrs. Crane! Lovely to see you! You haven't aged a bit!"

He waved with boyish enthusiasm, and she let out a scandalized gasp before yanking the blinds shut.

"Michael!" I elbowed hm.

"What?"

And once again he scooped me up and spun me in the air.

Behind us, John approached. Measured. Composed. His boots clicked once on the stone before he stopped.

"All right. All right. Put her down."

"John!" I leaped up and threw my arms around his neck. "I'm so glad you are here. Why'd you take so long?"

"I'm sorry . . . I'm just so sorry, Wendy."

Michael embraced us both, squeezing tight. And for just the flash of a moment, we were children again kicking a ball in the street. Chasing Nana in the garden.

The three of us stood bound together. A small circle of warmth in a city that felt colder than it should. A small family, but still, this was my family. Later we would talk about all things serious. But right now, we laughed. We reveled in our freedom. Michael complimented my hair, how it'd grown past my waist. And he and I teased John, so serious and so stiff but so clever. We huddled, recognizing between pauses how we'd survived something no one would ever understand but each other. Here we were now, John, a barrister. Michael, who'd completed his studies at King's College. How brilliant they both were. And the silent understanding that something had prevented us from having these lives and was trying to do it again.

Soon, the laughter faded and none of us spoke.

Silence stretched and filled with everything we hadn't said.

Every Christmas I'd spent alone.

Every letter I'd written and they hadn't answered.

Every time I'd seen John's name in the papers, successful barrister, respectable marriage, and I wondered if he ever thought of me.

"I'm sorry," John repeated. His voice wavered. "For staying away. For letting you carry this alone."

Michael's jaw tightened. "We thought if we discussed it like Father said . . . Pretend we were normal." He turned his face to the night sky and shouted. "Ha! Normal! Stupid!"

"We were scared," I said. "All of us."

John nodded. His hand found mine.

"Not anymore," he said. "Whatever happens next, we do it together. The three of us. Like it should have been from the start."

Michael placed his hand over ours. His palm was rough now, calloused. A man who went from university to bricklayer and soon to be off to war.

"Together," he said.

The word hung in the cold air like a vow.

The three of us laughed again, quieter this time, but real. Loud enough that the whole of the street seemed to flare awake.

Dogs barked. Front lights snapped on. Curtains twitched.

Faces appeared in windows, whispering behind glass about those troublesome, noisome Darling children gathered in the street at this hour. Of course it was those three. That raucous trio whose wild stories once filled newspapers and books and stages. Their names which still crossed the lips of London women over their tea.

Let them talk. Let them whisper.

I no longer cared what any of those useless people said, because now I had my brothers, and I had my purpose, and it was greater than all those who spoke about us.

Because while we were the ones they vilified and mocked, what they didn't know, what they could never know, was that the work my brothers and I had ahead of us was greater than all of them. Greater than any story any of them could ever tell.

Their children, and their children's children, would be able to sleep safely in their beds forever because on this cold night, on this London street, the Darlings had come together again to vanquish Peter Pan.

* * *

At the top of the stairs, John spoke. "We heard about the boy."

Michael swallowed. "Willie," he said quietly. "Beatrice's letters reached us this morning. We came straightaway."

Beatrice's letters? That sneaky and loving Beatrice.

"Beatrice's letters reached you? But I sent you letters, and you . . ." My voice thinned. "Did you not receive any of them?"

They exchanged a glance, brows tightening.

"You called me the other night, but the line disconnected, and when I tried to ring you back there was no answer," Michael said.

"No," I said, perplexed.

He stared. "You didn't?"

"No, not at night. In the morning, before school."

John exhaled. "Peter. He's crossed our lines and tampered with our mail."

A cold certainty slid down my spine.

"Of course he did," I whispered. He's a devil, and he knows we're stronger together."

We stepped inside.

The three of us stood in the parlor, the fire burning low, the silence stretching between us.

I made tea. The ritual of it seemed to steady us. Kettle. Cups. Saucers. Sugar bowl.

We had been children the last time we sat together like this.

John held his cup but didn't drink. His eyes moved around the room, cataloguing, assessing. The barrister's habit. I wondered what he saw. Worn furniture. Books stacked on every surface. Window latched and reinforced with extra locks. Did he hear the dripping faucet in the kitchen that kept me company on the nights when the silence seemed so loud?

This was what my life had become. A teacher's wages. A leaking house. And locks on every window.

Michael sat on the edge of the settee, elbows on his knees, hands clasped. He looked too large for the space. Too alive. In a few weeks he would ship out to Belgium, and all the horrors the newspapers dressed up in words like *honor* and *duty*. I wanted to remember his face like this, the way his jaw had squared, the stubble he hadn't bothered to shave, the lines around his eyes.

I didn't want to tell him about the hospital and all of the soldiers there and how their eyes had dimmed.

"You both look exhausted," I said. A stupid thing to say. We were all exhausted. We had been exhausted for twelve years.

"Thought I was going mad." Michael admitted. "Or maybe I'd always been mad and just gotten better at hiding it."

"You're not mad," I said.

"Neither are you." He looked up at me. "I should have said that years ago."

"You were just a baby . . ."

John set down his cup. The clink of porcelain against porcelain was too loud. "I should have said it."

I wanted to say that it was fine. That I understood. We were all children and scared and pressured by adults with what to say. But all of those years had calcified into something harder than understanding.

I'd grown used to being by myself. No one to write. No one to visit. Books kept me company at night, stories I could control, with endings that were written, solid, and could not be contradicted by someone else. I'd long ago resigned myself to the fact that people feared me for what I had experienced, as if getting close to me would transfer that suffering onto them. As if madness were contagious.

The fire popped. Shadows jumped. All three of us flinched.

Michael laughed, a short, harsh sound. "Look at us. Grown adults, scared of the dark."

"Because we know what's in the dark," I said.

The silence returned, but it was different now.

John spoke. "I think we're all afraid to say it."

"I'm not," Michael said. "He's back. We all know it. None of us are sleeping. We've got these stupid birds following us everywhere. And the shadows." He tipped his chin toward the window. "They're moving wrong. You've seen it too. Don't tell me you haven't."

"I've seen it," John said quietly.

"We know what we have to do." Michael's jaw tightened. "We go back."

I had known this moment would come.

"No," I said. "I go back. Alone."

John's jaw tightened. "Wendy . . ."

"You have Judith. The baby. She's just weeks old, John. If something happens to you—"

"If something happens to any of us, it happens," he said. "That's not a reason to let you face this alone. He's not going to stop. He's coming for all of us. We know that."

I turned to Michael. "And you. You ship out in days. England needs soldiers."

"The war will still be there when we get back." His voice was flat. "Or it won't. Either way, I'm not letting you walk into that place without me."

"You don't understand." I stood, moving to the window. The lamp lights dim. "I'm the one he wants. I'm the one who left. If I go alone, maybe I can—"

"Can what?" John was on his feet now. "Bargain with him? Reason with him? He's not a person, Wendy. He's a thing that wears a person's face."

"I know what he is."

"Do you?" John stepped closer. His voice dropped.

"There it is," I said. The anger. The blame.

"When we were children, you defended him. You made excuses for him. You said he was a child who never had a real mother, that he didn't understand."

"I was a child too!" The words tore out of me. "I was a stupid, lonely girl who wanted to be special, who wanted to be chosen, who believed him when he said I was the only one who understood him!" My hands were shaking. My whole body was shaking. "And before that my life was spent caring for the two of you!"

John went pale. "Wendy, I didn't mean—"

"Yes, you did." My voice cracked. "And you're right. I did believe him. I did make excuses. I loved him, for a time. And that's the worst part. That's the part I can never forgive myself for. I loved the thing that killed Roger. I loved the thing that killed those boys."

The room went silent.

Michael moved first. He crossed the space between us and pulled me into his arms. "It's not your fault," he said into my hair. "None of it was your fault."

I pressed my face against his shoulder. I could feel John behind me, his hand coming to rest on my back, awkward, uncertain, but there.

"I already got Roger killed," I whispered. "I can't get you killed too."

"Roger made his choice," Michael said. "He chose to save you. That was *his* choice, Wendy. Not yours."

"If I hadn't been there . . . wandered off in Kensington Gardens that day . . ."

"It doesn't matter."

Michael held me at arm's length. His eyes were wet. "You survived. That's not a crime. That's not something to be punished for. You lived."

John cleared his throat. When I turned to look at him, his composure had cracked completely. Tears streaked his face.

"I'm sorry," he said. His voice was wrecked. "I'm sorry we let you carry this alone. I'm sorry we didn't speak up more to Mother and Father before they sent you away. We were cowards."

"You were children . . ."

"Twelve years," John continued. "Twelve years you've been fighting this by yourself. Pretending that if we didn't talk about it, it would stop being true."

"I hate that you left me," I said. The words came out small. Broken. "I hate that no one believed me. I hate what he did to me, to those boys, to Roger. I'm so angry that sometimes I freeze up and don't know what to do with it."

"You don't have to make it stop," Michael said. "You just have to let us help carry it."

John stepped forward. Took my hand.

"He'll try to use you against me," I said. "He'll find your fears, your weaknesses. He'll show you things that aren't real. Make you doubt everything."

"We know."

"You might not come back," I said. "We all might not come back."

"We know that too," Michael said. "And we're still here."

I looked at them. My brothers. John with his cracked composure and his tears still drying on his cheeks. Michael with his soldier's shoulders and his boy's eyes and his arms still ready to catch me if I fell.

"You're certain," I said. "Both of you."

John squeezed my hand. "We finish this together, Wendy. No more running. No more hiding. No more pretending."

Michael placed his hand over ours. "Together."

The word felt like a door opening.

Outside, a crow landed on the lamppost. It tilted its head, watching us through the window.

Let it watch. Let it carry our words back. I didn't care.

"He murdered those children back then," I whispered, the words clawing their way up my throat. "He made sure to make it hurt. He started with the ones who played with us after we arrived. They all trusted him."

Michael flinched, as though struck. John's eyes narrowed on a spot on the wall, thinking.

"You remember them," I said. "Nibs. The twins. Curly."

"Jax," Michael added.

"So many," John said.

The truth hung between us, fragile, devastating.

Shadows trembled along the walls. The flame on the hearth bent low.

"I need to tell you something," I said. "My shadow . . . it's been acting strange. Wrong. Like he's . . ." The words stalled in my mouth for a minute. "Like he's trying to take hold of it."

John's head snapped toward me. "What does that mean?"

"I don't know."

Michael stepped closer. "Regardless of what it is . . . it's not good."

I reached into my satchel. The journal waited inside, its leather worn soft from years of being opened in secret, closed in fear, held in the dark like a talisman. "I . . . I checked and I don't have anything written about that, about my shadow acting odd."

"We'll have to talk to someone," John said.

I laughed, the sound harsh. "An expert in shadows?"

"No, an expert in—" he waved his hand toward the fire, "whatever this all is, a ghost, a monster . . ."

Outside, something seemed to brush against the window. A tree branch, but there was no tree close enough to the house.

I opened my journal and flipped through its pages trying to find something, anything to make sense of this all.

I read.

"'We arrived. The trees here hum when the wind passes through them. The boys are kind. Nibs. Curly. Peter says see, this is why I belong here.'"

The words drifted through the parlor. The fire flared, then dimmed. Its wavering light brushed across my brothers' faces: John, drained of color; Michael, lips parted as though hearing names he had buried beneath years.

"'Days have gone by. I'm beginning to miss home. Mother. Father. I think we had a dog, but I can't quite remember. I asked Peter when we could go back, but he ignored me. Instead, he invited John and Michael on an adventure. When I saw the boys packing things like spears and swords, I told Peter that Michael had to stay back with me. He's just too little. I don't think Peter liked that, but then I said Michael would help me with the pile of mending. All of those socks with all of those holes. And that seemed to please him.'"

My voice fractured. I turned another page. I read the first line to myself and then remembered. My voice fractured. I held back a sob.

"'They returned late this evening. Covered in red and mud, with cuts and scrapes. Peter laughed, said they'd battled pirates. I asked him where the twins were, and he said they'd be along soon. John sat in front of the fire, silent. The twins never returned.'"

John stood near the window. His fingers trembled against the fogged glass.

"It was all real," I said. "We weren't missing children. We were children who were taken."

"There are rules, aren't there?" John asked.

I flipped back through my journal.

"There's only two." I think. "Peter said that he can cross back and forth. That all of the children here had agreed to come with him. That not just anyone can fly, just him and whoever on the island is bound to him. Oh . . ."

"What?"

That word. *Bound.*

"He said our shadows were linked." That explains it. Why he's able to pull at me. Our shadows are linked and he's getting stronger, calling me back.

"What do we do now?" John asked with that same voice our father had used when things grew too serious.

I stared into the coals. They breathed with a slow, living glow.

"When do we go back . . ."

Michael's voice was rough. "How? How do we even get back there?"

"I think . . ." I spoke slowly. "If I'm thinking about this correctly, if I'm linked with him . . . then I can take us."

A knock on the door. And then another, and another.

We fell silent. Stared. Not knowing what to do next.

"I gather you're not expecting anyone at this late hour?" John asked.

"No."

Another three knocks, more forceful this time. Urgent.

In the hallway I could make out a figure standing outside the door. Dark hair. Coat. Brass buttons.

"Oh, my goodness . . ."

"Who is it?" Michael asked.

"I'll get it," I said, my feet moving to the door, everything feeling muffled as in a dream.

He stood on the step, a man weathered by years, not myth. He was tall, gaunt, and wrapped in a captain's coat worn nearly to threads. Salt stiffened the seams; one shoulder was patched with mismatched fabric; the collar sagged under the weight of exhaustion. His black hat, once crisp, was crushed slightly in his hands, the brim damp with evening mist.

He was not the swaggering tyrant from Mr. Barrie's stories. Nor was he a shadow from our nightmares. He was only a man, older, thinner. Hollowed by grief and miles.

James Hook. The adoptive father of my beloved Roger, himself a stolen child, who died saving me.

"Miss Wendy," he said quietly.

He inclined his head, not quite a bow, not quite a courtesy, something closer to recognition.

"Forgive the hour."

"James," I said, and leaned over and placed a kiss on his cheek. "Please come in out of the rain."

He trailed the sea and mist inside. His eyes were cold as brass. Quick. Restless. Eyes that once watched a boy fly and understood the terror in it long before we ever did.

We moved into the parlor.

John muttered, "Dear God . . ."

"Hook!" Michael stumbled back, hitting the wall. His eyes wide. Unblinking.

James Hook clasped his hands behind him. The posture of a sea captain measuring the room.

Michael swallowed hard. "How?"

James exhaled. "Because it's returned. You didn't kill it. Injured it. Made it mad. Twelve years it sleeps. That's its cycle. I imagine you all have seen it. So have we. It's angrier than all the years I've known it."

"I saw you," I said. "You were outside Marigold House. I was going to go find you, but . . ."

"I know," he said. "I saw the doctor arrive. And later, the constables. I thought it wiser to wait so this meeting could be held in private."

John stepped forward. "How did you find us?"

"I've been watching the signs. Crows gathering. Shadows moving on their own. When the patterns started again, I knew he was hunting. And I knew who he'd be hunting for."

"You came from . . . that place. How?" Michael said.

"I can come and go. It's not an easy journey to make. There are paths, if you know how to sail them. If you're desperate enough to try. One loses a bit of oneself when crossing the black waters between worlds."

He coughed—a wet, rattling sound—and continued.

"We all thought it died, but it didn't. It's back now, and it wants you three, especially you, Miss Darling. And each of us has our own reasons for wanting it dead."

"Why can't you do it yourself?" John asked.

James's jaw tightened. "Because I tried. Three times. And three times I failed." He held up the iron hook. "The first time, he caused me to lose my hand. The second time, he took most of my crew. The third time . . ."

He stopped. Swallowed. "The third time, he took my son."

The room went silent.

Hook's eyes snapped to mine. For a moment, something raw and terrible passed between us. Two people who had loved the same boy, who had lost him to the same monster.

Outside, the crows gathered on the rooftops. A black cloud rising against the darker sky, carrying word to their master that the game had changed.

James lowered himself into a chair, his face gray with exhaustion. "But first," he said, "you need to understand what he is. How he works."

He leaned back, wincing. His eyes went distant, seeing something beyond the walls of my parlor, beyond London itself. "He operates in cycles. Twelve years. That's how long the door stays closed between his world and yours."

"Why twelve?" Michael asked.

James shrugged. "I don't know. Old stories say it's tied to the stars; the second star to the right only aligns properly once every twelve years. Others say it's tied to him, to whatever he is. The fae have rules they can't break, no matter how powerful they become." He shifted in the chair, wincing. "What I know is this: Every twelve years, he crosses over. He gathers new children. He takes them back. And then the door closes, and London forgets, and the cycle begins again."

"But time moves differently there," I said. "We were gone for only three days. There, it was more like weeks."

James nodded. "Time is his to command on the island. A day here might be a month there. A year here might be a single night. He stretches it, compresses it, plays with it the way a child plays with clay." His voice hardened. "That's how he keeps them. The children don't realize how long they've been gone. They don't realize they're aging in hours what should take years. By the time they understand, they're too weak to leave. Too much of them has been . . . consumed."

"The boys," John said slowly. "How long had they actually been there?"

"Some of them? Decades." James's eyes went distant. "Curly was taken in 1872. The twins in 1884. They thought they'd been there a few months. They had no idea they'd already outlived their parents, their siblings, everyone who had ever known their names."

A chill ran through me.

"And Peter?" I asked. "How old is he really?"

James Hook laughed, a bitter sound. "He's not that old, but the one who made him is older than all of London."

"How can you help us?" Michael said.

"I can try to get you all back there somehow, but I have to consult with the thing that lives in the hollow in the tree. Humans can't cross the black waters with me. They can only get to the island with Peter, because he can fly."

James moved closer to the hearth, extending his hands toward the heat as if trying to thaw the cold from his bones.

"It's pleased by the war," he said. "It feeds on the happy ones. The innocent. Little children with big dreams. But war strips children of hope faster than anything else. And there's nothing that feeds it quite like stealing the hope of a child. I'm sure it's there, wandering your battlefields. Searching for boys playing soldier. Or slipping into the lives of those stuck in the in-between, between life and death."

Edward . . . that's how he's able to connect through Edward. He's not dead, just stuck someplace between the living and the dead.

"It's time you know its story," he turned to us, his face half lit by the fire, the other half lost to shadow.

CHAPTER

14

"THERE WAS A babe once," he began. "Taken straight from his pram in Kensington Gardens by a crow-man. Its real form is a crow, but it likes to make itself a man to blend in. Keep watch . . ."

I thought of the balloon vendor I'd seen who had not aged in years. It must be him.

"This crow, Solomon is its name. Heard the babe crying and reached into its pram and brought him up into the tree. It was there that Solomon gave the child passage to the island and gave him many of the gifts that birds carry. Solomon told this baby that he'd be betwixt-and-between."

"Betwixt-and-between? What the bloody hell does that mean?" Michael said.

The fire shivered. Shadows crawled higher along the walls.

"It means he belongs to neither world. Not fully bird. Not fully boy. Not alive the way you're alive, not dead the way the dead are dead. He exists in the space between things, between childhood and adulthood, between dream and waking, between story and flesh." He coughed. "It's what makes him so difficult to kill. He's not entirely real. But he's real enough to commit murder."

Silence fell around us, dense, cloying.

James turned toward the window and when he spoke again, his voice dropped to a frayed thread.

"And he has the girl," he said. "Agnes. There's not much time. And he will come for more. All of them."

Something in my chest seized. "We have to get her out of there!"

"You can't just run off and go get her. He will kill all of you. We have to plan this right."

"How long do we have?" John asked.

"She's much smaller than you lot were. I'd say three days."

Outside, the fog pressed harder to the glass, as if straining to hear.

John's voice cut through the quiet. "How do we kill him?"

"You don't kill him," James said. "You end him." His posture stayed rigid. "A creature like that, shadow-rooted, attention-fed, doesn't die. But his story can end."

Michael looked to all of us. "I'm ready. What do we need to do?"

"To end it," James said, looking at us, "you need to call it by its name. The name it was given when it was born."

My head spun. Everything lurched.

The fire crackled. Shadows jumped across the walls. John's. Michael's. James's. All stretching with the light. Except mine.

James looked at me with a sense of knowing. "I see it. He's taking your shadow."

"Wendy . . ." Michael was crossing over to me before I could tell him that I was fine.

I raised a hand. "I'll be all right."

"Your life is tied to his. If you go, I don't know if you'll be able to return here," James said.

"I'll worry about that later," I said. I had to save Agnes.

The coals hissed, then sagged. Their glow weakening.

Michael's gaze slid to John. "You're the barrister," he whispered. "Where do we even go to find a name?"

"Records," John said. "We'll have to move quickly. Figure out when he went missing. If Scotland Yard has any account of it. Missing persons. Birth records. Anything."

"You're going to ask me to walk into Scotland Yard?" I asked.

"We have to, Wendy," John said. "There's no time to waste."

And he was right.

The clock struck. The beginning of a new hour, of which we didn't know how many we had left.

"It's time I leave you." James lifted his hat, turning it slowly in his hands, rehearsing the weight of a farewell he had never learned how to give. At the threshold, he stopped.

"He'll appear gentle at first, Wendy. Apologize. It will say anything to keep you there. Remember everything he took away from you."

James adjusted the coat on his shoulders. I opened the door, and we watched the rain for a moment, before he turned around.

"In the life I imagined," he said quietly, "you and my Roger would be growing old at sea. Two children remade into something stronger than what hunted you."

Tears filled my eyes, and all I could do was thank him.

And as I closed the door and pressed my back against it, all I could think about was time.

Three days to save Agnes. Three days to save the children. Three days to save myself.

CHAPTER

15

WE STEPPED OFF the tram outside Westminster.

The stones were slick from last night's rain, and I nearly lost my footing on the curb. John caught my elbow before I fell.

Scotland Yard rose from the mist ahead. Gray stone. Gray windows. Everything about it looked muted and drained of color.

"What if someone recognizes us?" I asked.

"That's not going to happen," Michael reassured us.

John, who thought of all possibilities, just gave me a weak smile as he held the door.

Inside, John squared his shoulders. I watched the shift as it happened. Him transforming from brother to something else. The barrister. The professional. Spine straight. Jaw set. Eyes flat but purposeful. He had done this a thousand times in courtrooms, I realized. Put on a mask and become the person the situation demanded.

We all wore of masks of sorts. Peter had taught us, whether we wanted to learn about that or not.

The air was thick with tobacco smoke and damp wool. But there were more smells, that institutional smell of too many bodies in too small a space. Of ink and paper, and a particular staleness of rooms where bad news was delivered daily.

Men in uniform filled the lobby. Talking. Huddling. Consulting clipboards and shuffling papers. They moved with the sort of stern efficiency of people who had seen too much and learned to stop feeling altogether. So far, Michael was right. No one really looked at us. We were invisible here, just three more citizens with just another problem.

A clerk sat behind a high wooden counter. A fortress of ledgers and inkwells separated him from the public. He was older than I expected, sixties, maybe, with wire-rimmed spectacles perched on a nose that appeared to have been broken at least once. His hair was gray and thinning and combed carefully across a spotted scalp. When he looked up at our approach, his eyes were a washed-out blue.

"Help you?" His voice was flat. Practiced. The voice of a man who repeated these two words ten thousand times a day with nothing much interesting that followed.

John stepped forward. I hung back with Michael, letting him take the lead. This was his world. His language.

"We'd like access to missing children's cases," John said. "Approximately ten years back. Perhaps earlier."

The clerk's expression didn't change, but something shifted behind his eyes. A flicker of interest. Or suspicion. Hard to tell.

"We don't share files with the public." He picked up a pen. Put it down again. "You're going to need authorization. Proof of legal standing. A formal request submitted through—"

John placed his identification on the counter.

The card sat there between them. Cream-colored. Embossed. The weight of it somehow visible.

"John Darling," he said. "Barrister of the King's Bench. Historical inquiries fall within my purview."

The clerk studied the card for a long moment. Then he set it down and slid it back across the counter.

"No."

John blinked. "I beg your pardon?"

"I said no, Mr. Darling." The clerk's voice was cold. Dismissive. "Missing children's cases are not entertainment for bored barristers. They're not research material. Not fodder for whatever book or article or morbid curiosity brought you here today."

"This isn't morbid curiosity."

"Isn't it?" The clerk cut him off. "I've worked this desk for thirty-two years. I've seen every type walk through those doors. Journalists wanting a scandal. Writers wanting inspiration. Mediums claiming they can speak to the dead children if only we'd let them see the files." His lip curled. "You're not the first, and you won't be the last. The answer is no."

John's composure cracked. "Sir, if you would simply—"

"The answer is no." The clerk picked up his pen, already turning his attention elsewhere. "Good day, Mr. Darling."

Michael stepped forward, his hands balling into fists. I caught his arm before he could say anything that would make this all worse.

The clerk didn't look up. We had been dismissed.

I thought of Willie, the great pain he must have felt throughout his body. Of Agnes, and how scared she must be, wherever she was.

I thought of all the children at Marigold House, not knowing how much longer I could protect them.

"Children will go missing again." My voice came out harsher than I intended. Louder. The clerk's pen stopped moving.

"Right now," I said. "While you sit behind your counter and your ledgers and your thirty-two years of saying no. Children will be killed if you do not help us."

I leaned forward. My palms flat on the counter. My eyes locked on his. "I will make sure all of London knows your name. I will make sure everyone knows that we came here today begging for help, and you turned us away because you couldn't be bothered. Because we weren't important enough. Because children weren't worth your time."

The clerk's face had gone pale.

"Every child who dies after today," I said quietly, "will be on your head. Every single one. And you will carry that. For the rest of your life."

The ward had gone silent around us. I could feel the uniformed men staring. Could feel John and Michael holding their breath behind me.

The clerk's eyes flicked to the constables watching. He shook his head once and then returned his focus to me.

"You're the Darling girl," he said. His voice lost its edge. "The one who . . ."

"Yes." I didn't look away. "I'm that Wendy Darling." I straightened. "And we need your help."

The silence stretched.

Then the clerk reached beneath the counter. When his hand came back up, it was holding a binder. Thick. Heavy. The kind of weight that could only mean years of accumulated tragedy.

CHILDREN—MISSING/UNSOLVED, **1902–1905**

"God forgive me if you're lying," he muttered. "And God forgive me if you're not."

He turned the binder to face us. John leaned in first. Then Michael. Then me, though part of me didn't want to look. Part of me already knew what I would see.

Faces stared back at us from the pages. Charcoal sketches, mostly. Photography was expensive, and these missing children did not come from wealthy families. The drawings had a rushed quality to them, the kind of work done by police artists trying to capture a likeness from a weeping mother's description.

Eyes too large. Mouths too small.

Features blurred at the edges, as if the children were already fading from memory even as they were being recorded.

Some of them I recognized. I avoided making eye contact with John or Michael, because I knew they spotted some of the boys too.

Nibs. His name here was Ernest. But that was him, with his cocky grin translated into gray strokes on yellowed paper. Age eight, the notation read. Last seen Kensington Gardens, near Round Pond. Never recovered.

The twins, and that's what we called them over there, but here, their names were listed Archibald and Ambrose. In the sketch they appeared side by side, mirror images, even in death. Ages six and six. Last seen Kensington Gardens.

Curly. But his name wasn't Curly in the document. It was Stanley.

My fists clenched at my side.

His face looked up at me from a decade-old sketch, gap-toothed and trusting, and for a moment I was back in the tree-house, back in the clearing, back in that last terrible second before I left him behind.

Age seven. Last seen playing near Kensington Gardens.

"You know any of them?" the clerk asked. Not accusing. Just observing. "These children. You recognize them?"

I shook my head no, and Michael followed.

John's voice was tight: "Earlier. We need earlier than these."

The clerk studied us for a long moment. Whatever he saw in our faces must have convinced him, because he turned without another word and pulled a second volume from the shelf behind him.

CHILDREN—MISSING, 1898–1901

This binder was older. The leather was cracked and the pages brittle. John flipped through carefully. But even so, small flakes broke off at the corners and drifted down like dead leaves.

More faces. More children. So many interrupted and stolen lives.

I watched John's hands as he turned the pages. They were steady. Barrister's hands. But I could see the tension in his jaw, the way he kept swallowing like he was trying not to be sick. Knowing that there were many boys who'd gone missing over thc years. Not just the ones we knew.

"No," Michael said. He was looking over John's shoulder, his face pale in the dim light. "Further back. We need to go further."

The clerk reached for a lower shelf. This binder was ever older than the last. Crumbling to the touch. Pieces of it came off on his fingers, and he wiped them absently on his trousers before setting the volume on the counter.

FOUNDLINGS & INFANT ABDUCTIONS—1890–1898

John opened the cover. The pages inside were brown with age, the ink fading to rust. Some of the entries were barely legible. Damaged by water or time, sometimes both. Face blurred and smudged, as if time itself were conspiring to erase these children from history entirely.

"What exactly are you looking for?" the clerk asked. "If you could narrow it down . . ."

"A boy," John said. "Infant. Very young. Perhaps days old. Taken from his pram in Kensington Gardens."

The clerk's fingers trembled slightly as he took over the page-turning. "There were several," he said quietly. "More than people like to remember. Kensington Gardens was . . . there were stories, back then. Nurses afraid to take their charges there after dark. Rumors of someone snatching babies and little ones and dragging them into the trees."

Something in the trees.

He flipped through them slowly. One page. Then another. Names fading. Dates smudged. Some entries so damaged they were nothing but fragments: Male. Infant. Last seen. Never.

"Maybe he's older than we think," I whispered. "Can we go further back?"

Without a word the clerk disappeared into a room behind the counter. We stood there in silence, the three of us, surrounded by smoke and murmured conversations and the weight of all those children who'd gone missing in Kensington Gardens.

When he returned, he was carrying a ledger so old the binding was actively unraveling. He held it carefully, both hands supporting the spine, as if it might crumble to dust at any moment.

"These are the oldest we keep readily accessible," he said. "Anything before this would be in the archives. Weeks to retrieve, at minimum."

ABDUCTIONS & STRANGE OCCURRENCES—1887–1890

Strange occurrences. I almost laughed. If they only knew.

The first page cracked when he opened it. The sound was obscenely loud in the quiet that had settled around us. A few of the uniformed men glanced over. Curious for a moment, and then they looked away again.

The clerk turned the pages with agonizing slowness.

And there, halfway down a page so faded I had to lean in until my nose nearly touched the paper, in ink that had turned from black to brown to something barely darker than the page itself:

Unnamed Male Infant—Approximate age: 7 days. Last seen: Kensington Gardens, near the elm walk. Mother reported he went missing from pram. No body recovered. No ransom demanded. Case closed, 1889.

"Unnamed," Michael breathed.

"Missing baby," the clerk said. He was looking at the entry with something like sorrow. "Such a sad thing. These cases . . . they stay with you. Even after all these years."

Michael's hand found my elbow. I didn't know if he was steadying me or steadying himself. Maybe both.

This was him. We all knew it.

We could feel it in our bones; in the memories we'd spent twelve years trying to bury. This faded entry, this unnamed infant stolen from his pram years ago, this was the beginning. This was the moment Peter was born.

Or rather, the Peter we knew. Had he lived here, and been allowed to grow up, who knows what he would have become, but what took hold of him in Kensington Gardens that day made him something different. Something not dead or alive. Something not human or bird. It made him something that could cross between this world and the next. Betwixt-and-between.

The clerk looked at us again. Really looked. And I saw the question forming in his eyes before he asked it.

"Why the interest now? After all this time?"

"Research," John said. His voice betrayed nothing. But his hand, resting on the counter, had curled into a fist. "For a case I'm building. It's quite private. Historical precedents."

The clerk didn't look convinced, but he didn't press. "Is there anything else you need?"

John's eyes were still fixed on the page. On that word: Unnamed.

"Is there any way to identify the name?" he pointed. "Every other entry has a name. The family name, at least, if not the child's."

The clerk shook his head. "Doesn't look like we were given one." He reached to close the binder, and I had to stop myself from grabbing his wrist, from screaming at him not to take it away, not to close the door on the only clue we had.

James's voice echoed in my head: *To end it, you need to call it by its name. The name it was given when it was born.*

We needed his real name. Without it, we couldn't end this. Without it, the children would never be safe.

"Do you need anything else?"

"Yes." John hadn't moved. Hadn't blinked. "Is there a record of the parents? An address? Somewhere we might find more information?"

The clerk turned the binder to face himself. Flipped through the pages surrounding the entry, searching for supplementary notes, cross-references, anything.

Then he stopped.

His finger rested on a line of text I couldn't read from where I stood.

Without a word, he stood and disappeared through the door behind the counter. We heard his footsteps receding, heard the creak of what might have been a filing cabinet, heard the shuffle of papers being moved.

We waited.

The smoke seemed thicker now. The murmur of voices more distant. The whole world had narrowed to this counter, this moment, this terrible suspended breath between one truth and the next.

When the clerk emerged, he was empty-handed. No binder. No file. No paper.

My heart seized.

He took his seat slowly. Crossed his hands on the desk. Leaned forward, and when he spoke, his voice was barely above a whisper.

"The father's dead."

The words hit me like a physical blow. I felt Michael sway beside me.

"Died in 1891," the clerk continued. "Two years after the boy was taken. The file says heart failure, but . . ." He shrugged. A small, sad gesture. "Men don't usually die of heart failure at thirty-two. Grief, more likely. The kind that eats you from the inside."

John's voice was carefully controlled: "And the mother?"

The clerk's eyes met mine. Held them. "She's in Bethlem."

The word dropped into the silence like a stone into still water.

Bethlem. *Bedlam.* The Bethlem Royal Hospital for the treatment of the mentally ill.

Of course she was.

"Thank you," John said to the clerk. "You've been most helpful." He gathered up his identification. Straightened his coat, smooth and professional and utterly in control.

But as we turned to leave, the clerk spoke once more.

"The Darling children," he said softly. "I always wondered, you know. What really happened to you. Where you really went."

I looked back at him. At this old man who had spent his life filing away tragedies, cataloguing the lost and the stolen and the never found.

Somewhere magical at first, and then terrible, I wished I could tell him, but all I could offer was a weak smile.

He nodded. As if that was exactly what he had expected. "I hope you find what you're looking for," he said. "Whatever it is. I hope you find it."

We walked out into the gray London morning, and behind us, the doors of Scotland Yard swung shut.

Bethlem.

The mother was in Bethlem.

And she had been waiting for years for someone to believe her.

* * *

The British Museum smelled of dust and limestone. Old scents that settled into my skin and dragged me back to when Miss Eleanor brought us here. I remember Rosie and us being scolded for wanting to reach out and touch the statues.

Michael and I moved toward the reading room.

"I can't believe he works here," I said, my head craning to look at the dome overhead.

"For now," Michael said. "He and I leave for Belgium together, but I spotted him in the enlistment office, and we just carried on just like when we were in school."

John had to get home to Judith and the baby, but Michael believed something could come from this visit before leaving for Bethlem in the morning.

Just outside the reading room Michael gave our names to the secretary. Before dialing she repeated Michael's instruction.

"Folklore and Antiquities . . . are you quite sure?"

Michael raised a brow. "What, that doesn't sound like something a fine gentleman such as me would fancy?"

His expression didn't shift, but the silence answered for her.

I bit back a laugh. There was something thrilling in watching him bristle, just a little.

She lifted the phone handle. After a clipped conversation, she hung up and gave a polite, if perfunctory nod. "You may go in."

Michael flashed her a grin that was half charm, half challenge, and we stepped inside.

* * *

"Wendy? Michael?"

I turned.

George Hale stood beside the index drawers. He was still like the boy we knew from our neighborhood, fresh face with spectacles perched crookedly. George was a few years older than me, but as an only child he spent a lot of time with us outside playing and chasing after Nana.

He put his arms around us. "I'm so glad to see you. What brings you here?"

I eyed Michael, hoping he'd answer, but he held up a hand. "Wendy, what brings us here?'

I wished I could scold him, but that's what little brothers do, no matter their age. Put you on the spot.

"We're researching the children who went missing," I said. "At Kensington Gardens."

Something shuttered behind his eyes.

"Come," he said. "I have something for you both to see then. There are volumes you won't find on the public shelves."

He led us down a narrow corridor into a room marked STAFF ONLY. The air was colder here. We walked past older shelves with thick-spined tomes bound in cracked leather. Their titles obscured by dust.

George stopped before a case labeled FAERIE LORE: NORTHERN COUNTIES & ANTIQUATED BELIEFS. He slid out a volume whose pages were yellowed and set it on a table.

"Some scholars called it changeling logic," George said, as he opened the book carefully. "They believed fairies take what they desire. And that's not just adults or even children. They can take whatever it is that they want. That they're drawn to. Milk. Honey. Anything really. But they do prefer children."

He hovered a finger above a page, searching. "Ah, right. Here. See. If a child answers a fairy's call, that fairy then has the ability to take that child's name. Then it replaces it with a new one. A binding one that connects the child to the fairy."

That's what Peter did with the boys on the island. None of them had their real names. They were all given new ones after they'd arrived.

But he didn't do that with us. Or, with me. Still, he said it. He said we were bound.

"What do you know about an ash ring?"

"An ash ring? Hmm," he said. Straightening up and then standing in front of the shelves again. "Ash ring." He said those words like he hadn't heard them together in years.

"Ah," he said. Pulling down more volumes and setting them on the table.

The first one: THE SPIRAL PATHWAYS OF THE ASH RING

He opened it and inside there were diagrams wound in frantic spirals. Circles. So many different kinds of circles. Circles within circles. So many different patterns.

"Kensington Gardens," George said, tapping a sketch of a circular grove. "Before the city spread, was considered a crossing point. Ash rings were doors. One spiral leading deeper, another leading out."

"I am so confused. Ash rings. Doors. What are we talking about?"

"Fae," George said, matter of fact. "And where they live." He motioned to the diagrams.

"And the babies?" I asked.

George opened the second volume: THE CHILDREN WHO VANISHED IN THE NIGHT GARDENS.

"As you can imagine, missing children anywhere causes a lot of speculation about things, and these incidents at Kensington Gardens were no different."

Pages turned until he landed on a map. "It's been long speculated that in this section, right off of Round Pond, there's a natural ash ring."

"That's where the boys went missing," Michael said.

"Exactly. If you believe in this, it's a portal where one can slip and fall and disappear into another world."

He looked back to the page and corrected himself. "Well, maybe not slip and fall. Lured. Taken."

"By what?" Michael asked.

"Fairies, Michael. Please keep on."

We left the museum in silence. Outside, the fog had thickened. The lamps along Great Russell Street smeared their light across the wet pavement.

Black wings beat overhead. More of them settled onto lampposts and trees along my path than last night. Crows. There were just so many of them now. Watching me. Always watching.

CHAPTER

16

"SHE DOESN'T SPEAK much," the nurse whispered, the next day, at Bethlem.

I wondered if she had been here then too, when I had. Same time. Same walls. We might have passed each other in these corridors, a woman and a girl whom no one believed.

The floors were scrubbed white, but the grout between the tiles had gone gray with years of mopped-over filth. The walls were bare. And the windows, so high, so narrow. Iron bars behind the glass. No one could reach them. No one could get in or out.

That was the point, I supposed.

Doors on either side stretched on forever, each one identical, each one hiding someone else's nightmare. I kept my eyes forward. I didn't want to know what sounds came from behind those doors. I didn't want to imagine who else had been put away for telling the truth.

"She doesn't get many visitors," the nurse said. Her voice was flat, professional. "None, all the years I've been here."

The door to her room opened with a metallic groan.

It was dim inside. A single window, glazed with decades of grime, looked out over a courtyard of skeletal trees. They looked like hands reaching up from the ground, fingers spread, grasping at nothing.

The bed was stripped. No sheets. No blankets. Just an iron frame and a mattress stained dark with years of sweat and sickness. A wooden chair sat in the corner. A chamber pot beneath it. Nothing that spoke of comfort or care.

But there were books.

Everywhere.

Stacked along the walls. Piled beneath the window. Arranged in careful rows across the floor. I stepped closer, and my breath caught.

The Little White Bird. A first edition, spine cracked from reading.

Peter and Wendy. Three copies. Four. The pages soft and worn.

Playbills from the stage production, edges yellowed, illustrations of a boy in green tights flying across a painted sky.

Pamphlets. Newspaper clippings. Penny-press illustrations of fairies and pirates and children who never grew up.

All of them about him.

Her shrine. Her obsession.

I picked up one of the books. The cover showed a boy silhouetted against the moon, arms spread wide, shadow stretching beneath him. Inside the front cover, in shaky handwriting that might once have been elegant:

He is real. He took my son. He will take others. Someone must stop him.

The same sentence, written over and over, filling the margins of every page. The words grew smaller as they went, cramped and desperate, as if she were running out of room. Running out of time. Running out of hope that anyone would ever read them.

I set the book down. My hands were shaking.

"She collected them," the nurse said from the doorway. "Every story. Every mention. The doctors thought it fed the delusion, wanted to take them away. But she . . ." The nurse paused. Something flickered across her face. "She fought. Said they were evidence. Said someday someone would come looking for proof."

I looked at John. At Michael. Their faces had gone pale.

"Mrs. Bell." The nurse's voice was too bright for this sad place. "You have some visitors. They are your . . ." She eyed us, uncertain.

"Niece and nephews," Michael blurted.

He removed his hat and eased into the chair across from her. "Aunt Bell! It's so good to see you . . ." His voice faltered as his gaze swept the room. Cracked walls, peeling plaster.

Mrs. Bell sat facing the window. Her hair hung long past her shoulders. Silvered and unwashed. Both of her hands rested in her lap. Her knuckles swollen. Her fingers raw and red. Nails bitten to nothing.

"That's lovely," the nurse said. "I'll leave you then."

The door to the room remained open. Sounds from the hall drifted in. A scream. A sob. Somewhere deep in the ward, a woman shrieking "Get them off me, get them off me" until her voice gave out.

Mrs. Bell's eyes flicked to mine.

Green. They were so green.

She smiled. Not kind, nor cruel, but with the terrible certainty of someone who had been expecting visitors for a long time.

"Niece and nephews . . ." she said. The words slid out.

"I'm sorry for the deception," I said.

Outside a crow cawed, then another. Black spots fluttering in the sky and gathering in the trees just outside the grimy glass.

"What do you need?" Sharp now. "Why have you come?"

Michael shifted forward. "Your son—"

"My son is dead!"

The last word landed like a door slamming shut.

Silence, for a long time. And then she spoke again. Her voice flattening into a story she seemed to have rehearsed a thousand times alone in this room, waiting for the right audience to share it with.

"I took him to Kensington Gardens. I was so tired. It's hard work keeping a baby. And he would just cry and cry. Colic, they said, but I knew it wasn't colic. I was just so tired. So we went for a walk, and we passed the Round Pond. I set up his pram right next to a bench with this wonderful tree beside it. He liked it there. Quiet with lovely shade. The birds circling overhead," her voice dropped. "I was just so very tired. I closed my eyes. It felt like the first time I had ever truly slept. And when I woke . . ."

She stopped.

"He was gone. Instead of my baby I found a crow. This beastly thing. I've never seen a crow so large. It sat perched on the handle of the pram, just staring at me. I stood and screamed. He's taken my baby! He's taken my baby! So many people came. So many. But it didn't matter. He was gone."

Something brushed my ear. Cold. Weightless. Like a child's breath learning how to speak.

Mrs. Bell leaned forward, motioning Michael closer. He hesitated, then leaned toward her.

"When a fairy takes a baby," she whispered, "it's no longer a baby. Not anymore. All of those human parts. Those are all gone. It becomes something else. Timeless. Enchanted." Her lips pulled back from her teeth. "Dangerous."

I stepped forward. "Mrs. Bell. What was your son's name?"

"I told you. My son is dead. That thing that wears his face," her voice cracked. "That's not my son."

She stared at me with a grief so old it had hardened into something else. Madness, or maybe it was clarity.

Her hand lifted, trembling. "You don't understand," she murmured. "You're already his." Her eyes dropped to the floor. "You and him. Your shadows are combining. One bleeding into the other." She looked up, her eyes were wet. "There's no separating you from him. Soon. It will all happen soon."

She sat back. Her gaze drifted to the window, and she began to hum a soft lullaby.

"Mrs. Bell," Michael said, trying to get her attention.

Nothing. She continued humming.

I looked down at my shadow. It bent wrong. Too long. Stretching toward the window as if it were reaching for something I couldn't see.

"Mrs. Bell, please," John pleaded. "A child's life depends on this. We just need a name. That's all we need."

"Bell," she murmured. "Bell. Bell. Bell."

"Yes, Bell," Michael said. "That's his surname. What's his Christian name?"

She began to rock. Humming louder now. Drowning us out.

"Please," I begged. "Mrs. Bell."

But she was gone. Trapped somewhere in her own mind.

Michael touched my arm. "Let's go."

"What do you mean, let's go? Michael, we need this name. We only have two days to save Agnes."

He looked at her, at this small woman. Face gaunt. Humming to no one. He shook his head. "I don't think we're going to get it from her. Maybe there's another family member. If we don't have much time, then we should be out there looking for who can help us."

I wanted to argue. Wanted to shake him. But I looked at her, this woman who spent all of these years alone. It was as there was no one even there right now. Nothing behind those eyes and nothing behind that humming.

Please, I thought. *Wake up. Give us his name.*

She turned to me. Her eyes had sunk deeper into her skull.

"Peter Gideon Bell."

The window exploded.

Glass and iron burst inward in a shrieking wave, and through it came the birds. Black wings. Yellow beaks. Dozens of them. Then more, pouring through the shattered frame like smoke, like a swarm, like a curse brought to life.

They descended on her.

I saw the first beak strike, opening a red line from eye to jaw. I saw her hands come up, too slow. I saw the birds tear at her fingers, at her scalp. Ripping silver hair out in bloody clumps. Her mouth opened to scream, and a crow drove its beak into her tongue.

Her eyes, those green eyes, burst under stabbing beaks. Thick yellow and red liquid ran down her face.

She made a sound. Not a scream. Not anymore. A gurgle. Wet and full.

Then more birds, crowding in, fighting for space on her body. Pecking. Tearing. Shredding. Until there was no face left. Until there was nothing left that looked like a woman at all.

The nurse seized the door. Her face white. "Oh my God . . ."

Michael grabbed my hand and pulled.

We ran. Behind us, footsteps thundered, nurses, doctors, patients drawn by the screaming. All of them rushing toward Mrs. Bell's room.

Where they would find what remained of her. Where they would never find her again.

We ran until my lungs burned. Until the screams faded behind us. Until Bethlem was just another gray building against a gray sky.

Michael bent over, hands on his knees. "We got it," he said. "Wendy, we got his name."

I opened my mouth to answer.

And tasted blood.

My hand rose to my face. My fingers came away red. From my eyes. From my ears. From somewhere deep inside that had already started to pay the price.

I looked down. My shadow was fading.

We had to move quickly.

CHAPTER

17

Rain streaked the windowpanes. The street below had blurred to smears of gaslight and wet stone. Then, footsteps on the stairs. Slow. Heavy. The sound of someone dragging themselves up each step.

I rushed to the door and turned the latch.

James Hook stood there, hat gone, coat torn. His left arm hung at his side, a bloodied scarf wound tight around the forearm, already soaked through. He caught himself on the doorframe.

His hand left a dark smear down the wood.

"Miss Wendy," he murmured.

"James!"

I was under his good arm. He sagged into me, heavy and cold, smelling of rain and river, and something metallic underneath.

We made it inside to the foyer.

"Sit. Here . . . lean back."

"It's nothing," he said, though his jaw clenched as I lowered him to a chair. He gestured to the scarf on his forearm. "The demon caught me with an arrow crossing back through the gardens. A graze. I've had worse from barnacles."

But his face was pale, too pale.

"Let me see."

"Later." He waved me away with his hook. "There's no time. I didn't come here to be nursed."

"Agnes?" I asked.

His eyes half closed. For a moment I thought he'd lost consciousness.

"I tried," he said. "Found his treehouse." He swallowed. "She's there, Wendy. Alive. But thinning. Fading. Until she forgets she ever was Agnes at all."

He coughed. When he pulled his hand from his mouth, there was blood on his palm.

"There's more. I went to the Black Rock."

I went still. The Black Rock. Where Roger saved me. Where a rhyme was carved. And where words continued on the stone's surface into the sea in a script Roger could not read.

"The words on the rock tell a story, of those who lived on the island before us," James said. "They tried to kill him too." His voice dropped. "They carved their failures into the surface so that others would know. So that others wouldn't make the same mistakes."

"What mistakes?"

He didn't answer immediately. His gaze had drifted somewhere past my shoulder, past the walls of this house, past London itself.

"The carvings continue past the tideline," he said. "Down into the water. I dove to read them. Held my breath until my lungs burned and my vision went dark at the edges." He stopped. Swallowed. "I had to know how the story ended."

His eyelids fluttered. He blinked hard, trying to hold on.

"James . . ."

A feather slid under the door. Black and slick. Another followed. Then a third.

"He's followed me," James whispered. "Wendy . . . your shadow . . ."

I rose to my feet.

The glass hummed. Feathers shivered. Outside, the fog pulled back from the window.

I filled my lungs and then I said: "Peter Gideon Bell!"

Something screamed. The sound was almost a child's voice. Almost. The shadows fled to the corners of the room.

"Oh, Wendy." The voice came from everywhere. From nowhere. "You remembered my name. How sweet. How useless."

The fog surged forward again, darker than before.

That was his name. That was what his mother told us was his name. "It didn't work. Why didn't it work?"

"The name alone isn't enough. That is what I came to tell you."

The arrow came before James could finish.

I staggered back. Falling into myself. Into my mind. A similar image. So long ago.

He jerked. Made a small sound. Then blood began to run, dripping onto the floor. The arrow had struck him in the chest.

"James!"

I caught him before he fell out of the chair. His eyes were wide, unfocused, searching for something I couldn't see.

"Not enough . . ." he gasped. Blood bubbled at his lips.

"But I said his name. I said it!" Tears blurred my vision. *Why didn't it work?*

"Wendy . . . listen . . . The name wounds him. Makes him vulnerable." He drew a shaking breath. "To kill him, you must speak his name as you drive a blade through his heart."

His hand gripped my arm.

"It must be done in his home. Where he's real. Here, he's just a shadow. A shadow can lure children away. A shadow can convince a child to jump. And a shadow . . . can kill another shadow."

His breath rattled.

"You must . . . go back . . . Use your shadow." The words came slower now.

"James!"

His fingers pressed something into my palm. I looked down. A hilt set with rubies. "For Roger," he breathed.

The blood pooled beneath him, dark and still spreading.

I staggered back against the wall and slid down to the floor. His body shuddered. Eyes closed. Chest now still.

I stared at his hand, the one that wasn't a hand.

He was a myth. A villain in stories told around campfires. The great and vicious sea captain who sailed black waters in search of gold. But his greatest battle had never been with a whale or even a crocodile.

It had been with a boy, not really a boy.

And in this story Captain Hook had lost.

But he had also been a father. A father who buried his son and carried a dagger across worlds and years, waiting for the chance to put it in the hands of the girl his son had loved.

I sat there, the dagger cold in my palm, the blood reaching toward me across the floor.

The feathers under the door lay still, and Peter was gone. For now.

But he had left something behind. I looked down at my shadow.

It was smiling.

CHAPTER 18

I HAD PLANNED OUR escape after I promised myself I wouldn't allow him to hurt me anymore.

"What are you doing?"

I was sitting in the treehouse, writing as fast as I could before the sunset and I lost light.

His voice was summer-bright, boyish, but beneath it throbbed something older. Patient. Certain.

"Journaling," I said. "My memories."

He leaned closer.

"Why?" he murmured.

My hand tightened around the journal.

"Because I need to remember who I am."

The leaves rustled, too sudden, too synchronized.

Peter smiled behind me. I didn't see it. But I knew it was beautiful in the way knives sometimes are.

Before I could close the book, his hand flashed forward. Too quick. Too eager.

The journal slipped from my fingers.

"Peter, no. Those are mine."

He didn't look at me. He was already thumbing through the pages. Roger's voice. The sound of bells . . ."

"Stop." My voice came out thin. "You have no right—"

He shut the book with a soft, deliberate snap. Not violent. Worse, possessive. "You have no memories, Wendy." The words brushed the back of my neck. "I am your memory now."

He pressed the journal to his chest, the gesture tender in shape but wrong in weight.

"Your thoughts," he said softly. "They're mine. Your dreams. Your fears. The way you breathe when you're trying not to cry." His smile widened, and something ancient stirred behind his eyes, something that had watched me far longer than I knew. "All of it. Mine."

I had been a girl who believed in stories. Who followed a boy through a window because he made the dark seem like an adventure. And now I understood, too late, too clearly, that I had never been a companion to him. Never a friend. Never even a person.

I was a thing he had collected. A voice to tell him stories. A heart to feed his hunger for adoration. A soul he could carve out and wear like a coat when the cold crept too close.

"Give it back," I said.

The flames crackled once, sharp, expectant, and the forest leaned in to hear his answer.

From somewhere beyond the trees came the squeal of a boar, the whoop of boys in pursuit, the thrum of drums stretched tight over bone.

Peter's expression flickered. The boy slipped away, like a mask loosened by heat.

What remained was the thing that wore him.

"Get rid of it," he said, and hurled the journal into the sand at my feet. "You just need me."

"Peter . . ."

Then he stepped closer.

His hand rose, and I flinched. Eyes squeezing shut, bracing for a blow that didn't come.

Instead, his fingers found my chin. Gentle. Almost loving.

He turned my face back toward him, slow and deliberate, the way one corrects a child who has forgotten her manners. His palm settled against my cheek, warm, steady, certain, and held me there.

I was trembling. I couldn't stop. My whole body shook beneath his touch, and I hated him for feeling it, hated myself for letting him see.

"Look at me," he said softly.

I opened my eyes.

He was smiling.

"Your thoughts," he said, thumb brushing beneath my eye as if catching a tear I hadn't yet shed. "They're mine."

He didn't finish. He didn't need to.

The drums outside the clearing quickened, as if the island itself agreed.

I looked down at the journal in the sand. My handwriting. My memories. My proof that I had once been someone before him.

And I understood, with a horror that settled into my bones like winter, that he would take all of it. Every scrap of who I was. Every thought I dared to think. He would drain me of life until there was nothing left but a girl-shaped thing that existed only to adore him.

That was what he wanted. Not love. Not companionship.

Erasure.

And he would call it forever, and he would call it belonging, and he would smile that golden smile while he did it, because to him, there was no difference between loving someone and owning them.

There never had been. Not for him.

In the morning I would wake John and Michael early. I'd run and fetch Roger, and we would finally leave this place.

* * *

He had appeared out of the dark wood, like something risen from it. No footfall. No breath.

Peter's fingers clamped around my wrist, cold enough to sting and strong enough that I already felt the bruise blooming beneath his grip.

"Where were you?" His voice was bright and sharp like a snapped twig.

"Peter . . . please."

Behind me, the palm fronds shuddered.

He laughed once, a bitter note. "With Roger," he said, tilting his head, his smile stretching wide. "You're going to run off with Roger."

"Let her go," Roger said, firm. "This is no place for her."

Peter released me as if bored, and I pitched forward, falling onto the ground, my forehead striking a stone. Dirt lodged beneath my fingernails.

"You monster . . ." Roger said. And then I heard feet, a scuffling. I turned over and found them face to face, feet apart.

"You were always a coward!" Peter said, a sneer on his face. "Afraid of adventures. Afraid of choosing sides. Afraid to kill pirates because you'd rather become one."

Somewhere in the trees, branches snapped, shapes waiting for a signal. My legs trembled as I pushed myself upright.

John and Michael stared in horror. Michael pressed both hands over his eyes, as if Peter's face alone could ruin him.

Peter smiled at all of us. "Here we have the Darlings . . . and a boy I found begging for food behind a tavern. Hands torn from digging through rubbish."

Roger stood still. Showing Peter no emotion. "Let her go," he said. "Let all of them go."

Peter shrugged as if none of it mattered. "Fine." He slipped into the trees, and he was gone.

Roger brushed the hair from my face. "Wendy? Are you hurt?"

"I'm fine," I lied. My head throbbed.

The arrow hit him before I could draw another breath. A whistle and then a soft, wet thud.

The force knocked him back into the tree trunk behind him. The arrow drove straight through the left side of his chest.

Blood burst out in a hot spray onto my blue dress. My hands. My face. There was so much. Too much.

His mouth opened in shock. No scream, just a small, wounded exhale.

"Roger!" My voice broke. "No! No! No! Roger!"

I grabbed the arrow with both hands, unsure of what to do.

"Wendy, don't—" John said, and I wailed, because I knew.

Blood pumped around my fingers in steady, horrible pulses. Warm. Thick. It splattered onto my arms, and I looked from my hands to his face, losing color. Growing white.

John knelt beside me, his hand on my back.

My own screams filled the air, bouncing off trees. Filling my skull until I felt something inside me dislodge.

I wrapped my arms around Roger's shoulders. He sagged against me, breath catching.

"I'll write you into every story," I told him, because I knew he was dying, that he wouldn't be coming back with us. "All of my stories. Every single story. For as long as I live. You are my story."

"Wendy . . ." John's voice trembled. "We need to go. Peter . . ."

I pressed my cheek against Roger's hair. "You were going to come with me," I whispered into his skin. "I was going to show you my home, and all of the years you missed living here. We were going to take them back."

"Oh," Peter said behind us, bright as a child showing off a trick. "I'm sorry. I thought he was a boar."

Rage flooded me, drowning everything else. My hand slid to the dagger Roger had placed in my palm on Black Rock.

I stood on shaky legs, turned and drove the blade into Peter's chest.

His scream cracked the open air. High. Wild. Awful. Not human. Not a boy. Like the whole of the island was screaming through him.

"Run," Roger rasped. His voice was barely a thread. "Wendy . . . go."

Michael sniffled in the background. "Wendy . . . I want to go home."

I dropped to my knees beside Roger again. My hands slipped in the blood pooling under him. Soaking my skirt. Soaking into the earth.

"Stay," I begged him. "Stay with me . . . please."

I pressed my cheek against his, and I told him everything. I poured everything into him about me. Every memory. Every warm moment on the ship. Every laugh. Every glance from him and how that made me feel less alone in a place of nightmares.

Roger's lip twitched in the faintest smile.

"Forget me," he whispered. "Go."

"Wendy!" Michael cried.

Roger fumbled weakly at his coat pocket and pressed something into my palm. His pocket watch. Still warm from his skin.

"One day . . ." his breathing frayed, ragged. "I'll teach you how to read the stars."

"Wendy!" John shouted. "Now!"

I looked into Roger's eyes. I knew. He knew. This was the last time.

"Why?" I whispered. My throat felt torn.

"So you can live," he said. "Out there."

His breath hitched, then stopped. He . . . just stopped.

"Roger," I whispered. "Roger . . ." His head fell against my shoulder.

The pocket watch ticked in my head. Steady and alive, when he no longer was.

John grabbed my arm. Michael clung to the other.

And we ran.

Thunder rolled through the trees. The ground buckled. The air warped, as the world folded in on itself and that place behind us. An island. A forest. A land that never really had a name.

The ash ring glowed ahead.

I didn't look back. I could not.

Michael sobbed beside me. John pulled us onward with all of his strength.

The ash ring pulsed, sharp, white, collapsing inward like a dying star.

And then, we were through.

CHAPTER 19

JOHN FOUND ME in the hallway, standing in front of the family portraits. Mother and Father, so young before any of us existed. Then the three of us as children, John in his top hat, Michael clutching his teddy, and me in the center, hair ribboned, eyes bright with something I no longer recognized.

Hope, perhaps. Or ignorance. It was hard to tell the difference anymore.

"Wendy." His voice was careful. The barrister tone stripped away, leaving only my brother. "We don't have to do this."

"Yes. We do."

"Hook is dead. We have no guide. No map. No way to know if we can even find her once we're there." He stepped closer. I saw his reflection in the glass. "And your shadow . . ."

"I know."

His hand closed on my shoulder, turning me to face him. "If we go, if we cross over, and we can't find Agnes quickly enough . . ."

He didn't finish. He didn't have to.

"Three days," I said. "That's what Hook told us. Three days without my shadow and then . . . We have just a few hours left."

I looked down at my feet. My shadow was barely there now. Thin. In the portrait behind me, the girl I used to be cast a shadow whole and complete. That girl had never made promises in ash rings. Had never loved a monster. Had never left boys behind to die in a world that wasn't supposed to exist.

"If I go," I said slowly, "I may never come back. I'll just . . . disintegrate until there's nothing left of me. I'll forget I never was Wendy Darling."

John nodded. His jaw tight.

"If I don't go, Agnes dies. She fades into that place, while Peter takes another child. And another. For the next twelve years until he sleeps again."

I met my brother's eyes.

"Then I spend the rest of my life knowing I could have stopped it and didn't."

I focused on the portrait of young me. That Wendy's smile didn't look forced.

"She looks happy," John said quietly.

"Because she didn't know what was to come."

Michael appeared at the end of the hallway. He said nothing. He didn't need to. I could see it on his face. He already knew the choice I'd made.

"It's not really a choice, is it?" John said.

My life had belonged to Peter since I was twelve years old. To the ash ring. To the promise. To the guilt of leaving those boys behind. I had spent years making myself small, weighted by guilt, and protecting the children at Marigold House because I couldn't protect those I'd lost.

"No," I said. "It's not a choice."

I touched the glass. My fingers left no smudge. The young Wendy remained untouched. Unburdened. Forever.

"We need to leave," I said. "Now. Before Peter gathers himself again."

Michael nodded. John didn't argue.

At Father's old desk, now my desk, I grabbed the key. The one he'd left here years ago. I curled my fingers around it and met my brothers at the nursery room door.

For a moment I wondered what if I just ran away. Left. Went to Marigold House. Hid from all of this. Hid from myself. But I knew there was no running from this threat of destruction. It would follow me.

I turned the key and opened the door.

Inside the room held itself perfectly still.

Everything stood untouched. A museum of our childhood. As if time decided to stop here and never explain where it'd gone.

Toy soldiers held their formation on the shelf, their tin faces lifted in permanent obedient vigilance.

Picture books lay open where we'd left them. Animals smiled in their colored ink.

The curtains hung the same, faded by the sun. And then, on the window ledge our initials.

W M J

A trinity carved by small hands. Children who once believed in flight. In stories. In a boy who promised us that we'd never grow up.

Michael's breath hitched. John touched the back of a chair. When the old wood groaned beneath his hand, he flinched. As though he'd awoken something that should have stayed asleep.

"We were happy here," John murmured.

I laid my hand on the window latch. It felt like a flock of birds were beating their wings behind my rib cage.

Michael stood at my left. John at my right.

For a moment, we were the children we'd once been. Older now, but still, we were here. Together.

I pushed the window open. Cold night air rushed in. And beneath it, something sharp and sweet that didn't belong to London but to a land very far away.

"Ready?" I whispered.

They nodded.

I took Michael's left hand, John's right. Our fingers interlaced together, trembling.

"Wait," Michael said. "I thought only Peter could do this."

Bound. Together. One. Just like my shadow was merging into Peter's, his was merging into mine. What he could do, so could I.

"Trust me," I said, and I closed my eyes. I felt the pull. That tug. And I focused on it, the world around me and the world where I wanted to be. Gravity shifted. My stomach dropped. My feet left the floor.

For a moment, it returned, joy. That same joy I'd felt at twelve years old, when a boy told me I could fly and I believed him.

That was at least one truth he told me.

Stars winked out, one by one. In their place, jagged shapes coiled against black.

I glanced down and my shadow was thinner than just moments before. Still, it followed obediently as shadows should. Pulling toward the second star as if something on the other side was reeling it in.

Behind my eyes I felt something sharp, nails clawing.

That was him. I knew it.

Somewhere, a crow screamed. Then another. They came from nowhere, black specks rising from chimneys, falling from eaves. Their wings beat in the air.

They didn't attack.

They followed.

We were pulled forward. London tearing away beneath our feet and now crows flanking us on either side. Wind roared. The world blurred. I tasted copper and salt on my tongue, and something else, the familiar rush of falling upward.

* * *

Then, we landed.

The world around us had spoiled.

Trees hunched inward. Their trunks warped and their bark split into long vertical seams.

Ferns curled away as we passed. Fungi swelled beneath our steps, soft, wet, pulsing. Even the grass seemed to bleed when we stepped on it.

The crows landed in the branches above. They were silent now, but still, they were watching. Their heads tilted in unison as we moved, tracking us with an intelligence that didn't belong to birds.

My shadow continued to tug. Pulling me toward the heart of the island. Toward him.

Michael led. John kept close behind me, his breath shallow and quick. "We didn't bring anything to fight with," he muttered.

Michael looked over his shoulder. "Wendy?"

I reached into my pocket and drew the dagger. The rubies caught what little light remained. "Hook gave it to me."

John nodded. "Hold on to it tight. That's all we've got."

Michael stopped. "You hear that?"

Screaming. The sounds of children screaming or what sounded like children. Voices pitched high, stretched thin.

It all warped until the sound barely resembled anything human.

Vines lashed at our legs, whipping from the brush with a wet snap.

The path beneath us writhed, no longer a spiral but a labyrinth rearranging itself with every step, folding back on itself like intestines trying to digest us whole.

The pull strengthened.

I gasped.

My knees buckled.

The sensation wrenched through me, hot and sick, like a hand had reached inside my chest and tugged. Toward the treehouse. Toward him.

My shadow screamed without sound. I felt it. I felt her, straining ahead of me, pulling so hard my skin burned where she was still attached.

The edges of my vision blurred. My blood beat wrong, too fast in some places, too slow in others, as if my body were being returned to a frequency I didn't recognize.

Come home, something whispered.

Not a voice. A feeling.

Come home, come home, come home.

Somewhere behind me, Michael shouted my name, but his voice came through waterlogged. Drowned.

"Wendy!" John's voice behind me, ragged. "Can you continue?"

I nodded, catching my breath.

His hand found my shoulder, steadied me. "Where to now?"

"The treehouse," I managed. My tongue tasted like rust. "Agnes must be there."

The forest tightened around us. Each step felt heavier than the last, and the pull more painful.

I doubled over, bile rising in my throat.

"Wendy . . ." Michael's voice shook with fear.

"Keep moving," I gasped. "If we stop, I don't think I can start again."

The light changed. Colorless. Suspended.

Ahead, the trees split open, their bark peeling back in curling in shreds.

The ground beneath us turned pale. Grass gave way to splinters that jutted upward like broken bones.

And then . . . silence.

Not the absence of sound but more like a pressure. It settled over us. It pressed into my skull.

My heartbeat slowed.

I staggered sideways, tried to right myself again. *Keep going. You have to keep going. She needs you.*

But the pain . . . my insides were on fire.

I wanted to scream, if only to prove I still existed, but I could not. My breath came in haggard gasps, Michael followed close by, and up ahead John stopped.

What does he see?

I kept moving, closer to him. My eyes fixed on the space where he was facing. Where the trees disappeared and . . . there.

The treehouse rose before us.

It hadn't collapsed. It had caved in on itself and surrendered to its surroundings.

Timber ribs jutted through the gray sky like bones. The boards were split wide, not rotted but ruptured, as though something had forced its way out from the inside.

The pull yanked again, so hard I tasted blood.

Home, it said. *You're home.*

A rotted rope ladder dangled from a beam above, swaying though there was no wind. The entire treehouse breathed. Wooden boards swayed.

"Agnes!" I shouted. Listened, but there was nothing. We walked the ruins, searching.

Ivy crawled over the beams. Bramble punched through the floorboards. The wood had gone soft with rot, sagging under its own weight.

But still, I could see what had been done.

A wooden sword lay half buried in the fire pit, its handle carved with initials I couldn't read anymore.

Tin cups hung from hooks, six of them, rusted through. I brushed a finger against one of them, remembering how I used to serve the children pretend tea with these.

"She's not here," John said, standing beside a hammock. It sagged between two dead trees.

On what remained of a shelf, I found a row of figures whittled from sticks. Crude little men with acorn heads. The kind the boys made when they were bored.

One was missing an arm. Another had no face at all.

I called out. "Agnes? Honey, where are you?"

A blanket I had sewn from scraps of fabric rotted in the corner, covered in mud, and something dark that had dried long ago.

Beneath the wreckage of it all, there was something I mistook for stones. Small white shapes rising through the moss.

As my eyes adjusted, my stomach dropped.

Ribs.

Not animal ribs. Not chicken. Not boar. Not pig. Not even an adult.

These bones were narrow, delicate, no thicker than reeds. Pale arcs pushing up from the earth.

No.

Tiny arm bones lay half buried in the dirt. A skeletal hand, small, fingers curled inward, as if motioning *Come here, let me tell you a secret.*

I spun around. They were everywhere. Michael and John were both still, shocked by what we were standing on.

"A graveyard," John said.

"Not a proper one. They weren't buried," Michael said. "It looks like they just died here."

Skulls . . . there were skulls scattered throughout. Too small. Too round. One had a crack straight through its middle. Another, its eye cavity pulverized.

"He murdered them," I said. "He massacred all of them."

John caught me before I fell back, and he held me there. Michael put his arms around us. And none of us knew what to say.

Our boys. They had been left where they fell. Left to molder and rot. To sink into the earth. Piece by piece. Bone by bone. Parts of themselves covered in moss, and cavities became worlds to insects that made their nests in their caverns.

Bones settled into the earth. Seeds that could never sprout.

But this land, it didn't just take children, I had learned. It split them. The dreaming self stayed on the island, forever young, forever dying. The waking self returned to London as desiccated, mummified shells. Found in riverbeds or fields or alleys with no marks of violence, no explanation. Just empty.

Two deaths. The one that fed the island and the one that broke their mother's hearts.

They were left as offerings to his arrogance. A testament to his self-importance. Arranged without ceremony. Without mercy. Reminders to him, and to us, that everyone who entered this land was meant to serve him. And when he tired of one, he ended them.

A sound tore out of me. Not a word. Not a cry. Something older. Something animal. It ripped through my chest and shredded the air, and I couldn't stop it. I couldn't push it back down. My whole body convulsed, as if my bones were trying to reject what my eyes had seen.

"Why?" I screamed it at the sky. At the trees. At nothing. At no one. At me. "I SAID I'D COME BACK!"

Tears streamed down my face. John and Michael hugged me tight, both of them sobbing. All of us mourning what had been done here.

"I told you," I sobbed. "I promised . . ."

But I was too late.

Every single one of them had died waiting for me. They died believing I would return for them.

This is what it means to lose to him. This was what happened to children Peter keeps.

I thought of Agnes. Agnes with her bird-quick laugh and her questions that never stopped. I thought of her in that treehouse.

I thought of her thinning.

I thought of the children at Marigold House.

Willie, so grievously injured.

Grace with her drawings.

Frederick, who still believed in happy endings.

All of them.

If I fail, this is what becomes of them. Bones scattered atop a garden. Skulls too soft to hold the weight of what was done to them. Offerings laid at the altar of a boy who called it love.

"I'm sorry," I choked. "I'm so sorry. I—"

You left them.

The thought was a knife.

You flew away and left them here with him, and they died calling your name.

The grief was tectonic, too large to feel all at once.

Somewhere above me, in the rotted ribs of that treehouse, Agnes was running out of time.

A breeze moved through the clearing. Bones shivered. A faint rattle. Teeth clicking in a skull.

Michael dropped to his knees. Or his legs simply gave out.

We were all so tired already, and we'd just begun.

His hand hovered above the nearest skull, small, fragile, the jaw hanging open. He did not touch it. Could not. He didn't speak. His shoulders hunched forward, trembling. His breath came in quick, sharp bursts.

Michael, who'd played war with these boys. Who'd called them brothers. Who now, as soon as we returned to the real world, if we returned, would be off to a real war.

John stood rigid beside me, his face gone pale. "We have to keep searching. She can be somewhere else, but she's not here."

He was right.

The air changed.

Trees leaned inward. Not swaying. Leaning. Folding forward. Branches creaking as they bent low.

A tremor moved through the canopy. Dead leaves spiraled down around us.

Then we paused when we heard a sound. Thin. High. Like breath drawn through teeth.

I wiped my eyes.

"Let's keep moving," Michael pressed.

We moved.

CHAPTER 20

WE OBEYED THE forest's push.

The path had already decided where we would go, and we let it, our feet sinking into damp moss with each step.

The bones watched us go. I felt their gaze on my back long after the treehouse was no longer in sight. In the forest, every now and again I'd think I'd hear their voices, shushing one another, giggling. Singing.

The forest shifted around us. Colors and light changing with each step. Trees groaned as they twisted into new shapes on our approach Shadows leapt ahead in quick bursts, stretching and multiplying until I couldn't tell which darkness belonged to us and which belonged to something else.

"Agnes!" I called. "It's Wendy. I've come to take you home."

I called again, but everything was so quiet. There were no sounds of insects or animals or birds.

The path dissolved. The ground beneath our feet softened, then hardened again. The pain returned in my center, bright hot, and then . . . I stumbled. Michael caught my arm.

"We've got you, Wendy," he said.

The forest walls peeled back, all at once, into a clearing.

"That can't be . . ." John said.

It was our nursery.

It was whole. Intact. Golden with dusk-light, as if the sun had been trapped inside that room for twelve years, waiting for us to return.

"That's not really our room." My voice trembled. "Be careful. Just . . . don't believe anything that you see."

The windows were open, and from outside we heard birdsong. Sweet. Lilting. Clean.

Wallpaper shimmered with rose patterns. Their petals flushed as though freshly painted that morning. Dust motes drifted lazily through the air, catching the light in soft, deceitful halos. Pretending to be magic. All of this was pretending to be home.

"Do you smell that?" John asked.

I opened my mouth to say that I didn't . . . but now I caught the scent he was talking about.

"Liza's lemon cake." The smell, fresh and bright.

The room breathed familiarity and dread in equal measure. Each inhale was a reminder that this place looked safe but that underneath it was untrustworthy. A lie.

At my feet, spongy moss dissolved into carpet. Fibers swelled up through the green like memory seizing control of the world, weaving themselves into the pattern I had traced with my fingers as a child.

John's hand tightened on my sleeve. His fingers trembled.

Both of my brothers scanned the room waiting for something to leap out at us.

I knew the truth before I let myself see her.

Some truths announce themselves by the way the air changes. By the way a room holds its silence. By the way your heart recognizes a shape it has mourned for years. But some things are just not real, no matter how much you want to believe in them.

No matter how much we all wanted to believe what we were seeing now.

Mother.

Standing at the window.

"John. Michael." I whispered.

Her posture was too perfect. Spine too straight. Shoulders too stiff, as if she were suspended from an invisible string. A marionette waiting for the hand that controlled her to decide what came next.

Her head tilted at an angle necks just can't angle. Just a few degrees past normal. Past human.

But what made it seemed real was that she hummed the lullaby that once carried us to sleep. Each note arriving a fraction of a second too late. That melody I knew by heart, but here, it was distorted. Like a music box that played with a broken gear. All of her seemed shaped by a memory in which someone never lived.

"My darlings," she said.

That voice was warm. That voice was soft. That voice was a lie, emerging from a costume of my mother.

Her smile was flawless. Every tooth in place. Every crease around her eyes exactly where I remembered them. But her eyes . . .

Her eyes were empty in a way that eyes in some paintings just are flat.

"You've come home," she said.

Michael made a sound beside me. John's grip on my sleeve tightened until it hurt.

"That's not her," John breathed. "Michael. Wendy. . . . That's not her."

"I know."

I stood in shock, staring at the thing wearing my mother's face.

She opened her arms. "Come," she said. "Let me hold you. I've waited so long."

None of us moved.

Then somewhere, behind her, in the shadows beyond the window, a boy began to laugh. His sick and twisted games knew no limits. The pain and the terror were the point.

Her fingers drummed lightly against the windowsill. A beat that sounded disjointed. Disconnected. Impatient that none of us ran to her, to it.

"Mother?" Michael whispered.

"Michael. No." I reached for his shoulder, but he slipped from my fingers.

"John!" I hissed. "Do something!"

"Michael," John said quietly but with force. "Stop right there. That thing. It's a trick. This is him. It's not our mother."

But Michael was the baby of the family, so spoiled and nurtured that even the thought of her being real, being here, even for an instant, was enough to put him under a spell.

Mother's head rotated like an owl's.

That is not our mother. That is not our mother. That is not . . .

"Start backing up," John whispered.

"Mum . . ." Michael whispered, and he sounded like he did so long ago. A little boy who was just so scared of the dark and wanted his mother.

That thing wearing our mother's face tilted its head. "My darling boy," it said. "Come here. Let me hold you."

It extended its arms and the illusion rippled.

The nursery began to melt.

Wallpaper slipping off the walls. Roses curling and blackening. Floorboards splitting open.

Mother's features slid downward. Eyes pooling into cheeks. Mouth stretching wide, revealing rows of teeth with points.

John lunged and snatched Michael by the back of his jacket and yanked him back.

Mother reached her arms out. "Darlings . . ." The word morphed into a series of trills and chirrups.

Chunks of Mother collapsed in piles of flesh and bone, but there was no blood. In its place were black shadows writhing like eels.

We stumbled out as with a screech, the forest engulfed the false nursery.

The three of us stood surrounded by trees, our hands trembling, reaching for one another, as if lost in a nightmare.

"Are you all right?" I asked Michael, and all he could do was nod. Tears filled his eyes, and he turned to look at the spot where the unreal nursery had appeared.

Mother's lullaby lingered in the air, sweet and putrid. Like perfume sprayed over something dead.

This was what Peter does. He discovers what we love the most and he forces us to watch as he takes it away. Our childhood, our friends, more.

He used our memories as weapons against us. He could show us anything he wanted. As long as we were here, he could reach into the deepest chambers of our hearts and pull out things we loved the most. Things we buried deep to keep them safe. Our hidden treasure. He'd steal it. Twist it. And torture us with it.

Nothing was safe here.

"We're close to her," I said. "That's why it's doing all of these things. To slow us down. Or get us to stop."

"We keep going then," John said. He led the way.

Ahead, the trees cracked open.

The world shifted and the ground dropped out from beneath us. I stumbled. My boots hit something wet. Something that squelched and sucked at my ankles.

Mud. Mud everywhere. Thick, gray, brown. Churned to the consistency of old porridge. It reached past my ankles. Now, past my calves. Cold and clinging.

I turned around, and Michael's face grew pale. Mud flecked across his nose.

"What is it?" I asked.

"That smell . . ."

Sweet, then sour. I could taste it in my mouth, like bile. Sulfur, gunpowder, scorched cloth, and burnt hair.

The decay of humans.

I gagged and pressed my hand to my mouth.

We were standing in a trench.

Earth rose on either side of us, walls eight feet high, shored up with splintered timber and sandbags that had burst their seams. The wood was black with damp. Water pooled at the bottom, gray-green, covered with a film of oil and floating debris. Cigarette butts. Scraps of cloth. A single boot, still laced, with something pale inside.

"Wendy . . ." John pressed against the trench wall, his face the color of bone. "Wendy . . ." he repeated. "Where are we?"

A shell screeched overhead.

I threw myself down, hands over my head, mud splashing into my face, into my mouth. My stomach flipping from the sickening taste of it. The explosion hit somewhere to our left, rocking the ground. Dirt and rocks sprayed across us.

My ears rang. Buzzing. Humming. Unable to hear what Michael was shouting. His mouth open. Lips moving. Arms waving overhead to get my attention.

It felt like the air was sucked back into the world and Michael came into hearing. "Aisne! Aisne! This is Aisne!"

Aisne? The Battle of Aisne. We were in the war. In France. I remember reading about this battle in the newspapers. Both sides dug along the Aisne River. Steep ridges. Limited crossing points. Shredded shrapnel rained down from above.

Bodies. Dozens of them. They were in the walls. Pressed into the mud and timber, limbs jutting out at angles.

Another keen in the sky. John closed his eyes and covered his ears.

Debris sprayed and the world shook.

A hand emerged from the dirt, fingers curled, reaching for something. Its flesh gray-green. Nails peeling back and black from their beds.

My chest locked tight.

A face pressed out from the mud. Mouth open. Eyes collapsed inward. Jaw hanging loose where something had chewed through the tendons.

Further down, a torso without legs. A leg without a torso. A helmet still strapped to a head that had its face blasted off by enemy fire.

British uniforms.

I could see the khaki beneath the mud, the brass buttons, belts rotted to leather strips. Boys. They were just boys who'd never return home.

It wasn't real here, but somewhere a version of this was.

"John! Michael!" I tried to reach for them, but my feet felt connected to stone. The mud held me. "It's Peter. He's doing this. He's making you see it."

"But it is real, Wendy. This is real!" John shuddered.

Michael watched on, stunned. Tears streamed down his face. Cutting pale tracks through mud.

A sound cut through the trench. A whistle. Short. Sharp.

The bodies in the walls began to move. Not all at once. A twitch here. A shudder there. Fingers flexed in the mud. Heads turned with wet, grinding sounds.

"Time to go, lads," a face in the wall said, its mouth working through mud.

Then the dead were pulling themselves free, arms reaching, legs kicking, bodies lurching upright.

They didn't stand apart. They pressed together, limbs stacking, flesh merging, until I couldn't tell where one soldier began and the other ended.

The mass of them spoke as one: "Time to go over. Time to meet the wire. Time to feed the guns."

They were all looking at my brothers.

"Come with us," they said. A chorus of ruined voices.

John dropped to his knees in the mud.

"No, please. I'm so sorry. God, I'm so sorry . . ."

"Coward," they began to chant. "Coward. Coward. Coward."

A boy slipped out from behind the advancing dead. Young. Too young for any war.

The little boy's smile widened. "I can take you back. Years ago. When you were a little boy. I can make you forget all of this. The shells. The screaming. You'd like that, wouldn't you? To be a boy again? To never remember? To never worry about work or wife or baby or a war you avoided enlisting in, for which they all called you a coward."

John looked up, and for a moment I dreaded that he was considering it.

"John, no!" I wrenched my foot free of the mud, trudging through and grabbing his arm. My fingers digging into his shoulders.

"It's a lie," I said. "He can't take the memories away."

The dead soldiers stopped. They stood in a ring around us, me and my brothers. The soldiers' eyes were empty. Fixed. Waiting.

Michael whispered, "Wendy, I can't do this anymore."

John remained silent and stunned. "I don't know. I just don't know."

"Please, help me. Don't abandon me." My voice was pleading. Then it was as if they could see again, and they each took one of my hands.

"How boring!" the little boy said. "You're all boring, the three of you!"

Corpses and scattered limbs sank into the mud. The trench evaporated into mist.

The gray sky cracked apart like a broken shell, and through the fissures poured a sickly light. Not quite twilight. Not quite dusk.

We stood in that forest again, gasping, trembling, covered in mud that was beginning to fade like morning frost.

My brothers stood silent, faces wet with tears and rain, and a lingering fear that I don't think any of us could ever name.

John wiped his face on his sleeve. "Any other ideas of where she may be? Where he could have taken her?"

I thought for sure they'd be at the treehouse. There were so many places here. Too many to name. Peter could create them on a whim. The river where we'd danced. The hollow tree where we'd hidden from the boys. The moonlit pool where he'd held my hand and promised me I would never grow up.

"We've already checked the treehouse," Michael said, his eyes rimmed with exhaustion. "He's not in the clearing. I . . . I don't know."

A memory emerged. Stone. Salt. The rhyme carved into black rock.

"Maybe . . ." My breath hitched. "Maybe he could be at the Black Rock?"

"Let's go then."

CHAPTER

21

BEHIND US THE trees halted abruptly at an invisible line. Their trunks leaned forward, straining toward the shore. Unwilling or unable to cross. Roots curled at their face like fingers. We stepped through the last veil of branches, and the sea appeared.

Or what remained of it.

The shoreline stretched into a long, blackened scythe beneath the starless sky. No moon. No light. Just where that sickly glow seemed to rise.

The water did not move, not really. It quivered, slick as tar, thick like oil. Reflecting nothing and swallowing every stray glimmer. Small ripples spread across its surface in patterns that had nothing to do with wind or tide. Something was breathing down there. Waiting.

The sand beneath our feet glittered with what looked like crushed glass. It wasn't sand. As we continued moving through it, something deep within me kept saying: *Bone, Wendy. These are pulverized bones.*

Movement crossed my vision. Something in the sky. I blinked. Feathers, dancing in the wind. He was here and he knew we were as well.

The shore came back into focus. Michael stepped forward first. His boots crunched in the bone-sand, and the crunch was so loud in the silence. "All of it, it's nothing like I remember," Michael said.

John looked at me as if I had all of the answers. "For all the horrors that happened here, it was beautiful once."

"I don't know. Maybe this happened while it's been asleep. Maybe it needs to feed in order to make this place alive again."

The hook behind my chest tightened. The ache of being reeled in. I took a deep breath, exhaling through the pain, knowing that regardless, it would end somehow.

"Agnes!" Michael shouted, her name ricocheting off the strange sky.

"She's here. Somewhere." I just didn't know where that somewhere was.

Above, more black birds. Crows. Circling. Dozens of them. Maybe even hundreds. Their wings beating in unison, making no sound. Just that steady, patient circling, tightening each time they passed us.

Beneath my feet, the ground hummed. A vibration felt more than heard. Thrumming up through my bones.

The tide moved backward, pulling inward, not out.

I watched the water shiver and retreat. We continued walking. The crows continued following. All until we came upon it.

The Black Rock.

It rose from the retreating water. Massive. Ancient. A point where the people who lived here long before Peter visited. It was on that rock they shared their warnings about a shadow eater who could be stopped with its name, a knife, and a punctured heart.

The rock gleamed wet and dark. So much water had retreated that I could now make out shapes and symbols carved across the surface the sea previously obscured.

And . . . something else. Handprints.

The former island inhabitants.

Just don't ever repeat the name carved on the Black Rock, Roger had told me once. *Its name is the source of its power.*

But the truth was clear now, a truth even Roger didn't know. It wasn't that warning, that rhyme, *Peter, Peter, shadow eater*, that brought him back to life. He lived in cycles of twelve years. Me thrusting a knife into him so many years ago just started that cycle sooner, because he wasn't really dead.

To end something completely is to face it and call it what it is.

"What is this place?" John asked.

The letters, the children's handprints seemed to glow faintly.

"I don't remember ever coming here," Michael said.

"That rock tells us how to end this story."

"Agnes isn't here, Wendy," John said. "What now?"

Black feathers fell from the sky.

Something tugged inside me. Not forward. Inward. Toward a hollow where an old ache slept. The world flashed black and I screamed.

When my eyes opened, I saw my shadow stretching long across the sand, warping, thinning, bending away from me like an animal testing the limits of its leash.

"Michael, help me." I heard John, who took one of my arms, and Michael took the other, helping to keep me steady.

"What hurts?" Michael said, panicked. Searching for a wound.

"Everything," I gasped, unable to catch my breath.

It was as if sharp talons scrabbled their way inside of me, digging beneath my skin, behind my eyes and into my skull. Nails hooked inside me, behind my flesh and then dragged down the length of my body. Invisible tears.

My vision blurred. I coughed. Blood hit the sand, flecked with glitter and black dust.

I coughed again, harder, and something caught in my throat. I choked. Gagged and clawed at my neck, doubling over.

My fingers clawed at my mouth, scraping against my teeth, reaching deeper, searching for the obstruction.

I felt them. Quills. Slick and sharp against my fingertips.

I caught hold and pulled.

My hands broke away; they were so slippery. I dug in again. Coughing, hacking. Tears rolling down my face.

My fingers hooked on them and I pulled.

They resisted.

Rooted somewhere deep in my chest. I yanked harder and harder, and they came loose with a wet ripping sound.

A bundle of feathers. Black and matted with blood and mucus.

I tossed them onto the sand. They twitched. Once. Twice. Flapping like live fish.

I dropped to my hands and knees, gasping. Heaving. Searching for breath that wouldn't come. My throat felt like I had swallowed knives or fire.

On the ground beside me, my shadow moved. Not with me, against me.

It spun and twisted. Its spine arched upward. Vertebra by vertebra. Like a cat bristling in defense.

Its head turned. Its mouth stretched open, wider and wider. Mocking me in that silent laughter.

All I could do was watch. I couldn't move. I couldn't scream. I couldn't do anything but know that he and I were merging as one in the world of shadows.

Michael was beside me now.

John shouted, "The sea! Something's coming!"

And it was.

Small. Pale. Covered in a tangle of seaweed. A child. A boy. No older than six or seven. His body bloated and blue. He dragged himself up onto the Black Rock. Water streamed out from his body, pouring out from his eyes, nose, ears, mouth. Dark red liquid splashing onto the Black Rock. He sat on the edge, feet dangling over the water.

He waved at us.

A small, cheerful wave. The wave a child gives when he spots his mother across a crowded room.

His mouth opened wider now, more water gushing out. Words strangling in his throat, but I could read his lips: *Come away.*

Another head broke the surface. Then another. Small bodies rising from the deep. Blue hands climbing the rock, sitting in a row. All of them waving. All of them smiling. Skin sloughing off their bodies in some parts, and in others, parts of them were missing. Lips and noses nibbled away by fish.

"Let's go." Michael's chin quivered. "Let's go back to the treehouse."

A child's laugh echoed across the still water. "Wendy . . ."

John supported me, holding me upright. "We're leaving," he said.

Above us, the sky tore open.

Birds spiraled downward, a storm of black feathers, and a thousand glossy eyes. Michael swung through the chaos.

The words on the rock flared gold. Then vanished.

Something inside me snapped. My shadow slammed back into place. Hot pain shot down my spine and I fell to my knees.

John and Michael dragged me up. Wind screamed. Birds gathered in the sky, their bodies shaping a single silhouette.

A boy in flight.

And then, through the pain, somehow, we all ran.

* * *

I don't know how far. I don't know how long. The forest blurred around us, branches clawing at our clothes, roots rising to trip us.

When we finally stopped I looked down at my shadow.

It was there. Whole again. Attached.

But it wasn't mine.

Its shape didn't match my body. Its edges were too sharp. And when I raised my hand, it didn't move.

It smiled.

Every sound doubled. Our boots squelching through the muck. Michael's and John's breaths strained, too fast, too shallow. Even the boom in my chest. My heartbeat. A war drum. Keeping time as we marched back.

The trees parted without warning.

And there it was again. The treehouse. Leaning out of the darkness like a child's lost toy waiting to be found.

Worn boards creaked and groaned. Shadows pooled at its base. Everything was as we left it before—but not.

The rope ladder hung in the same place. The tin cups, including the rusted ones, were still there. The same vines crawled up the supports, thick and slow.

But something had changed. A change I couldn't quite name.

Not a leaf moved. Not a branch swayed.

Everything was frozen still. Holding its breath. Waiting.

Air sat heavy in my lungs, warm and wet. It was harder to breathe here than just moments ago along the path. The air tasted different too. Metallic. Old. Like touching a copper penny to the tip of my tongue.

Before, the treehouse had smelled of rotted wood, damp and decay. Now it smelled alive. Sweet. Almost too sweet, but underneath that scent there was something else. Burning.

My body knew before my mind did. My hands started to shake. My heart raced. I knew I had to face him, but I hadn't seen him since I was a girl.

All I'd encountered in the days leading up to today was just a shadow. I was scared of how I'd feel when I looked into his eyes. Here I was, a grown woman about to face a child's face, with a monster beneath.

"He's here," I said.

"What is that?" John pointed.

Agnes's hair ribbon. Tied to the rope ladder. Pink silk stained dark.

"Agnes!" I shouted. My voice cracked.

Nothing.

"AGNES!"

The crows came first.

They erupted from the treehouse in a shrieking black mass, pouring from windows, gaps in the wood, spiraling upward into the sky. Their cries filled the air, sharp, relentless, circling overhead. Gathering like a storm cloud.

The door opened, and he stepped out.

Breath escaped me.

I had prepared myself for the boy. The eternal child with his cruel smile and dismissive eyes. The Peter I remembered, small and golden, but terrible.

This was not that Peter, but . . . it was him.

He was tall. Broad-shouldered. A grown man. His jaw was sharp, his cheekbones high. His hair the same wild tangle of red-bronze curls, but longer now, falling across his forehead and past his ears. He wore a loose white shirt, open at the collar, and his skin glowed faintly gold in the dim light.

He was beautiful.

He was the most beautiful thing I had ever seen.

My breath caught. My heart stammered. Somewhere beneath my ribs, something old and buried stirred, the girl I had been, the girl who had loved him, the girl who wished he could be what he had promised her.

The raging, burning pull and tug of my insides, the scrape of claws deep within me, was gone. Alleviated, cooled. Healed.

He smiled. Soft. Sad. I felt my brothers behind me, one on either side, each of them trying to measure how this was him.

Peter smiled, his teeth so white. It was a smile I've seen the children make when they were caught staying up late or stealing biscuits from the pantry. It was a smile that said, *I knew what I was doing was bad, but I'm sorry. I didn't mean to hurt anyone. Please forgive me.*

He scratched his head. "I know . . . I've put you through a great big fuss."

A great big fuss? All of this? This was more than just a mistake.

"Wendy," he said, pleading. His voice was low. Warm. A man's voice now, rich and deep, and hearing my name in it felt like I'd been caressed.

He descended the ladder slowly. Gracefully. The crows screamed overhead.

"You can ignore them," he said. "They're not a bother."

I glanced over my shoulder to John and Michael, their looks of confusion matching my thoughts. *What was going on here?*

Something in the space between us changed. My brothers were still there, I knew, but it was as if they were being pulled away. Miles. Another world altogether.

"Where . . ." I reached for my thoughts. My memories. They all seemed clouded now, covered by a veil.

Peter approached, one hand in his pocket, the other gesturing as he spoke.

"I was a child," he said. "I didn't understand what I was doing. You understand? Of course, I know you understand these things. Because you've always been the better of us. My better half, if I'm allowed to say that. Always so smart, my darling girl."

In the distance I thought I heard someone shouting something. A word, but I couldn't quite pick out the letters.

"I didn't know how to love without hurting," Peter continued. "Thank you so very much for giving me a second chance. I've waited for you, Wendy. All these years. I've waited for you to come back to me."

Again, a word. A sound So far, but . . . something. Someone calling.

Peter stopped a few feet from me. Close enough to touch. His eyes, those impossibly green eyes.

"My darling . . ." He reached a hand out but pulled it back. "You look hurt. Are you all right ? Don't worry. We'll make sure you get your rest."

"I . . ." I reached back into my mind. *Wendy. Darling. Peter.* What else?

He reached his hand up again, slowly, holding it steady there by his temple. His eyes churning. "You'd like to stay here, right? That's what you told me. Don't you remember, my darling? I asked if you would come away. You agreed. You were very excited when I asked. Do you remember, my love? Come away?"

My body began to tremble. Not from cold. Not from fear. From something much worse. It started deep in my chest and spread outward until my hands shook and my knees threatened to fold beneath me.

He stepped closer. I should have stepped back, but I didn't. I couldn't.

"Oh no . . . shhhhh. My love." His voice poured over me. "My love. My Wendy. You're shaking. You must be cold. We'll get you inside. You'd like that, right?"

His hand came up. I watched it move toward my face as if from very far away. As if I were trapped behind glass, watching someone else's body, someone else's life.

His fingers touched my cheek. Warm. Gentle. Real. And then, something inside me slipped.

A memory, gone before I could grasp it. That feeling when you wake from a dream and wish to catch it but just can't.

Something about a house. Children. A woman with kind eyes who had told me something important. I tried to reach for it but found nothing. Just smoke and shadows in its absence.

"You'd like to come away with me," he said. Not a question. A truth. Certainty. "You want to come away with me. We discussed it. Don't you remember?"

Did I? I tried to think. There had been a reason why I came here. A name. A little girl with . . . what color hair? I couldn't picture her face anymore. Had there been a girl?

His thumb traced along my cheekbone. Down to my jaw.

Another memory dissolved. Brothers. I had brothers. Didn't I? Their names were . . . their names . . .

"I remember," I heard myself say. My voice sounded strange. Distant.

He lowered his voice. "Shhhhh, of course you do, darling." His touch left trails of warmth that sank into my skin and spread. "You're tired. I'll help you. I'll tell you what you remember. You remember the second star." He nodded yes, encouraging me to do right.

"That's good," he said. "You remember that. You also remember what the wind feels like. What it feels like to be free."

His voice. His hands on my skin. Everything else but him seemed to fade from my mind.

"Peter . . ." I said.

"Yes," he nodded again. "Peter and Wendy. That is the story. That is the only story you ever need to know."

But there had been a building. Red brick. Children running in a yard. I had worked there. I had . . . I had . . .

Gone.

"You've been so tired, for so very long." He murmured. "So alone. Carrying all that weight by yourself."

What weight? I couldn't remember what I'd been carrying. But I was tired. So very tired. My whole body ached.

"Guilt," he said, "and grief. They're difficult things to process. I understand that so very well, which is why you need me to take care of you. No one can take care of you like I can. No one can give you the life you need but me."

Guilt over what? I searched for it and found only fog. There had been something. Something terrible. Small shapes in the dark. Bones? No. That didn't make sense. Why would I remember bones?

"I can take it away," he whispered. "The aches you're feeling. Loneliness."

His other hand came up. He was cupping my face now, both palms against my cheeks. Where his skin touched me, I felt pieces of myself lifting away. Floating up like ash. Like the names of the children I had . . . the children . . .

What children? Did I have children? I wasn't a mother . . . was I?

"You don't have to be strong anymore, Wendy. You don't have to fight. You can rest."

My name. He said my name. *Wendy.* Yes. That was me. That is me. That was the only thing I knew for certain anymore. Wendy. And Peter. Peter and Wendy. Our names . . . on the cover of a book.

A book? Where?

Had there ever been anything else? Have we ever been anything else?

I opened my mouth. There was something I needed to say. A word. A name. It had been important. It had been the reason I came here.

But I couldn't remember coming here. I couldn't remember anything before this moment. Before his hands on my face, his breath on my skin, his eyes filling up my entire world.

"I can give you everything," he whispered. His lips were so close to mine now. "The island. Eternity. A home where you'll never grow old, never grow sick, never be forgotten."

Behind me, someone was shouting. A man's voice. Two men. Different voices. They were saying a word over and over again. Wendy? Was that what they were saying? My name? Were they calling me?

Was that me? It didn't feel like me anymore.

I moved to turn toward the voices, but Peter's hands held my face firmly in place.

"There's nothing to worry about over there. You just need me," he said. "That's the old world you're leaving behind. Remember? You don't want that world. You told me yourself. That's why you agreed to come away with me."

Come away . . .

He was right. It was all fading. They were all fading. Their faces. Their voices. Even the sound of my name in their mouths was growing distant, tinny, like a radio signal dying.

"Say yes," Peter breathed. "Wendy, do come with me to Neverland."

His forehead pressed against mine. His nose brushed mine. I could feel the heat of him everywhere now. His chest almost touching mine. His breath warm against my lips. His fingers sliding back into my hair.

Above us, crows erupted. They spiraled overhead. Wings beating the air into a frenzy. The sound was deafening.

The treehouse door opened again, and a little girl stepped out.

Thin. Pale. Her eyes ringed with gray. Standing on the platform staring down with something that looked like confusion.

He turned. Smiled at her and then looked back at me.

"Our daughter," he said. "We can be a family. Wendy. The family you've always wanted. The family you never had."

His hands slid to the back of my head, fingers curling there, tight.

"I've waited so long for you," he whispered. "Do you know how long? Do you know how many nights I watched your window, wanting you, needing you to come back to me?"

His lips grazed my cheek. My jaw. The corner of my mouth.

"No one will ever want you the way I want you, Wendy. No one will ever know you the way I know you."

I was dissolving. Melting into him. I could feel myself emptying out. Thought by thought. Memory by memory. But it didn't feel like loss. It felt like relief. Like setting down a weight I'd been carrying so long I'd forgotten I was holding it. I'd forgotten that I could abandon it.

His lips hovered over mine. Not quite touching. Not yet.

"Say it," he murmured against my mouth. "Say yes. Be mine. Let me take care of you forever."

Soon there would be nothing left. Nothing but his hands in my hair and the green of his eyes and the sweet aching promise of his mouth so close to mine.

I wanted to never be alone again, in this land or any.

"Yes," I whispered.

And he kissed me.

Soft at first. Tender. His mouth moved against mine and I felt myself falling, falling into him, falling out of myself, falling away from everything I had ever been.

It was beautiful. It was perfect. It was everything I had ever wanted.

Then he inhaled.

Not breath. Something deeper. Something that tugged at the center of my chest, the place where I kept the things I loved most. I felt them tear loose.

My mother's face. Gone.

The smell of my father's pipe. Gone.

John teaching me to read. Gone.

The weight of my newborn brother in my arms. Gone.

Michael's first word, *Wendy*. Gone.

Gone. Gone. Gone.

He was drinking me. Swallowing my life in long, slow pulls, and I couldn't stop him because the kiss still felt like love, still felt like coming home, even as he hollowed me out.

And behind my eyes I saw them.

Hundreds of them. Their faces pale and thin, mouths open in silent screams.

They reached for me, small hands grasping, desperate.

"Wendy!" they called.

I sensed them all, every child Peter had ever consumed.

They were inside him. Trapped. Still conscious. Still screaming.

And I was about to join them.

"Wendy!"

Curly.

His face surfaced through the sea of lost children. That gap-toothed smile and those trusting eyes. The boy who had tugged at my elbow in the dark and told me he was sick and missed his mother.

Something split.

Deep inside me, beneath the fog, beneath the forgetting, something cracked open like ice on a frozen lake, and the cold rushed in.

I remembered.

Agnes. John. Michael. Marigold House. Hook dying in my arms. The dagger at my belt. The name that could unmake him.

And Roger . . . Roger, the one who really loved me and who Peter killed.

I remembered who I was and then I bit down.

Hard.

My teeth sank into Peter's lower lip and I tasted blood. His blood. Wild and formed from this island. Thick like tree sap, fresh like leaves, and bitter like ash.

He jerked back with a hiss, his hand flying to his mouth. In that instant, I saw his true face beneath that mask.

Ancient. Void of life. Starving.

The face of something that had never been a little boy.

"You," he breathed. Blood, golden blood, dripped down his chin. His eyes had gone black. Completely black. "You bit me."

I staggered backward. My legs barely held me. My mind was full of holes. So many memories gone. Pieces of myself I would never get back because he had stolen my happiness and replaced it with suffering.

But I remembered enough. I remembered my name, and I remembered his.

My hand found the dagger at my belt.

"Yes," I said. My voice came out ragged. Broken. "I did."

All softness vanished from his face. What replaced it wasn't just anger. It was hunger. Raw and ancient and endless.

His hand shot forward.

I didn't see it move. One moment he was standing there, golden blood dripping from his lip. The next, his fingers were locked around my wrist, not the hand holding the dagger, but the other one.

He squeezed.

I felt bones in my body shift. A wet grinding sound. Stones rubbing together.

Then the pain hit. Bright, blinding. A scream that started in my wrist tore through my whole body.

I could not pull away. His grip was iron.

"You bit me," he said again. Offended that I would defend myself. His voice changed. Losing the sweetness and finding something else darker beneath. "You actually bit me."

He smiled. Not the tender smile. Not the loving smile. This smile showed too many teeth.

"I was going to make it gentle," he said. "I was going to let you fade slowly, sweetly, dreaming of our life together until the very end." His fingers tightened. Another bone cracked.

I screamed.

"But now I think I'll take you piece by piece. And I'll make sure you feel every single one."

My shadow lurched.

What little remained of it, that thin, tattered shred still clinging to me. It tore toward him like a dog straining at its leash. I felt it ripping. Tearing at my insides to break free.

"*Wendy*!" Michael's voice, somewhere behind me. "John, he's killing her!"

John shouted something. I couldn't hear the words. The world narrowed to Peter's face and Peter's grip, and the terrible sucking emptiness spreading through my chest.

More memories tore free.

My first day at Marigold House. Gone.

Beatrice's voice telling me I mattered. Gone.

The faces of the children I'd taught to read, to hope, to believe they mattered.

Gone, gone, gone.

He was finishing what he'd started with the kiss. Draining me dry. And this time there was no tenderness to hide behind. No seduction to soften the theft. Just his hand on my wrist and his smile in my face and the slow, agonizing dissolution of everything I had ever been.

My life only had two points. Before I met Peter, and after.

"I told you." He whispered. "You don't need those memories. You don't need that pain. You don't need anything but me."

The dagger. I still had the dagger.

My fingers tightened around the hilt. The rubies bit into my palm. Real. Solid. Something to hold on to.

Peter saw my hand move. His eyes flicked down to the blade.

"Ah," he said. "Still fighting. I always loved that about you. Your fight."

He released my wrist.

I stumbled backward, gasping, cradling my broken hand against my chest. Bones ground together with every movement. The pain was extraordinary. But the dagger was still in my other hand. The dagger was still mine.

"Come then," Peter said. He spread his arms wide. Welcoming. "Let's see what you remember to do with one of those."

The crows descended.

Not one or two. All of them. The entire spiral collapsed inward, folding down from the sky like a black fist closing. The first one hit my shoulder. I felt the impact before I saw it. A hard, heavy thud, talons punching through fabric into flesh. I swung my arm to knock it away and two more landed on my back.

Their claws dug in, hooked, held.

They were everywhere.

Wings beat against my face. Beaks stabbed at my arms, my neck, my hands. I couldn't see, couldn't breathe, the air turned to feathers and fury. A talon raked across my cheek and I felt the skin split, felt blood run hot down my jaw.

I slashed with the dagger. Hit something. A crow screamed and fell away, but three more took its place.

"*Wendy*!" John's voice, muffled by the chaos.

A beak drove into the back of my hand, the one holding the dagger. I felt it punch through the skin, scrape against bone. My fingers spasmed. The dagger slipped.

No. No, no, no . . .

I grabbed for it. A crow dove at my eyes. I threw my head back and its beak caught my forehead instead, opening a gash that poured into my vision.

The dagger hit the ground.

I dropped to my knees, scrambling for it, and the crows followed me down. They covered my back, my shoulders, my head. Their weight drove me forward onto my hands. Their claws shredded my clothes, my skin, everything they could reach.

My fingers found the hilt.

I grabbed it, rolled onto my back, and swung blindly at the black forms above me. The blade connected, once, twice, three times.

Feathers exploded.

Something wet and warm splattered across my face.

For one moment, the crows pulled back. Just a few feet. Just enough for me to see the sky.

Peter stood exactly where I'd left him. Arms still spread. Smile still in place. He wasn't even watching the attack.

He was watching Agnes, still on the treehouse platform, frozen. Eyes fixed on me. On the blood. On the birds, circling for another strike. Tears streaking her face.

"You see, love?" Peter said to her. His voice was gentle. Instructive. "This is what happens when Wendy doesn't listen."

Agnes's lips trembled. "Miss Wendy," she cried.

The crows dove again.

This time I was ready. I got my feet under me, raised the dagger, and started cutting. Hacking away. A crow came at my throat. I caught it with the blade and threw its body aside. Another went for my eyes. I ducked and felt it tear a chunk from my scalp instead.

Blood ran down my face, my neck, my arms. I couldn't tell how many wounds I had. Didn't matter. Couldn't matter. The only thing that mattered was staying alive long enough to reach him.

I pushed forward. *One step. Two.*

The crows battered me from every angle, but I kept moving, kept slashing, kept bleeding toward the monster who had taken so much from me.

"John!" I screamed. "Michael! Get Agnes!"

I didn't know if they heard me. Didn't know if they could move. Didn't know anything except Peter was ten feet away and I had a blade and I remembered his name.

Eight feet.

A crow latched onto my wrist. I shook it off and it tore skin away as it left.

Six feet.

Another went for my throat. I caught it with my free hand, felt its beak tear into my palm and crushed it against my chest until it stopped moving.

Four feet.

Peter's smile flickered. He was not afraid.

He should be.

Peter's hand came up. Fast. Casual. Like he was swatting a fly away.

The blow caught me across the face and sent me spinning. I hit the ground hard, the dagger skittering from my grip, and for a moment the world went white. All I knew was pain and the taste of blood in my mouth.

"Wendy. Wendy. Wendy." His voice came from above me. "This hurts me as much as it hurts you."

I tried to get up. My arms wouldn't hold me. I collapsed back into the dirt.

Disappointed. Gentle. "You really thought it would be that easy." He placed a finger on his chin. "I suppose it was that easy for me with . . . what was his name?"

Footsteps. Slow. Deliberate. He was walking toward me.

"I've lived a long time," he said. "I've killed things that you can't imagine. Pirates. Mermaids. Fairies. Children." He said the last word like someone would say breakfast. "And you think one little girl with a dagger handed to her by a grungy dead sea captain is going to end me?"

His boot pressed down on my broken wrist.

I screamed. My arm shook. I tasted bile and blood. The pain whited out everything. Thought. Memory. Hope.

"I'm going to take my time with you," Peter said. "And then you're going to stay with me here forever." He leaned down. I could see his face through my tears, through the blood and dirt.

I saw John. Bleeding. Pale. But moving. Crawling toward where the dagger had landed. His hand stretched out, fingers brushing the hilt.

Keep him talking. Keep him focused on me.

"You're afraid," I spit blood.

His boot ground down harder. Peter's smile twitched. "What?"

"You're scared of me." The words came out broken, bubbling through tears and mucus. "That's why you want me to beg. That's why you need to make it slow. Because if you kill me fast, you won't get to play pretend and think you're still in control of me."

His boot pressed harder. Bones grated. I sobbed.

"I'm not afraid of anything," he said. But his voice had changed. Tightened.

"You are. You're afraid of growing up." My lips shivered. I could barely see now. Just shapes and shadows. "Afraid of being forgotten. Afraid that one day children will stop believing in you, and you'll fade away. Like you never existed at all."

"Shut up!"

"That's why you keep them, isn't it? The children. That's why you can't let them go." I laughed and choked back blood. "You're not keeping them young. You're keeping yourself alive. You're a parasite. A leech. Without them you're not the great Peter Pan. Without them, without me, you're nothing and you have no story."

"I SAID SHUT UP!"

He grabbed my hair. Yanked my head up. His face was inches from mine, and it wasn't beautiful anymore. The mask was cracking, and I could see the darkness underneath.

"I am forever," he hissed. "I am stories. I am every child's dream and every parent's nightmare. And everything to Wendy Darling, and you don't get to tell me otherwise."

Behind him, John's hand closed around the dagger.

"You're right," I said.

John rose. Staggered forward. Raised the blade.

"I get to tell you your name."

Peter's eyes went wide.

John drove the dagger into his shoulder. Not his heart. His shoulder. But the blade sank deep, and Peter screamed, a high, inhuman sound that split the air. He backhanded John.

Somewhere I heard Agnes scream. Cry.

"Get her away from here, Michael!" I called out.

"Come on," I heard him say. "We'll meet you on the path. Please. Hurry."

John lay crumpled where he hit a tree. But the dagger stayed where it was, buried in Peter's flesh, its ruby hilt sparkling in the light like fresh blood.

He looked at the dagger. Looked at me. His face twisted with rage. "You think this changes anything?" He withdrew the blade and threw it at my feet. "You think a little cut is going to stop me? I've been stabbed a thousand times. I've been shot. Burned. Drowned. Nothing kills me. Nothing can kill me. I am—"

"Peter Gideon Bell," I said.

The name came out quiet. Almost a whisper. But it struck him like lightning. He staggered. His hand flew to his chest. His eyes, those beautiful green eyes, went wide with something I had never seen in them before.

Fear. Real fear.

"No," he breathed. "No, you can't. You don't get to write my story . . ."

I got to my feet. I don't know how. My wrist was shattered. My face torn. Blood oozed from a dozen wounds. But I stood.

"Peter Gideon Bell," I said again. Louder this time.

He screamed. His hands clawed at his face, and where his nails dragged, light spilled, green light, sick and pulsing, like something poisonous trying to escape.

The crows went mad. They cawed and crashed into each other overhead. Some fell from the sky, dead before they hit the ground.

"STOP!" Peter howled. "Stop saying it!"

I walked toward him. One step. Two. My broken wrist hung at my side. The dagger was sturdy in my other hand.

"Peter Gideon Bell."

Cracks spread across his face. Down his neck. Across his arms. Green light blazed through every fissure, brighter and brighter.

I heard Roger. *"Stab him in the heart and tell him he's nothing. He's only a story, one that feeds and lives off the lives of others."*

This is for Roger. This is for Hook. This is for the children. This is for me.

"You're nothing, Peter Gideon Bell," and I drove the blade deep into his heart.

The name struck like a hammer brought down on glass.

He staggered, not from the blade in his chest but from the sound. From hearing the truth of himself spoken aloud after so long hiding behind a boyhood that had never belonged to him.

His hands clawed at his chest. His breath broke into wet, panicked gasps. The sounds of a drowning man.

His shadow convulsed. I watched it writhe, twisting, folding in on itself, a creature trying to crawl out of its own skin.

It opened its mouth and screamed. Not sound. Void.

Peter looked down at the dagger buried to its hilt. At the rubies pressed against his shirt. At the golden blood already spreading through the fabric.

He looked back at me.

"Wendy," he said. Almost gentle. Confused. As if he couldn't quite believe I had done it.

His hand came up, not to grab me, not to fight. Just to touch my face. His fingers trembled against my cheek.

"Why?" he whispered.

His voice cracked. His green eyes filled with tears. "I don't understand. I thought . . . I thought you loved me."

Something twisted in my chest. Something old and stupid and twelve years old.

"I told you I'd give you everything," he said. His voice was shaking now. Small. Wounded. "I gave you the stars. I gave you flight. I showed you magic when everyone else wanted you to be ordinary."

A tear spilled down his cheek. Golden. Glowing.

"Was it not enough?" he asked. "Was I not enough?"

My hand trembled on the dagger.

"I waited for you," he whispered. "I never stopped believing you'd come back to me."

His fingers curled against my cheek. Desperate. Tender. "And now you're killing me." His breath hitched.

A sob. A real sob, broken and small.

"Wendy, please. Please. I'm scared. I don't want to die. I don't know what happens when I die."

My vision blurred. Tears. My tears. Mixing with the blood on my face.

"I'm sorry," he breathed. "Whatever I did, I'm sorry. I didn't mean to hurt anyone. I just didn't want to be alone. I just wanted someone to stay. I'm stupid. I'm sorry."

His hand slid down to cover mine. The hand still gripping the dagger in his chest.

"You're the only one who ever really knew me," he said. "The only one who ever really saw me. And now you're . . ." His voice broke. Shattered. "Now you're leaving me again. You're all leaving me. Everyone always leaves."

I felt myself wavering. Felt the certainty crumbling.

Maybe I was wrong. Maybe he really was just a frightened boy who didn't know how to love without hurting. Maybe I was the monster here. Maybe . . .

No. Wendy. No. Don't let him do this to you.

"Take it out," he whispered. "Please, Wendy. Take the blade out and hold me. Just hold me. That's all I ever wanted. For someone to hold me and tell me I'm not a monster."

His tears fell faster now. His whole body trembled. "Am I a monster, Wendy? Is that what you think of me? Is that why you're doing this?"

I opened my mouth. To say what, I didn't know. To apologize. To comfort him. To pull the blade free and gather him in my arms the way I'd gathered so many frightened children . . .

Then I saw it.

Behind the tears. Behind the trembling lips and the wounded eyes.

He was smiling, and then I remembered.

"He'll appear gentle at first, Wendy. Apologize. It will say anything to keep you there. Remember everything he took away from you."

The corner of his mouth curled up in that old, familiar smirk, the one that said, *I win, I always win.*

I understood. Even now. Even dying. Even with my blade in his heart. He was still playing a game with me. Still manipulating. Still trying to turn himself into the victim and me into the villain. Still trying to make me feel guilty for the monster he is.

"You're not scared," I said. My voice came out steady. Cold. "You're just angry that it didn't work."

His eyes flashed bright green. The mask shattered.

I twisted the blade, hard.

And Peter Gideon Bell began to break.

His mouth opened. His hands came up, clawing at the blade, deep in his chest. The cracks spread down his neck, across his collarbone, and raced along his arms.

His skin flaked away in bloody, fleshy patches. Underneath, there was no muscle or bone. There was just light. Sick, green light. The color of a stagnant pond and of things that glow in swamps.

His hands grabbed my shoulders. His grip was still strong.

"Please," he whispered.

His face was a ruin. One eye had gone dark. The other still held mine.

Terror. That's what I saw in him, in it. Not rage. Not hatred. Terror.

Good.

His body held for a moment longer. Light spilled from every crack, every seam, every place where Peter Pan had been stitched together from stolen children and stolen years. His mouth moved. No words came out. Just golden blood, thick and slow, running down his chin.

His chest caved in first.

Then his face.

Then he was falling, not backward, not forward, but inward. His body collapsing, folding into itself like paper crushed in a fist.

The light blazed brighter. I covered my eyes with my good hand.

I heard him screaming. Heard the crows screaming. Heard the island groaning beneath us, the ground splitting, the trees cracking, the whole rotten world tearing itself apart because the thing that held it together was dying.

Then silence.

When I lowered my arm where Peter had stood, there was nothing. Just a scorch mark on the ground. Just ash, already scattering in the wind. Just the faint smell of honey and rot, fading.

The crows hung motionless in the air for one long, frozen moment.

Then they fell.

All of them. Hundreds of black bodies dropping from the sky like stones, hitting the ground with soft, final thuds. Dead before they landed. Dead the moment their master died.

I stood in the clearing, the dagger dripping gold in my hand, and I felt nothing.

Just empty. Just done.

Behind me, I heard movement. Groaning. The wet sound of someone dragging himself upright.

John. His face was gray with pain, his shoulder soaked red, but he was standing.

Michael was beside him, and Agnes was tucked under his arm. Her eyes were fixed on the scorch mark where Peter had been. On the ash still swirling in the air.

"We saw the light," Michael said. His voice came out hoarse. "The green light. It shot up through the trees like a flare. And we knew that meant you'd won."

He couldn't finish.

Agnes pulled free from Michael. She took one step toward me. Then another. Her gray-ringed eyes searched my face, the blood, the wounds, the tears still drying on my cheeks.

Her chin quivered. "Miss Wendy . . ." She wrapped her arms around my waist.

"He's gone," I said. "He's never coming back."

Agnes nodded. Once. Twice. Then she cried.

John's eyes met mine over her head. He didn't smile. Didn't speak. Just nodded once, as if to say, job well done.

Then Michael's voice, thin and strange: "Wendy. Your shadow."

The ground beneath me was empty. Bare. No dark shape stretched from my feet. No silhouette traced my form against the ash-covered earth.

"Wait." John pointed. "It's right there."

Then we all saw it.

It drifted at the edge of the scorch mark. My shadow. Loose. Unattached. Floating just above the ground like a dark silk scarf caught in a breeze that touched nothing else. It rippled and folded, tattered at the edges, thin as old paper, but whole. Still shaped like me.

Still mine.

"Don't let it get away," John breathed. "If it drifts too far . . ."

The shadow trembled. Lifted higher. Started to float toward the jungle, toward the darkness between the dying trees.

Michael moved.

He lunged forward, wincing, stumbling. His hands closed around the shadow's edge. It writhed in his grip, trying to pull free.

"I've got it," he said through gritted teeth. "God, it's cold. Wendy, I've got it, but I can't . . . it keeps trying to . . ."

The shadow twisted. Fought. It didn't recognize him. Didn't want to be held by hands that weren't mine.

Agnes stepped forward. "Let me," she said.

He handed her my shadow.

It went still in her hands. Quieting. Almost like it knew her, remembered. Or maybe just that it recognized the hands of a child, someone who knew how to hold fragile things.

Agnes looked at me. Her eyes were serious. "I can sew it back on," she said. "When we get home. I'm good at sewing. Mum taught me before—" Her voice caught. "Before."

I knelt in front of her.

"You would do that for me?" I asked.

She nodded. Fierce. Determined.

I blinked back tears. "Hold on to it tight," I said. "Don't let go. No matter what happens."

Agnes clutched the shadow to her chest. It curled around her arms, settled against her, as if it knew it had found safekeeping.

"I won't," she said. "I promise."

I looked at my brothers. At this brave little girl. At the shadow that would be carried home in a child's arms, to be sewn back into place.

We had come here to save Agnes.

But she wound up saving me too.

The treehouse groaned behind us. A crack split the air, wood splintering, supports giving way.

"We have to go," John rasped. "Now. The whole island is coming down."

It sounded like a dying animal. The screeching. Without Peter that meant this land would no longer exist.

Trees toppled over.

"Let's go," Michael said.

We ran.

John grabbed my arm and pulled me forward. Michael scooped Agnes up, shadow and all, and we plunged into the jungle as the world behind us ruptured.

The ground heaved. Split. A fissure opened three feet to our left, and I watched a tree disappear into its hole, roots and all.

The air filled with the sound of cracking, groaning, dying—the island was dying.

"Don't stop!" John shouted. "Whatever you do, don't stop!"

I couldn't have stopped if I wanted to. My legs moved on their own. Moving. That's all I could think. I needed to move. We needed to get home. Before we were trapped here.

A palm crashed down behind us. I felt the spray of dirt and leaves. Michael stumbled, nearly falling but finding his balance.

"The hollow!" I gasped. "We have to reach the hollow tree!"

The jungle fought us every step. Vines lashed at our legs. Roots erupted from the ground and tried tugging at our feet. The trees themselves seemed to lean inward, trying to trap us, hold us, keep us here to die with the rest of it.

Then up ahead. Movement.

A boy between two ferns. Pale. Translucent. Watching us with hollow eyes.

Then another. And another. Peeking between trees and bushes.

Children. Everywhere. Stepping out of the dying jungle like dreams surfacing from deep water. They lined the path ahead of us, dozens of them, hundreds, their small bodies dressed in animal skins, crowns made of leaves, necklaces fashioned out of vines.

I knew their faces. So many of them. The twins, holding hands. Nibs with his crooked grin. Tootles, so small, holding his wooden sword high.

And Curly. Standing at the front. Smiling that gap-toothed smile.

I slowed.

"Wendy, we can't stop—" John started.

I couldn't help it. I wanted to say something, wanted to say sorry, that I was just so very sorry that they would remain here, lost boys forever.

The ghosts of the children weren't blocking our path. They were clearing it. They were bidding us all farewell.

* * *

Curly reached out his hand and I reached out mine. Our fingers brushed against one another. I felt him. He was real. When I looked over my shoulder, he had moved to the middle of the path, waving goodbye.

The jungle parted before us. Vines pulled back. Roots flattened. Trees that had been falling seemed to pause, to wait, to hold themselves upright just long enough for us to pass.

The path widened into a clearing. And there it was, the hollow tree. The fork in the road. Go right, and we did.

The children kept step on either side of us, following.

"Goodbye, Wendy!" One shouted, and then another.

"Bye, Wendy Darling!"

I brushed tears from my face and continued running, faster and faster.

The island continued to moan, scream, suffering as it died.

I turned around once more.

The jungle was folding in on itself. Trees collapsing inward, pulled toward some invisible center. The mountains in the distance, those jagged peaks I remembered from childhood, were crumbling, sliding, disappearing. Somewhere beyond the trees, the Black Rock split with a crack like thunder.

"They're not coming with us," Agnes shouted.

"No," I said. And I saw it in her face, the questions she couldn't ask. Why weren't they coming? What would become of them? Would they be alone forever?

We reached the ash ring, and I stopped, bent double, gasping for air.

Michael set Agnes down but kept hold of her hand. She held my shadow with her free arm, clutching it tight like a precious item.

"I don't know if I can," I said. My voice came out in rasps. "I don't have my shadow attached. I don't know if I'm whole enough to . . ."

"You can. You're still here," she held up my shadow. "A little broken. But you're still you. You just have to believe."

Believe.

"I don't even know how to anymore."

Agnes shrugged. To her, the answer was so simple. "Just let go."

I looked at my brothers. Their bruised faces. Their clothes covered in dirt and blood and mud and leaves.

"Let go," I whispered.

I reached for John's hand. He took Michael's. Michael took Agnes's, and Agnes took my other hand.

I closed my eyes and repeated. "Just let go."

I thought of this chain of broken people, and how we had come together to protect one another, and I repeated those words in my head over and over again: *Believe. Let go.* And the noises of this dying world, trees crashing, mountains imploding, all of it, began to fade away.

The darkness swallowed us whole. Cold. Complete. For a moment there was nothing, no ground beneath my feet, no air in my lungs, no sense of up or down.

Light. Faint at first. A pinprick in the sheet of black. Growing.

Agnes gasped. Michael swore. John's grip tightened.

Then silence, past space, leaving behind the second star toward home, and whatever would come next.

CHAPTER

22

We stood in the nursery. Our nursery. The window still open behind us, curtains stirring in a breeze that smelled of London, coal smoke, and rain.

"You're bleeding," John rasped. He'd slumped against the wall.

"I know," I said. "So are you."

Michael sat on the floor beneath the window, staring at his hands as if he didn't recognize them. The wounds the crows had left were already scabbing over, impossibly fast.

Agnes and my shadow were already at play with my old dolls.

John reached for me. Not to restrain. Not to urge. Only to steady.

"Wendy," he said, softer than I'd ever heard him. "It's over."

I looked down at my hands. I hadn't realized, this whole time, running toward the ash ring, I still clutched the dagger in my hand.

"I can't keep it," I said. "I need to be rid of all of it."

"I'll be back. I'll get the fire ready."

At the fireplace, we knelt in front of the hearth. I handed Michael the thimble, John the dagger, and in my hands, I held my journal and Roger's watch.

We watched the flames, not saying anything. I imagined in that moment, we each were bidding farewell to parts of ourselves, parts of our past, and to all we loved and lost on the island.

Michael tossed the thimble onto the logs, and John did the same with the dagger. I let go of my journal and watched the pages blacken and curl, and for a moment I hesitated before adding the watch. "You told me to forget," I said. "To move on . . ." And with that I added the pocket watch.

Agnes tugged at my hand. "Miss Wendy? Can you read me a story?"

"Of course, love, go find a book on that shelf."

"Wendy." John's voice. Quiet. Strange.

"Yes."

He and Michael were both staring at the hearth, at the place where we laid our items.

My journal had turned to ash, the thimble burned, but the pocket watch and the dagger, the two items that came from Neverland, were gone. Disappeared.

"It's like they vanished," Michael said.

All of them. Vanished. As if the stones had swallowed them whole, or they had never existed at all.

"This one," Agnes said, holding out a green book with gold letters.

PETER AND WENDY

"I've never read it, actually," Michael rubbed his hands together. "Let's see what this Mr. Barrie knows about Neverland and Peter Pan."

"You're all really expecting me to read this?"

"You told Agnes to pick out a book. Those were the parameters, and I think we're all waiting to hear this story."

"All right then," I said.

I turned to the first page. The paper was yellowed, the ink faded with age, but the words were clear. I read:

"'All children, except one, grow up. They soon know that they will grow up, and the way Wendy knew was this.'"

I thought of the boys, their bones in the dark, their voices finally freed. I thought of the mermaids and shores and waterfalls. I thought of Hook, dying in my arms with Roger's name on his lips.

I thought of Agnes, small and trembling but here and alive.

I thought of Beatrice's voice: *Your life belongs to you.*

As I read, Michael wiped his eyes. John stared out the window. Agnes held my shadow's hand.

Outside the window, London stirred. Carriages clattered. Voices called. The world went on, oblivious to what we had survived, what we had lost, what we had finally, finally escaped.

I decided in that moment that I didn't care if they read Mr. Barrie's version of the story or knew mine. Let them believe in the boy who never grew up, the magical island, the adventure that never ended.

We knew the truth.

And the truth was this: The monster was vanquished. The children returned home and their story continued.

Epilogue

THE CHILDREN AT Marigold House had forgotten about the shadow that consumed their nightmares.

They remembered nightmares, of course, bad dreams about birds and bells and a boy who smiled too wide. But children's memories are kind. They blur the edges. They soften the dark.

I was grateful for that.

Agnes slept in the bed farthest away from the window now. She still woke sometimes, gasping, reaching for a shadow that wasn't there. But each morning, when the light came through the windows, she smiled a little wider. Ate a little more. Laughed a little louder.

She was coming back to herself. Slowly. The way all healing happens.

I was in the garden when I found it.

The roses had finally bloomed, late this year. I was cutting stems for the dining hall when my shears fell and struck something hard.

I knelt. Brushed away the soil.

And there, nestled among the roots like something the earth had been keeping safe: Roger's pocket watch.

I lifted it with trembling hands. The case was clean now. Polished. As if someone had wiped away the years of tarnish and neglect. And the crack in the face, it was gone. I turned the pocket watch over in my hands, believing for a moment this was not real, but there they were, his initials: R.H.

"I'm so sorry, my darling," I said. Tears welling in my eyes. "I thought maybe I should be rid of it all . . . all of the memories, but no matter how hard I tried to forget that place, I could never forget you. No matter how hard I tried. I'm so sorry. I don't want to forget you. Not ever."

I pressed the watch to my heart. The metal was warm against my palm. It wasn't ticking, but still, it was here, and it was real.

Inside children were laughing. The kettle was singing. The world here was warm, and mine.

"Good morning, Rosie," I said as I entered the kitchen.

A great wail greeted me instead, little Jane in Eleanor's arms, her face red and furious.

Rosie was gathering bowls and spoons for the children's breakfast.

"She'll quiet now that Wendy's here," Rosie said.

And she did. Jane's cries softened to hiccups, then silence as she extended her fingers toward me.

"Hmm," Eleanor said, looking from Jane to me. "You're right, Rosie. Wendy could pass for her mother."

"I'm nobody's mother," I said.

"This is true," Rosie said. "But who knows, maybe when John finishes those repairs on your house, little Jane could go with you."

"And who would take care of her while I was at work?"

"We've got to find Wendy a husband, then," Eleanor said.

The pocket watch began to tick. I hadn't wound it.

"You two . . ."

"And Michael?" Eleanor asked.

"John and I received letters this week. He's made it to the Western Front."

I said it lightly, as if it meant nothing. As if my heart didn't seize thinking of him in the trenches, but all I could do was hope for him to return home safely as he had done before.

I washed and readied for lessons, and the classroom greeted me like an old friend.

The air smelled of chalk dust, lemon oil, and paper. I opened a window and a breeze moved slowly, teasing books stacked beside my desk, fluttering their pages.

I moved toward them without thinking, fingers brushing the spines. The covers bore faint fingerprints, smudges of coal and breadcrumbs, the traces of children who would one day forget this room entirely when they grew up and left us.

I reached for my papers when a knock came at the door.

"Yes?" I called, thinking a child may have woken early. "It's quite early. You should be preparing for breakfast," I said without looking at the door.

The door creaked open, and through the narrow sliver, Beatrice appeared. She looked beautiful, her red curls pinned up but still spilling out from beneath her hat. "Aren't you an absolutely lovely surprise this morning! What are you doing here?"

"I've got the day off and wanted to spend it with you."

"You're so sweet."

"Plus, we miss you at the hospital," she said with a smile.

"I know . . . but more children are staying with us, so they need me."

"I'm glad you've living here."

"For now," I said.

"Regardless, I'm glad you're here now. I don't want you all alone in that big house of yours." She paused, her smile turning mischievous. "But maybe we can change that, eventually?"

"What are you talking about?"

"I have a surprise for you."

"A surprise?"

"You have to cover your eyes first."

"What are you up to?" I laughed. "You're just like the children."

"Those are the rules. No peeking."

I covered my eyes with my hands, the same as I had before Lillian presented me with a green ribbon in my hat.

Footsteps approached. Heavier than Beatrice's. Someone else entered the room.

"Your surprise is a visitor," she said. "You can look now."

I lowered my hands.

He was standing in the doorway. No hospital-issued shirt or trousers. Just a man in a handsome suit. Standing upright and here. The soldier.

"Edward . . ." The name came out as barely a whisper. My hands found the edge of my desk to steady myself.

He was there. Standing. Whole. And he was looking at me like I was the only person in the world.

Beatrice stood behind him, her eyes darting between us, smiling with satisfaction.

Edward's cheeks flushed. He shifted his weight from one foot to the other. His eyes kept finding mine, then darting away, as if afraid if he looked too long, I'd disappear.

"Well," Beatrice whispered. "Aren't you going to say anything?'

He smiled, bashful. "Hello."

She rolled her eyes. "Oh, my goodness, you two are ever so boring. You're perfect for one another. Where is the dramatic greeting?"

"Beatrice . . ."

Edward stood like a man newly arrived from a long voyage, upright but uncertain. Our eyes met, and it was like looking into a mirror after grief. Slow. Hesitant. Disbelieving that safety could be real.

He crossed the room with careful steps, as though testing the floor's willingness to hold him. He stopped in front of my desk, hands uncertain at his sides, when something caught his eye.

"Your pocket watch . . ." His voice was lower than I expected. Gentler.

"Yes." My heart leaped. How much had he remembered.

"It belonged to your friend."

I opened my mouth to speak, but I felt a sting behind my eyes.

"I'm sorry," he said quickly. "I didn't mean . . . I just remember some things you said. The stories you read."

I looked at Beatrice, my dear friend and lifeline to this outside world, outside of Marigold House. I'd lived my entire life under the care of someone else, my parents, then Peter, then this house, then my own guilt. I had been too afraid to move forward for fear of being hurt. Or worse, for fear of losing someone again.

Beatrice gave me a single encouraging nod, and in that small gesture she told me it was all right to jump.

"Miss Darling," Edward said. "You read to me every day for months."

"I did."

"I wanted to thank you," he said. His eyes softened. "Thank you for sitting with me so I wasn't alone in the dark."

"You're very welcome."

Edward looked over his shoulder to Beatrice, waiting for her encouraging nudge. She smiled and shook her head at the ceiling.

He exhaled, gathering courage. "If you have time, could you tell me a story?"

I smiled, because of how sweet the request was. "Of course. You can join me for class. The children would be delighted to meet you, if you don't mind."

"I'd love to meet them."

He sat. Carefully. Like a man who had forgotten how.

Down the hallway, Jane's cries reached us, then faded.

Beatrice watched us from the doorway; her hand pressed to her chest. She caught my eyes, nodded once, then slipped out, pulling the door closed behind her with a soft click.

Edward and I sat in the quiet classroom, the empty desks waiting for children who would arrive within the hour.

"I don't remember much," he said, after a long moment. "From before. Just pieces. Flashes of light in the dark. People shouting. But I remembered your voice. It was like it reached through to find me. Telling me I would be all right. The stories you told." He looked at his hands, turned them over as if checking they were real. "They helped me to remember."

My throat tightened.

I thought of all the stories I had told him. The silly ones. The brave ones.

"Stories are like that," I said. "Sometimes they can pin us down to this world, and sometimes, other stories, they take us away. Elsewhere."

In his eyes, I saw something I recognized, the look of someone who had been somewhere dark and was still navigating his way toward the light.

"Will you tell me one now?" he asked. "Before the children come?"

It didn't take me long to figure out what story I should tell a man who had been trapped in the darkness for so long. I thought of my own story, and how I had been trapped there too.

"Once upon a time," I said slowly, "there was a girl who learned that growing up wasn't a tragedy. It was a gift. But in order to learn that lesson, she would first have to meet a boy who would never grow up."

He leaned back in the chair. Closed his eyes. Not sleeping, just listening. Trusting.

Outside, birds sang. Inside, the watch ticked slowly.

Edward smiled.

The door opened. Small faces appeared, and like every morning I felt so happy to be surrounded by the spirit of childhood. The children gathered around me and Edward, asking him all sorts of questions, what was his name, what was he doing here, how did he know me.

Willie entered last, navigating each step on his crutches, Agnes at his side. She gasped.

"Oh, Miss Wendy has a friend!"

I rose from my desk, smoothing my skirt, tucking a strand of hair behind my ear. Edward looked delighted as he responded to each of the children's questions.

And as the children settled, chattering and curious, I felt something I hadn't felt in a long time. Wonder. Surprise. Adventure. And the best part was, I had found all of that right here at home.

ACKNOWLEDGMENTS

THANK YOU so very much to Sara Henry, Julia Abbott, Dulce Botello, Mikaela Bender, Alexandria Mitchell Pressman, Kaitlyn Kennedy, Dana Kaye, Matt Martz, Thaisheemarie Fantauzzi Perez, Lane Heymont, Gerardo Pelayo, Little C, Little B, Christina Henry, Daniel Kraus, Becky Spratford, Hailey Piper, Mathilda Zeller, Maxwell Ian Gold, Jamal Hodge, and Linda Addison.